© TY FITZMORRIS

MICHAELA CARTER is an award-winning poet and writer. She studied theater at UCLA and holds an MFA in creative writing, and her poetry has been nominated for two Pushcart Prizes, won the Poetry Society of America Los Angeles New Poets Contest, and appeared in numerous journals. Recently she cofounded the Peregrine Book Company, an independent bookstore in Prescott, Arizona, where she works as a book buyer and story-teller. Carter lives in Prescott with her partner and two inscrutable children and teaches creative writing at Yavapai College. This is her first novel.

FURTHER OUT THAN YOU THOUGHT

MICHAELA CARTER

WILLIAM MORROW

An Imprint of HarperCollins*Publishers*

"Not Waving but Drowning" by Stevie Smith, from *Collected Poems of Stevie Smith*, copyright © 1957 by Stevie Smith. Reprinted by permission of New Directions Publishing Corp. and Estate of James MacGibbon.

HarperCollins books may be purchased for educational, business, or sales promotional use. For information please e-mail the Special Markets Department at SPsales@harpercollins.com.

FIRST EDITION

Designed by Diahann Sturge

Library of Congress Cataloging-in-Publication Data has been applied for.

ISBN 978-0-06-229237-7

14 15 16 17 18   OV/RRD   10 9 8 7 6 5 4 3 2 1

For Kurt Valore, and for Hannah, my dearest palindrome

FURTHER

OUT

THAN

YOU

THOUGHT

IT HAD HAPPENED. She'd crossed the finish line.

The transformation was complete. She was no longer her body. Her body was not her. The separation was palpable.

Had you been there, she'd have told you to come closer.

Closer, she'd have said. I'll demonstrate.

Can you feel my nipple, the taut nub against your lip, your tongue, your teeth?

I don't know you?

No, I don't.

Is that a problem? It feels wonderful; it means nothing— nothing more than the fact of itself. It just is, this meeting of flesh.

Is there anywhere else you care to touch?

One

THE CENTURY LOUNGE was warm and red, like a womb. The walls were red, and the curtains—everywhere there were curtains; between the main stage and the backstage, between the private dance booths and the showroom—red velvet curtains. Day and night were a constant gloaming, and always the room smelled of perfume, of sweat, of pussy and cigarettes. The red and lilac lights lining the main stage sent rays through the smoke as the dancers walked the room with their lit cigarettes, as they leaned toward the ears of the men, also smoking, or eating a burger and fries, but watching, all eyes, as the girls, in passing, whispered, "Wanna peek, up close, twenty bucks," the chiffon and black lace like forgotten wings waving behind them.

It was a late night in late April, but it could have been any time, any day, any season.

"Mr. Cooper," she said, standing, pushing in her chair, "I'm up."

Already Joe the DJ was pitching her dance over the loudspeaker: "And next it's Stevie. Girl next door like you've never seen her before."

Looking up from his Coke, Mr. Cooper pushed his spectacles up the bridge of his nose. "She's been gone since last night. Didn't even leave a note." Lost in his personal drama, he'd been repeating himself. Stevie had stayed to listen, but now Devotion was gathering her cash and Stevie was onstage next. He reached into his pocket for the flask of rum and poured. "White girls," he said, shaking his head. "They just do what they want. Not you, but . . . Think she'll come back?"

"I hope so," she said.

He opened his wallet, handed her a twenty. "You here tomorrow?"

"Ten in the morning."

Backstage, she saw Devotion through the smoke, sitting cross-legged on the carpet, flushed and out of breath, the wad of bills in her pink silk slip. Sweat trickled down her hairline and between her breasts, and she pulled her long blond hair off her neck to let it cool. "My mother's out there," Devotion said. "Came all the way from Wisconsin."

"To watch you?"

Devotion shrugged, lit a joint. "She doesn't like it," she said. "But I just gave her a grand."

In the chair before the mirror sat Brett. Brett had been gone for what seemed to Stevie like months, and now she was back. Stevie watched her lick a fingertip and slick the thin dark arches of her brows.

"Lady Brett," Stevie said.

"Ms. Smith," Brett said, and she held her eyes in the mirror, Stevie thought, a second longer than her usual quick glance, before she returned to her reflection, lifting her chin and assessing. Her smooth, black hair framed her dark eyes, her cheekbones, softening the angles. In only her black bra and G-string—what she always wore—her long brown body was easy. Satisfied, she leaned back. "Damn slow night," she said, talking to herself.

"It's been slow. The recession and all," said Devotion. "How were things in Portland?"

"The place was crawling with strippers. We thought we might move there, but I couldn't get work."

Stevie had a hard time believing her. If Brett, with her high curves, couldn't get work, then the men in Portland had to be blind, or else society really was on the verge of collapse. But she was here. She was back. That was all that mattered.

At the club, there were those girls who chose beneficent abstractions for their pseudonyms—Devotion and Mercy, Charity and Love. There were the girls who named themselves after sky-nouns—Heaven, Angel, Star, and Rain. And then there was the small faction of those with literary pseudonyms, consisting of Brett—Lady Brett Ashley out of Hemingway—and Stevie, after the London poet Stevie Smith. They were the minority, and for too long Stevie had been holding the torch on her own.

Devotion put the joint to Stevie's mouth. "Indica," she said. "Not Sativa. From Mendo." It was spicy sweet, Turkish, Stevie thought, and smelled like ripe apricots.

Exhaling the smoke, Stevie slipped between the curtains and floated onto the stage. Richie Havens was singing "Lady Madonna," and the room was a dark and hazy abyss, but something was different. Let go, she told herself, drift, forget yourself in the music. But something had changed. Lights in her eyes. And, closing them, there was the quivering ghost—what a flash does when you get your picture taken.

The photographer was her mother. Always. Smile, she'd say before the flash. Think of peanut butter. Think of whales.

Whales don't eat peanut butter, she'd tell her now.

Through the ghost, she could see, at a front table, the woman who had to be Devotion's mother, with her big hair, a floral-patterned dress, and a cigarette.

As Stevie began her dance—her hands clasped behind her back, her chest out, her lips in a schoolgirl pout—she thought of her own mother, who would be wearing a black T-shirt and jeans, her hair in a ponytail, camera around her neck. Yes. Simone Griffin would be in the far back, taking the scene in a frame at a time—the slant of light made visible by the smoke, the value of the perfect shot, chiaroscuro, the light like spoken words against the dark, wherein lay the silence, the mystery she had liked to say was necessary for art.

Only Simone Griffin wouldn't be here. Were she alive, she'd have no idea how her daughter earned money these days. Stevie would make sure of that.

Devotion's sense of flagrant continuity seemed so simple. Her real name was Justine, she'd told her once. But if her mother was here, it meant she had no need to hide this world from the other one, the real one. The concept baffled Stevie, who couldn't imagine working here without its being a secret from her family.

She twirled her plaid gingham dress up and smiled, but the room was vast and barren. A toothless mouth, it swallowed her whole. Night after night, it digested her slowly. This red room without any escape, this stomach with its lining of eyes. She unbuttoned the dress, let it fall.

There he was, at his usual table. The little wave. Tony. He was late. This was her last set. She hadn't thought she'd see him tonight.

She unhooked her bra, looking his way. Ran her hands around the curve of her breasts, over her stomach and hips. The move had become mechanical, but she watched his blue eyes flicker, his lips curl to a puckish smile. And when he raised his glass to her, she felt, for that instant, the power she'd possessed when she first started stripping. That rush of gratification. Like standing at the edge of a cliff and feeling the wind off the ocean. Knowing you could jump. She returned his smile and slipped back through the red curtain.

Backstage, Devotion was talking. About the army, how they'd whip her into shape. "Three years of stripping and where am I going? Too many drugs. And the men." So the army was her newest savior. Stevie laughed. She hadn't heard this one before.

At the mirror, Brett toked what was now a roach. Stevie could see the ring of tattoo around Brett's upper right arm showing through the makeup and powder. One of the rules at the Century Lounge was no tattoos, and she had to cover it when she danced. Stevie could just make out the head of the snake eating its own tail. Ouroboros, Brett had told her once, what the ancient Egyptians had seen in the Milky Way—a great serpent encircling the universe, the eternity of time in constant re-creation.

Brett leaned over Stevie, handing the roach to Devotion. Stevie could feel her nipple graze her shoulder, and she caught her breath.

Devotion laughed and took the roach, held it between her long red nails. "I read the encyclopedia. I crave knowledge. After the army I'll go to college," she said, and took a hit.

Stevie envied her easy certainty, even if it was just the pot talking. She had never been able to think, much less to talk, like that. She questioned every decision, weighed the positives, the negatives. The world was too full of possibilities, the choices were too many and each choice had its repercussions. You could go crazy thinking this way, she knew, but how could one be sure of any future? If conviction was a kind of blind stupidity, maybe it was the good kind, in which you rule out alternatives and the world conforms to your thought. You choose the life you want and then you create it. Simple.

Stevie pulled off her white G-string. Each girl danced two songs—one with clothes and one without. The songs were back-to-back, but she wanted to linger here a second longer, with the women who had become her sisters. She reached for the roach. She didn't have long nails—her nails were bitten and bare, like Brett's—so the roach burned her thumb and finger and, before she could smoke any, she dropped it in the ashtray.

"Christ," said Devotion, looking up at her. "Your tits."

"What?"

"They're huge."

Devotion picked up the roach with her nails and held it to Stevie's lips. She breathed the smoke and her throat burned.

Brett looked her over in the mirror. And Stevie, too, assessed her own reflection. With her green eyes and her pale skin, her shoulder-length hair dirty blond and messy, she was almost Brett's opposite. Brett was staring at her breasts. "Do they hurt?"

"Well," Stevie said, and held them up, deciding. Her breasts seemed heavier, but then, she'd filled out since she'd started stripping. Her body had more muscle, but a little more softness as well.

"Probably just that time of month," said Devotion. She picked up her white boa from the carpet and put it around Stevie's neck.

Her next track was playing, and the stage was empty, waiting for her to animate it with her sad sway, with her silent siren song. In only feathers and fake pearls and heels, Stevie moved past the curtain, feeling it skim her thigh, her tender nipple. What time of the month was it? She wasn't exactly sure. Nights and days ran like watercolors, one into the next, so fast, months bleeding into months.

She entered the light, her hips swinging as she walked. Taking the boa in her hands, she ran it along the edges of her breasts. Rickie Lee Jones sang, *Just walk away, Renee. You won't see me follow you back home*. Her favorite song. Cold pole in her hand, she twirled, as if she could become white whirling smoke, could dissolve into air.

Like her teenage anorexia, that longing she'd had to be without hunger, to defy even gravity. She was fifteen, her scapulae protruding like incipient wings, her body going backward, her boy-girl body intent on not becoming a woman.

Eat, her father had said. Eat.

Down to the bones, yet hidden, an eel in its hole, she stayed put. Her mother was gone, and no bait he offered could lure her from the safety of her resolve. Her life was up to her now. She was dancing ballet, eating a hard-boiled egg and a Saltine cracker a day, maybe a grapefruit, or an orange. If she chose to vanish, that was what she would do. She didn't need food. She didn't need people. Not even her father, who had begun to notice her again. When he held her in his arms like a child and set her on the bathroom scale, she pushed up on the underside of the countertop, adding false weight. Victorious trickster, she held her head high—queen of a world not entered, but overcome.

Around the pole she spun, and the tiny lights whirled like planets as she hurled herself through the universe. She tried to feel them whirl inside her like chakras. Red at the tailbone, her connection to home, to mother. And lilac at the top of her head, open to the stars, to the poetry of her thoughts.

Be in your body, not in your head, Brett had told her the night she'd auditioned. It was when the stripping felt best, like dancing with your eyes closed, feeling the music move you—a breeze across a field of wheat.

She had been new then. Hair short, spit curls at her cheeks, she was trying herself on, her new self—Stevie. Like Stevie Smith, Stevie the dancer would dress like a little girl: white church socks with turned-down ruffles, short white cotton gloves, Mary Janes with heels, the blue-and-white dress straight out of *Alice in Wonderland*, pearls. That first night, she'd worn real pearls, the last gift her mother and father had given her together, her present when she'd turned fifteen. She never wore them here again. Her costume, she realized, had to be just that—clothes and accessories that made her into someone else. As Stevie, she was innocence willing to go the distance, never tainted by any one thing she did, because she was only playing. This was a game of hopscotch, of jump rope, skipped to a nursery-rhyme beat. One, two, buckle my shoe.

Three, four, shut the door.

She was late this month. She knew that much. But how late?

Stop it, she thought. Stop thinking. She felt her feet, how they ached from being all night in her secondhand Halstons with the four-inch heels. She felt the muscles in her thighs and back and waist as her hips rocked from side to side. She felt the heat of the lights, felt a drop of sweat slide down her neck. Only how could she be just a body, if that body might be changing, already beyond her control?

The empty sidewalks of my block are not the same, Rickie Lee sang. *You're not to blame.*

Stevie walked the rim of the stage, bending here and there to gather the green. She bent at her waist, her legs straight. She'd learned that from Brett, too. Every move a chance to exhibit her sexuality. No waste, no shame. To the men behind the dollars, to their late-night TV gaze, she smiled, saying, "Thank you, thank you, thank you, thank you, thank you." A distant echolalia.

One boy clapped in appreciation and smiled back. Korean possibly. Spiked black hair and white teeth.

"The Way We Were" was playing, and here was Joe's voice over the loudspeaker. "Next on the main stage it's the luscious Miss Love."

Stevie stood up, walked quick to the curtain. She brushed past Love, her cheek against Love's breast, and the world went white. She turned an ankle and grabbed Love's arm. "Hey, darlin'," said Love in her southern drawl, holding her up. She guided her backstage, helped her sit on the carpeted step. "Y'all right?"

Stevie focused her eyes.

Long legs and hair, her dark skin showing through the pink gauze of her costume, Love was stately and steamy, like an orchid.

"Honey?"

"I'm fine," Stevie said, and smiled to assure her.

Alone, Stevie lay on the carpet, caught her breath. Love's pink veils would be moving in circles as she pirouetted from one corner of the stage to another. *She moved in circles, and those circles moved.* Roethke said that. Like Brett's Ouroboros. No escape from ourselves.

Stevie sat up, brushed the filaments of carpet from her sticky back. She opened the bottle of water she'd stashed in a corner, put it to her lips and felt the liquid slip down her throat and fill her. She drank the entire bottle, as if to purify herself from the inside out. *Water cleans the soul* was what her mother had liked to say. She'd never leave the house without bringing a mason jar of water with her, and she'd dubbed the pool in their backyard her "reservoir of sanity." Stevie was born in Phoenix in late August and her mother had spent the last three months of her pregnancy in the water. She'd even slept on a raft some nights, floating under the stars. It was no wonder Stevie required water, needed it like air. If she didn't have a bottle nearby she couldn't relax, and this bottle was gone. But she was almost off. She could last, and she could always get a glass from the bar.

Folding the money into her purse—a beaded half-moon evening bag, the one token from her real life she allowed herself here—she thought, again, of her mother. The purse had been hers, and she'd given it to Stevie when she was twelve. It had seemed magical at the time, when Stevie had placed it over her shoulder and imagined who she might be at twenty-five, imagined all she'd know then. She'd pictured dinners and conversation. A whole other kind of dancing—not for, but *with*. What she'd pictured was elegant, easy, streamlined. As if wisdom could arrive cleanly as mail, or the newspaper on one's doorstep. As if wisdom didn't come from getting dirt under one's nails.

Two

SHE MET TONY at the private dance booth, their booth, the one on the side—the corner pocket, he called it. Behind the red curtains, in the dark, she put her moon purse on the high shelf, fed the token into the slot. It made a lighthearted clink when it hit bottom, like a quarter fed to a pinball game at a rusty boardwalk arcade. Now there was the heat of the red light, like a warming oven, and she sat still as a mannequin on the ledge the size of a child's desk that separated her from Tony. He was supposed to sit with his hands folded in his lap like a good boy. This to adhere to the club's *No Touching* rule: he wasn't to touch her, and she wasn't to touch *anything pink*. And there was the lurker behind the curtain, peeking through the cracks, making sure the dancers and their patrons followed the rules.

Since her first night, Tony had what the man behind the curtain called wandering hands. Though Stevie had denied it. When confronted, she had told the man he hadn't touched her. She'd kept their secret. Tony had paid for ten private dances in a row that first time, and that made two hundred dollars he'd spent. Of course, there were the tokens she had to buy at the bar at eight bucks each, the club's take of each dance, so she'd only brought home one hundred twenty. Cash she wouldn't have had otherwise. The money didn't hurt—car insurance had been due, rent and tuition—but she'd turned down cash before. The truth was she liked Tony, liked his Spanish accent, his thin body and bald head, liked the fact that, at sixty-five, he was exactly forty years her elder. And she liked how his eyes shone with life— their flash of sun on ice.

They had chosen the corner booth because here the lurker couldn't see quite so well. Here, on her knees, she could lean toward Tony, letting his knuckles brush her nipples. Standing, facing Tony's image in the back mirror, she could lower herself, quickly, letting her labia graze his hands. With her back against the mirror, she could open her legs and touch herself.

She was shaved completely. It had been a gradual thing—the removal of hair. That first time, before her audition, she'd shaved just her labia, or rather her boyfriend, Leo, had. On a towel on the coffee table she'd lain back, her head on a pillow, and let him shave her. There was the warm soapy water, the blades of the virgin razor, Leo, cautious and precise, taking his time. Cool air on her labia, she'd felt that part of her come to life. After a few months, the triangle narrowed to a landing strip. And then, to be seen, to be that much more vulnerable, that much more seductive (and because it went with her Alice dress), she shaved it all off, the whole brown tuft. Utterly bare, she knew in that very lack of defense there was power—the trust that comes of ownership. And she knew her little-girl act was one reason Tony had taken so strong a liking to her.

Tonight, she let his pinky trace the lips on her face as if he were glossing them. His pinky stopped and her lips opened, taking it in. Tony's little finger in her mouth sent through her body a new thrill of contact. She nibbled the tip and let it go, reveling in the ease of her actions, her mouth parted, ready. And then she thought of Leo, home alone, waiting for her, and wondered if her guilt amplified the thrill. The thought frightened her, and the blood quickened in her veins.

She moved to the back of the booth, sat with her shoulder blades pressed to the cool mirror, legs spread, and watched him look. Her availability vast as the sea drew him in. His face glowed.

"Baby. You're wet," he said. "Really wet, like in the beginning."

At his table, in her plaid dress again, she sat across from him. They drank cranberry juice and club soda. It was Stevie's drink at the club, where all choices were nonalcoholic, and Tony had decided it was his now, too.

She could hear Brett one table over, introducing herself. "No. Not Brat, Brett."

Tony was saying he'd had dinner with some literary friends and pulled out Stevie's poems, told them some escrow agent had written them. They'd gone on about how sensual the poems were, and asked if the author was a sensual person. Tony insisted she was bookish, shy.

"I am, you know," Stevie said.

Tony laughed. "And then they began to analyze the poems," he said, "and I got bored. But listen. I want to patronize the arts. So here's the deal. A thousand dollars. But no dancing, we'll just go out to dinner. Bring anyone you like. Bring Leo."

He'd offered her a grand before, for a private dance at his house in the marina. Said she could bring a chaperone. And so she'd told him about Leo. How he was dressing up as an American revolutionary and selling tapes of his album on a street corner in Century City. Tony had bought one. It was the only tape Leo had ever sold.

She mulled over this new offer. Should she break her rule and take the club outside, into the real world? When she'd first started dancing, Brett had warned her about that. The rule was a good way to keep things safe, lives separate. But this was Tony. She'd known him for months.

He leaned back, crossed his legs. "I listened to Leo's tape," he said, and pulled it from his pocket. "*Fourth of July Address*, huh? Who's the girl on the front?"

"Liberty," said Stevie. It was a pencil sketch of a woman's face. Leo had drawn it.

"She looks like you," Tony said. He turned the case over to the list of songs. "That 'Freedom Song' is as good as any I've heard. Ever. But why does he do all that talking? Who wants to listen to that?"

She tucked her hair behind her ear. She blushed. Why explain Leo's discourse on liberty, or his refusal to pay taxes because they were unconstitutional?

Maybe she would go to dinner with Tony. Maybe she'd go alone.

The Asian boy with the white teeth and spiked hair tapped her on the shoulder.

"Go ahead," said Tony. "I'm calling it a night."

The boy followed her past a few occupied dance booths to one that was open. Passing Brett, she lingered, watched hot jazz spread from her like the sweet reek of night-blooming jasmine, watched it spread from that blur of fold and soft black fuzz. Hands on her thighs, knees open, torso trembling, her neck long, her lips grazing her shoulder, she inhaled her own heat, held it.

Stevie forced herself to stop looking.

She stepped into the next booth, put her purse on the ledge, the token in the slot. Brett dancing on in her imagination, she thought of all she wanted to say. Or maybe it wasn't really talk she wanted.

Six private dances later, the twenty-one-year-old Korean named Danny bought her a club sandwich for a late-night dinner. Mild eyes, refined voice and hands, he talked of Rumi, and the role of the beloved in Persian poetry, the beloved being a metaphor for God. God as immanent and transcendent, within all and outside all. "God," he said, "is the Self in everyone, in spirit and in matter. These bodies"—he patted his smooth arm—"they're made of God."

"And what I shall assume, you shall assume. For every atom belonging to me as good belongs to you," said Stevie.

"Whitman," the boy said, surprised. "One of my favorites."

ONE LAST PRIVATE dance before the club closed. This time, her crotch was close enough to tantalize. Her pelvis tilted like a plate, her sex near his nose, his mouth.

His lips brushed hers. No tongue. Just a closed-mouth peck of a kiss.

She pulled away, caught her breath. This had never happened, and for a moment she was stunned. She hadn't seen it coming. The lurker was there. She glimpsed him between the flaps of curtain, but she didn't holler for him to throw Danny out. After all, it was God kissing God, lips to lips, immaculate. And she had offered her sex. Like an ice cream cone on a summer day, she thought. As if she were the ice cream and the sun. It wasn't his fault. In his position, were Brett dancing for *her*, who was to say she wouldn't have done the same?

Still, she didn't offer herself to him again.

Three

IN THE DRESSING room, Brett was the only dancer left. Stevie could smell the musk of her sweat mixed with the sandalwood oil she wore. She was naked, her legs crossed at the ankles, her bare feet on the countertop as she counted her cash. Her breasts, small enough to fit in her hands, were as brown as the rest of her. Leaning back in the wooden chair, she seemed as comfortable topless as any man. Maybe she was part Egyptian, or Native American, thought Stevie, with her straight dark hair and her almond eyes.

"Hey, Stevie, walk out with me?" Brett grinned, Marlboro Red between her teeth, and struck a match.

"Sure," Stevie said. She was alone with Brett, she could say anything, and all she said was "Sure."

Brett turned, opened her locker. Her coccyx, Stevie saw, was worse than she'd remembered. The perpetual bruise, from her being so often on her back, was the size and color of a small plum. Stevie wanted to kiss it, to make it better, and at the thought, her heart began to race. Pulling on jeans and a small, thin, men's white T-shirt, she could feel her cheeks flush, though the mirror showed only a white mask. Under the cover of the makeup and powder, she found her voice.

"Mind if I bum a smoke?" she said.

"Go for it."

Stevie lit the cigarette. She'd been with women before, but they'd been the ones to make the first move. Brett had a boyfriend, one to whom she was engaged. He was young, a writer. And that was fine. After all, didn't she have Leo? No, she didn't want anything real with Brett. Just contact—taste and touch. She'd watched her for six months now, minus those months she'd been gone. Watched her bend at the waist and inch her G-string down her thighs, watched her spank her right cheek until it was crimson.

It wasn't so much what she did as how she did it. She moved like a cat, sprung, the tension of contraction in the taut muscles of her abdomen. On her knees she arched her back, her hair skimming her feet, her rib cage an altar for her open heart.

But it was her detachment that had fascinated Stevie from the first night she saw her dance, an aloofness Stevie aimed for, but could never quite achieve.

That night she had come to the club with Leo, as a customer, to see if she might work there. And she had worshipped Brett from their table at the back of the room. She had taken her last five dollars from her pocket and placed it on her stage. A token. And Brett had smiled down at her. Aphrodite, sending with her eyes a blessing—benevolence, light. Brett was above the club, beyond it—beyond the money and the men. And the bruises, on her knees and her tailbone, those places where she had touched the wooden stage floor—where gravity had pressed her body against it again and again—were proof of her night of work, proof that her body had, in fact, been here

at the Century Lounge. The bruises made her human, and all
the more beautiful.

Brett put on a Derby hat, jodhpurs, and boots, buttoned a
vest over her black bra. Stevie noticed the pendant hanging from
her black velvet choker between her collarbones—a silver crescent inlaid with stones. Before she could think, she took it in her
hand.

"I made it," Brett said. "I'm starting a company."

Some of the stones were the blue of deep ocean and some
were milky, mysterious.

"Lapis lazuli," she explained, "to help you remember your
dreams. And moonstone, for intuition and new beginnings."

"It's beautiful," said Stevie, letting it go.

Brett slung her bag over her shoulder, gave her hair a small
flip. She shone, as if with her own light, Stevie thought, as if she
were a star and paparazzi were waiting in the parking lot to catch
her in their flash.

Stevie unlatched the thick back door and together they pushed
it wide. She felt the night move through her in one clean gust.
The air seemed warmer than usual, and the moon surprised her
with its brightness. She'd missed the moon without knowing it.
Low cloud cover must have kept it from her. And now it was full,
and it made of the parking lot a lake. Walking on water, on air,
she felt giddy, and a little witchy.

They stopped midlake, between their two cars. It was perfect. She should kiss her right here, right now, while they were
wading in moonlight. Quick. She should catch her off guard.
Before Brett kissed her cheek and squeezed her arm, before she
turned. She felt her heart lurch, and she couldn't move, couldn't
cross the distance between them, between friendship and something else.

The moment was gone. She'd missed her chance. They were moving again; they were back in time. They kissed cheek to cheek. Brett squeezed her arm and disappeared into her old black Mercedes.

Stevie's own car, a silver Nissan—more of a dull gray, really, with its coating of dirt and city grime—was under the sign big as a billboard whose red letters read XXX LIVE NUDES!!! *Live* with a long *i*, as in live bait, in which you aren't rooting for the bait to outlive the predator fishes; no, you're appealing to the fishermen who want to catch a goddamn fish already. On Century Boulevard, the main drag to and from LAX, the sign attracted plenty of those hungry men with their empty lives.

Inside her car, she locked the doors and started the engine. Two quick lefts and she was heading north on the 405, windows down so she could feel the night. She loved driving the L.A. freeways late at night. It felt like flying. Past Arbor, Hillcrest, Manchester. She could take South La Cienega, a straight shot to Fairfax; but since it had streetlights, it was only worth taking when the freeway was slow. On the stereo, Bing was singing, *Would you like to swing on a star, carry moonbeams home in a jar, and be better off than you are, or would you rather be a—*

She turned it off. It was Leo's cassette. He'd left it in when he'd borrowed her car last.

And anyhow, she'd heard music all night long; now she wanted to listen to the wind. She wanted it to erase things, especially tonight. Tony's finger in her mouth, the boy's lips on her labia. She'd let things go too far. And it had been easy somehow, far too easy. She was slipping. She didn't recognize herself.

Come June it would be one year that she'd worked at the Century Lounge, and at the start she'd sworn she'd strip for a year, no more. To put herself through graduate school, to not yawn her life away in an eight-to-five desk job—filing—which was what she had been doing, to enter this world that had intrigued her, this other side of life, the underbelly. To fear nothing, to walk right up to the edge and peer into the depths. To know what she couldn't know without going there. She'd hoped this world would fuel her creativity, wake her up with its strange terrain, give her something compelling to write poems about and the time in which to write them. She'd had reasons and purpose and entered this life of a stripper with her head on straight, or so she'd thought.

But now the lines that marked what she would and would not do, the lines she'd drawn to keep herself safe in—and separate from—this other world were vanishing. It was like stepping into a dark room. After your eyes adjust, it's just a room. The shadows lighten and what had seemed to lurk there becomes familiar. And if the Century Lounge had become familiar, where would she then need to venture to find herself? How much further would she need to go to draw that exacting line and keep well enough behind it?

She exhaled her fears, let the wind take them. She imagined the night air combing the smoke from her hair, rinsing the salt from her skin. With each passing mile, she left further behind her the cave of eyes and music and the red light that cast the scene in unreality, made it all a dream she could wake up from. By the time she got home, to their apartment in the Miracle Mile, to Leo, she would be herself. She would be Gwen.

Gwen was quiet. She spent her time reading, filling notebooks with her inky scrawl. Gwen was faithful.

Stevie was an invention, sprung from Gwen's imagination. She was shameless, free as the sky, or death—those curtains that enclose us and that we cannot touch. Stevie did things that would make Gwen blush to watch, things that would mortify her, were she to dwell on them.

Stevie could turn her back on a man, and with a quick arch she had him. There. Turning around to stare him down, Stevie would cross her legs. He'd reach into his pocket, pull out his bulge of a wallet, float her a ten. She'd lean close, let her tits graze the metal bar between them, catching her breath as if he had been the one to touch her. She'd uncross her legs, and with a hand she'd open them. Tension. The leg resisting the hand. And her mouth open. Breathing in, she'd toss her head back. Another ten and she'd be on her back, arching, her knees up and spread.

The mound of Venus.

Stevie would do this for anyone who had cash. Gwen had created her for this very act. Before the man left the club, he'd scribble his number on a book of matches. Stevie would thank him, and Gwen would toss it in the nearest trash can.

But now there was Tony and his offer. A grand for dinner. Jesus.

She felt her breasts. Devotion was right—they were bigger. And they hurt. Her nipples felt sensitive, tingly.

Different.

Her heart quivered, and her mind was a dark expanse—as if she were beyond the earth and its draw, beyond oxygen. Floating, frozen. She'd never had a scare. Not like this.

What if she was pregnant?

Her face and hands were hot. They were burning.

But this sort of thing happened to people all the time. Didn't it? How many girls at the club had been worried when it was nothing?

She took a breath, let it go.

The sooner she bought the test, the sooner she'd know. The

sooner she'd be free. Yes. On her way home she'd stop at Jin's. Buy a goddamn test.

The 405 to the 10 East and off at Fairfax. The streets seemed quieter than usual, even for the middle of the night. The air was charged. As if, with a single match, it would explode.

But inside the charge, floating right through it, a sweetness laced the Los Angeles air. At first she couldn't place it. It was heavy, heady, as if from a dream. And then she knew. It was the smell of citrus blossoms—orange, grapefruit, lemon. The smell brought back her childhood in Phoenix, and an affection she'd stuffed in some dark chamber of her heart when she'd left town for good. The feeling evoked images—the long white Easter dresses of her young aunts, still in their teens, the dresses trailing the Bermuda grass in her grandparents' backyard, as her aunts walked barefoot past the white Victorian iron bench and chairs, past the swimming pool, past the grapefruit trees with their trunks painted white, their branches bent with fruit, and her own white dress a miniature of her mother's. Her mother with her long dark hair and her bare feet seemed breezy in this memory, happy holding Gwen's hand. Even her green eyes were laughing. The image had the feel of Super 8 film—jumpy, too quick, then slow, fuzzy, and without words. Perhaps it had been filmed—by her grandfather—and that was why she remembered it . . . this feeling of belonging, of being adored.

A block from their home, Gwen searched the street lined with cars for a parking spot. Nothing. Passing their apartment, she saw the light still on. One thirty in the morning, and Leo was awake, as usual. She should get him, so as not to walk home alone. He would want her to. But she had to buy the test—something he didn't need to know about. Not yet, at least.

Yes. She would find out on her own.

Three blocks away, she parked her car in the nice, predominantly Jewish neighborhood with houses and carports and no parking problem. Still, she didn't dare lock her car, didn't leave a single thing in it that could be stolen. She'd learned the hard way, found her car in the morning with its windows smashed and the lock on its trunk drilled out—her cassettes and her Walkman, her books of poetry and her Rollerblades gone. They'd even taken her journal.

The sidewalks were quiet. It was called the Miracle Mile, this section of town. Brand new in the thirties, the buildings were eclectic, each one different from the next. She passed a castle with turrets and stained-glass windows, a hacienda with wood beams and stucco and a red tile roof, an Italian villa—all of them tiny, fit to the size of their small lot, and all of them with barred windows, dark at this time of night.

She turned the corner and a loud bass of a voice rattled the night and made her stop. *Leave Earth, Leave Earth, Leave Earth, Leave Earth, Leave Earth.*

She crept in her sneakers toward the source of the booming, insistent chant—a man black as space at the street corner, directly in front of Jin's 24-Hour Mini-Mart and Donut. Jin's Joint, they called it. She could smell the just-fried old-fashioneds, their vanilla heat thickening the air.

Leave Earth, Leave Earth.

The man was dressed in layers—a T-shirt, a long-sleeved button-down shirt, a jacket, a knit cap. His bottom half was thick, too, as though his pants were doubled, and she wondered if he was wearing all he owned. His clothes were blackened. His skin was obsidian dulled by soot. His hair was matted black wool. His eyes did not seek her out, although she was all that moved, apart from the occasional car, in the world to which they seemed to be open.

Leave Earth, Leave Earth—his mantra, the mantra he shouted to no one in particular, to bird and to dog alike—*Leave Earth, Leave Earth.*

She would buy the test tomorrow. Along with an old-fashioned. Her feet moved in time to his beat as she passed, her gaze fixed further on, down the street.

A half block past him and she found herself chiming in as she jogged home. *Leave Earth, Leave Earth.*

Their brick Gothic building was just across Sixth Street, which was always empty at this hour, and yet she stopped at the red light, looked both ways for cops, before she dashed to the other side. She'd been frisked before, written a ticket for jaywalking at two in the morning, on an empty street.

She listened. The night was still again. Or was it? She heard the rhythm, the words, but she was unsure if the voice was his or hers—that incessant voice in her head now tuned to his channel.

Four

THEIR BUILDING WAS called the Cornell. The apartment
had been Leo's until she'd let her own studio go a month after
they'd met to move in with him and save money. In the thirties,
when the area was posh, Mae West had owned the Cornell, and
the third floor had housed a brothel that serviced the Brooklyn
Dodgers when they'd come to town.

Gwen pushed open the heavy iron gate. The courtyard
fountain dribbled past stone angels into the rectangular stone
pool, flickering with koi fish. She adored the courtyard. It was
what she'd first fallen in love with when she'd come to Leo's
apartment.

In the brick walls were windows open to the night. And between the windows in horizontal rows were faces of white stone.
There was the row of young sailors, schoolboys dressed in sailor
hats. Then, further up, the row of maidens presided, braids
framing each oval face. And way up at the top, the row of ho-
munculi rubbed their potbellies like African fertility gods. Over
the lobby's glass doors at the center of an archway was a man's
face—the face of a Viking, bearded, gaunt from his travels, a
poet Viking, purged of his lust for the world and with his heart

pure as the heart of a saint, looking for land from the prow of his ship and seeing an island shaped like a woman.

From one of the windows, a man peered down at her. "Lookin' fine, Gwendolyn," he called, mispronouncing her name, so it rhymed with *fine*. *Gwendo-line*. It was Barry sitting at his window, naked—at least from the waist up—and smoking. He was the son of the owner of the Cornell and he lived there for free. Leo had dubbed him Psycho Barry, since most nights he spent naked and alone, chain-smoking and talking to himself. Tonight, though, he was quiet. He must have taken his lithium.

"Hey, Barry," Gwen called up. "Get some sleep, you hear?"

"Yeah, yeah. Sleep is good. You like sleep? You like sleep, Gwendolyn?"

"I love sleep, Barry. Good night."

"Sleep tight, sleep tight, Gwendolyn. Don't let the bedbugs bite."

Unlocking the door, she could hear the news on the TV coming from their ground-floor apartment, echoing off the high brick walls, as if Leo had just cranked the volume. *Today in East Los Angeles, at the corner of Florence and Normandie, thirty-three-year-old Reginald Denny was pulled from his truck and beaten.*

She wasn't sure she could take it. Another night of news and ranting.

With a small key she opened their mailbox, along the wall with all the others. A few collection notices for Leo's long-ago maxed-out credit cards. And for her, a bill from her master's program. The second half of this semester's tuition, twenty-five hundred dollars, due in a couple of weeks. One more semester and she'd graduate. All without loans or money from her father. There was—*hallelujah*—a check for Leo, a residual check from some voice-over gig or other. And at the bottom of the stack was an invite to the AA meeting Greg, the manager of the Cornell, held in the lobby every day at noon. Even after Leo had told him to mind his own business, he still slipped an invite into their box on a weekly basis. Whenever Greg saw Leo, he'd tell him he was praying for him, to which Leo would retort that he was an atheist. These days, however, since they were late with their rent, Leo avoided him completely, exiting the building through the back door.

Walking down the hall, she flipped through the mail again. Nothing from the literary journals to which she'd sent her poems—three, four months ago.

She opened the door to the cloud of their apartment. It smelled like the good stuff. Might as well put the smoke to use. She took a deep breath and dropped her bag, went into the bathroom and started the bath.

When she'd first started stripping, Leo had drawn baths for her, warmed her towels in the oven and rubbed her dry. It had made her feel like a baby, loved for merely existing. Those were the nights she'd bought red wine and steaks, which he'd fried up with green onions. Those were the nights they'd feasted.

Sitting on the edge of the sofa, Leo exhaled, filling the room with more of the skunky-sweet smoke. His white Lhasa Apso, Fifi, was curled up beside him, snoring. Leo was wearing his white caftan, open at the neck, without anything on underneath. It was what he always wore these days, except when he was on the street corner dressed as a soldier from the Revolutionary War.

"I told you," said Leo, pointing at the television as if identifying the culprit. "Did I not tell you this would happen? Man, you could feel it. The unrest, the tension." He tugged at his beard. She stood a minute, taking him in.

He was as beautiful as he'd been when they met, maybe even more so, because he was freer. In their time together it was almost as if he'd become more himself. A riotous mane of curls, his brown hair was streaked with sun-bleached strands, as though he'd spent the day at the beach instead of on his street corner. His Mediterranean skin glowed in the TV light, the muscles in his neck and face flared with elation, and his hazel eyes were bright. She was struck by how like a child he was, bursting with life, even at this hour of the night. It made her realize how much her feet hurt. She slid off her shoes.

"Every generation needs a new revolution. Jefferson said that."

The wall behind him was covered with note cards. These were new, another scheme.

Gwen handed him the residual check along with the collection notices. He tossed the latter, still sealed, with their bold *Final Notice* warnings, into a waste bin in the corner of the room and tore the envelope with the check open. "Sixty-two fifty, not bad."

It wouldn't begin to cover what he owed in back rent, but at least it was something.

Gwen turned on the kitchen light and the cockroaches scattered. The sink was full of dishes. On the stove was a pot of bay leaf soup with garlic and eggs—Leo's daily fare, because at pennies a bowl it was what he could afford. In another pot was fettuccini Alfredo, a splurge—what he'd bought with the grocery money she'd given him.

She opened the cupboard, and more roaches scurried for the dark. One was longer than the rest, and it moved slower. Gwen saw the egg sac at the end of its body as she watched it flicker into a crevice. She took a mason jar and rinsed it as best she could in the full sink. In the refrigerator she found the water filter and poured the few drops that were left. She'd have to fill it. She'd have to wait.

On the counter sat the DustBuster, full of roaches. Live roaches. They were crawling its plastic sides, tracking it with their sticky black turds as they searched for escape. It was Leo's Relocation Program. He'd vacuum the roaches into the DustBuster, and when it was full he'd dump them, still alive, into the trash bin at the back of the Cornell. "Switch two letters in 'pest' and it becomes 'pets,'" he'd said just that morning. He refused to kill a single roach. For his compassion, Gwen loved and hated him.

She watched him pace the living room, pace the aisles of carpet foxed with dog piss, between the waist-high stacks of books and notebooks and newspapers, between the towers of his record collection and videocassettes. On the antique coffee table, the table he'd grown up with, his childhood drawings inked on its underside, there was the Ziploc bag of pot, the eye-shaped ashtray Gwen had made of clay, the purple bong.

Water pipe, the salesgirl had corrected. We don't sell bongs.

Gwen had thought it might be fun. Getting high now and then, watching movies. A way to relax. She didn't foresee how he would take to it, need it like a kite needs wind. High and higher. How far off the ground could he go?

She filled her jar with water, drank it down and filled it again.

"This is serious," Leo was saying. "Gwen, watch." He took her arm and sat her down. A black man was pulling a white man from his truck and beating him on the pavement, bashing his head with a cinder block. It had happened early that evening.

"It was the Rodney King trial. The bastard police that beat

him got off. All of them white, by the way. And now this. You can't hold a people down," Leo said, his eyes blazing.

How long had they been showing this? How long had Leo been watching?

Gwen's stomach turned. She felt sick. "Can we switch the channel?" she said, snatching the remote from the table and clicking.

"Damn it, Gwen." Leo took it from her, but on his way back to the news, he stopped on the Home Shopping Network. A woman turned her hand, and the ring on her finger sparkled in the studio light. A man was talking fast. If you called in the next five minutes you could purchase this ring for only $59.99.

Gwen watched Leo pick up the phone and dial. "What are you doing?"

His eyes shone. "My mama's always wanted a diamond."

"It's cubic zirconia."

"They say you can't tell the difference. But can I use your card?" he said. "I'll pay you back."

"What about rent?"

"This is important. My mom thinks I have a record deal. She believes in me."

He was standing on the sofa, bouncing up and down and wearing a hopeful smile, dimples and shiny teeth. She could hear her bathwater running. It had to be getting high. She tossed him her wallet.

In the bathroom, she closed the door that didn't lock, turned off the water and peed.

No blood. Not even a tinge in the toilet, and on the paper, nothing.

She wiped off her face—the creamy whitish base that made

her look like a china doll, the mascara, the eye shadow and the residual lipstick—with Luvs Baby Wipes, unscented. It took three towelettes, both sides, to get all of it. She washed her face five times with the good soap her father had given her at Christmas—the last time she'd been to Phoenix, her yearly two-day visit. She undressed, lit the blue devotional candles at the head of the bathtub and slid into the hot bath.

The purple-and-black art deco tiles around the tub were coming loose. A few had fallen off. Mildew spread from the faucet. The shower didn't work. And to the side of the window facing the street, the plaster was bubbling and the cream-colored paint was peeling off.

Leaning back, relaxing, she noticed faces in the peeled paint. In the candlelight they wavered, a circus scene. The thin male profile by the faucet had whispered something to the ringmaster, his face a twist of a smile. And, up in the corner, two girls were waiting—one with her eyes lowered, the other gazing out the window at the night.

What were they waiting for? If they didn't like the circus, why didn't they up and leave?

She closed her eyes and the bruises on both her knees were a vague ache that seemed, as she soaked, to spread over her whole limp body, as if to combat her apathy. To feel pain, she thought, was to be alive.

Leave Earth, the man had said. Maybe he was right. Maybe that was the answer.

She slid under the water and let her breath bubble up.

Isn't that the test?

When you think you want to kill yourself, you take a bath instead and, under the water, let go of all your air. You hear your heart in your ears. And then, you feel it—your survival instinct, alive and well in every cell, pushing you up. And by the time you take your next breath, you love the air that saves you.

It was the Count's philosophy. Worked every time.

Leo knocked once and opened the door. "The Count called." He held up the Ziploc. A few fuzzy green buds left. "He's out." It was no surprise the Count was up, too. He liked the nighttime best and, like Leo, had nowhere he had to be in the morning. "He asked if you were coming," Leo said. "He wants you to pay your respects."

"He's dying again tonight?" she asked, the water up to her chin. It happened once a month. He'd call in a state of fervent agitation, sure that night was his last, and Leo or Gwen or both of them would hold a bedside vigil until he fell asleep. And then he'd wake up the next day and somehow keep on living.

Leo shrugged. "He's dying, and he redecorated."

"What's the new theme?"

"It's a secret. He wants you to see it."

"I have to work tomorrow. I have to sleep," Gwen said. She ran her hands over her body—over her calves, between her legs, under her arms. Smooth enough to last through tomorrow. And anyhow, her razor was dull, she needed a new one.

Sure, she could go.

Leo didn't move. His eyes were distant, as if staring through her he could see a desert of sand he could walk and walk until he remembered and—"Leo?"

"Zero," he said, coming back.

She wouldn't ask him where he was. What it was he'd been thinking. She just didn't have the energy. "I'll meet you at the Count's," she said.

Leo left. She heard the door close behind him.

Why did it feel so good to be alone?

Alone, she could feel the world ebb, taking with it the boy's lips, Tony's hands, her swollen breasts and lack of a period, taking the fact of their being months late on the rent. Two, to be exact. She'd paid her half all along, but other than a few voice-over gigs, Leo hadn't worked in a year. She could pay his half. She had the money, but that was enabling his lifestyle, his choices. And wasn't she doing that already? Buying their groceries and paying the utilities, letting him borrow her car.

She unstopped the drain and the water swirled down it. Counterclockwise, slow. How had she come to be in—out of all the baths of Los Angeles, of the world—this one, the bath of the slipping art deco tiles, of the peeling paint and plaster circus men, the women in waiting? Watching the water whirl down the hair-clogged drain, she remembered. That first afternoon.

She lay back and closed her eyes. She used her heel to stop the drain, to keep the warm water a little longer around her.

SHE WAS SOMEONE else when she'd come to this apartment. Fresh out of college, in her cutoffs with the white eyelet trim she'd sewn by hand along the hem, her hair in a ponytail, a bag of sweet white corn in her arms. It was summer, the afternoon of the solar eclipse that was full in Baja California but only partial in Los Angeles, so that those who cared to caught the crescent sun in a shadow box, where it appeared no bigger than a baby's fingernail.

A phonograph played a young Pavarotti in *La Bohème*. The bedroom's manila curtains billowed in the open French windows and turned the light to sepia. She'd felt tired, tired of running— from actor to unemployed actor, from one audition to the next, from herself. She lay on the bed and he lay beside her.

He slid the elastic from her hair and took his time pulling his fingers through the thick mass, working out the tangles. His lips seemed softer even than the night before—their first kiss, by his car. And on the bed their kissing led to holding. In his arms, she had drifted.

The light through the curtains dimmed. They jumped from the bed. He made the shadow box from a shoe box and she cooked the corn, and armed with these they climbed the stairs to the roof, the sky cloudless but eerie, like a black-and-white dawn.

He peered into the eyehole at the end of their shadow box. She pressed her cheek to his smooth cheek. "Can you see it?" he said, letting her eye have the whole eyehole.

"What should I be seeing?"

"Here." He lifted her hair and the sun shone through the pin-hole beside the eyehole. "Can you see the crescent at the end of the box?"

She could see it. It was like a tiny moon; only it wasn't the moon but the sun, partially blocked by the moon and captured in this shoe box like an insect. Fragile, so easily extinguishable.

As the sun regained its strength, in his dusky living room, windows open, curtains drawn and flapping in the breeze, they threw clothing to the carpet—their shirts, her bra.

Her torso on the arm of the sofa, her nipples between his teeth, her body had warmed and woken. He kissed his way down her skin as if to learn every inch of her, as if she were a text to which he would return, as if she were scripture. He opened her cutoffs with his teeth, buttonhole by hole. He slid them off. Her white underwear was next, and halfway down her legs before she said, "We shouldn't. Not yet."

"We won't," he said, leaving her underwear at her knees as he unlaced her sneakers and slid them off with her socks. He held her foot and licked between her toes. He sucked them whole like hard candy. He licked a line up her leg and stopped, his upper lip so near her sex it touched that brown tuft of hair as he spoke. "You're exquisite," he said. There were tears in his eyes, in hers.

Sliding a finger inside her, he moved the way she imagined his cock might, its rhythm slow and even. His tongue touched where the tuft gave way to flesh and, finding its right place, began to flicker, as if smoothing some roughness. She closed her eyes, becoming the heat of his persistence.

She could feel the pillowy center of his upper lip where it puckered and pursed, could feel his saliva drip from her sex, over that silky barrier reef and down the other side. Its tickle made her self-conscious. He removed his finger and, seizing the slick opportunity, did what no one had ever done, what even she had never dared. The muscles of that other orifice tightened in defense. Yet, as he slid just a fingertip out and slowly in, she succumbed to the sensation and became simultaneously the bull's-eye and the arrow that pierces it.

Her first time—first orgasm with a boy anyway. Coming. It came down to trust.

He kissed her lips and she tasted Christmas—orange spice and pine.

Sweet white corn sustained their play for days, their private harvest.

Midnight. Leo's candlelit bedroom, French windows open to the courtyard, curtains drawn. Between his paisley-patterned sheets they were naked. Should they or shouldn't they? She'd hovered, with the question, over him.

They'd waited a week. It had seemed forever given the lust they felt, or was it love? They'd said as much. At least he had, on the sofa, her ear to his heart.

"I know it's crazy, so soon and all, but it's true and I have to say it or I'd be a liar."

"Do you? I think I—" The words had stuck. "Love—" She'd never said it, except to family. And looking into those hazel eyes that looked so unflinchingly back, she couldn't think of a single good reason not to say the words "you too."

But between the cool sheets, she couldn't trust herself. On top of him, naked, she was seeing ghosts. The ghosts of past lovers like vultures circled, their caws raucous, insidious. Here, where she ached to be filled not once, but again and again by the same man, they attacked, marked her with what she was: undeserving of more than a night, a week at most. Loved and left. Had there been one or two—but ten? Twenty? Who knew how many: men she'd been desperate to surrender to—her willing body like a white flag long raised before the battle had begun.

His voice was sweet as the strokes of his fingertips, brushing her hair from her forehead. "We don't have to."

"I want," she said. "I need you." And she sat on him further, all the way. A good fit. They stayed like that, swaying, like an anchored boat in a bay.

Still, the ghosts wouldn't leave.

"Tell me," he said.

"All the others," she said. He stiffened. "I'm afraid you won't want me in the morning."

"I want you for a hundred mornings, for a thousand, for as long as you want me."

Their boat capsized and he was on her. On a chain around his neck, the charm his grandmother had given him when he was baptized grazed Gwen's lips, rhythmically. The image was an angel, a gold boy with wings. She took it between her teeth, onto her tongue like communion.

The morning after, she woke to cool red rose petals falling in handfuls over her body, her face. He kissed her and left her to bask, returning with a bowl of deep reds and blues, berries. "Open your mouth," he said, kneeling next to her. And he placed the fruit on her tongue—raspberries, blueberries, their sour and sweet mingling as she swallowed.

Five

SHE PULLED HER heavy body from the tub, dried it with a thin towel. She took her toothbrush out of the Ziploc bag that protected it from the roaches and brushed.

She, too, could feel something coming. She turned up the lamp in the living room so she could see the note cards—read the writing on the wall. *Zero for President*, one said. Around it were cards on which Leo had drawn himself in his minuteman costume—from the front and the side. One in pencil, and one in ink—red and black. Another card read, *Agency of the Resident President's Program You. Join us and have the job of your dreams.* Amazing. How, exactly, was he planning on employing others when he wasn't employed himself? *THE JOB OF YOUR DREAMS* was in capitals.

His job—the one he'd hired himself for, the one he worked at incessantly, without any pay—was dreaming. All night. All day. Pipe dreams.

It had begun one Saturday morning when, polishing off the last of the week's quarter ounce, he decided he'd walk across America barefoot, without a penny in his pocket, to see if he could make it by depending solely on the kindness of strangers—a test for the Blanche DuBois theory of survival. As a trial walk, he headed to Venice Beach where, with blistered feet, he called for her to pick him up.

Or perhaps it'd started after he quit his job as set sitter on a sitcom, because he wanted to do more with his life. He'd been driving the youngest boy on *Growing Pains* to and from the set, and then hanging out in the dressing room, smoking pot and writing songs as they filmed. It wasn't much of a job, but it was a job. After months of not working, he went to the Catholic church around the corner from the Cornell and laid his past-due credit-card bills on the altar, asking the priest to forgive him his debts, like Jesus said. I can't do that, the priest had told him. Leo had turned and walked up the aisle, leaving the bills behind him. The priest had yelled for him to come back, but Leo had kept walking.

And now he was Zero, full-time. Zero is nothing, so it includes the all. When you give up possessions, said Leo, everything becomes yours. Zero is the Fool in the tarot deck, pictured as a young man holding a white rose, walking the cliff's edge, a little white dog yipping at his ankles, perhaps to keep him from stepping off the cliff, from falling. Gwen had told him this, and he'd thought the image perfect.

She dimmed the lamp, blew out the candles. It was a matter-of-fact action, blowing out the candles, an action not full of magic, as it had been when she was a kid and a grown-up let her blow the candles out after dinner, or before bed. She'd always made a wish first, in case it counted. She wondered what it was she'd wished for.

She put on a black silk slip that had belonged to her mother, the straps of which she'd stitched back on more times than she knew.

The Count's apartment was three flights up, on the top floor. She walked the dingy gray-carpeted halls in her slip and socks. It was after three in the morning. No one would be up but them. She rang his bell and yawned. Fifteen minutes, she told herself, a half hour at most.

After a glamorous wait, he unlatched the little barred window and stooped to look at her through the crisscrossed metal. His dark eyes looked larger than when last she'd seen him, and he wore a black turban on his head. He unlocked the door. "If it isn't the lovely Miss Gwendolyn. Glad you could come, kid." His speech was slow, methodical. Was it his body giving out, or was it alcohol? The smell of vodka clung to him like an atmosphere, medicinal, and so potent it made her eyes sting.

His aqua satin robe gleamed in the blue light of his hallway. He was walking with a cane. A curtain of red plastic beads from Chinatown made a cheap nostalgic music as he walked through it and she followed him into his bedroom.

Sinatra crooned from a radio made in the fifties. Candles lit the room. In his black silk pajamas and his robe, the Count lay back on his leopard bedspread and propped black satin pillows behind his back and head. An overflowing ashtray and pill bottles crowded the bedside table. Once her eyes adjusted to the low light, she saw that his room, formerly decorated like an old Hollywood-style screening room, was, indeed, transformed. The eye of Ra, big as a headboard, was painted in gold behind his bed. Protection in the afterlife. Beside it he had tacked a poster of Liz Taylor in a gold headdress.

"*Cleopatra*," he said, following her gaze. "Most expensive film of all time." He was breaking a bud into flakes in the open Zig-Zag. "You know how she died."

"Liz?"

"Liz? Heavens, no. Darling, don't give me a heart attack. Liz can't go before me. Cleopatra. She held a cobra to her breast and let it bite her. How gorgeous is that?"

The windows facing the alley, which he'd long ago painted black, had figures on them now, outlines in gold paint. One, Gwen knew, was Anubis, guard dog to the afterworld. The other was a man in a tunic holding a scepter.

"Anubis and . . ."

"Anhur. God of the sky. He led the way to heaven." The Count rolled the joint, licking the edge of the paper and twisting it closed. He rolled the tightest joints of anyone she knew.

"Behind you," he said. "I made those, too. Out of clay."

Pell-mell, across the top of a bookshelf, scarabs shone in the candlelight among other Egyptian trinkets—a tin sarcophagus, a pyramid of blue glass with *Luxor Hotel, Las Vegas* engraved on one side, a rubber sphinx key chain. Gwen picked up a scarab and held it to a candle. He'd shaped and etched the gray clay and painted it black. It was detailed. You could see the wings and the carapace. She closed it in her fist. Scarab beetles lay their eggs in dung—life from excrement, life everlasting.

"Take it," Valiant said, his face flickering. Even by the candle-light, she could see he'd grown thinner, and his dark skin was tighter, more—somehow—transparent. On his neck, just above his collarbone, a purple-black, dime-sized lesion had appeared. It was shaped like a kidney bean. When had that happened? How long had it been since she'd seen him? One week? Two? She looked away. She didn't want him to see her tears.

"Where's Leo?" she asked.

"Jin's Joint. For cigarettes and a little vodka. Will you do the honors?" he said, handing her the joint and the lighter.

What the hell. Maybe it would help her sleep.

Count Valiant wasn't really a count. And yet the title fit him. He had been, since Gwen had known him, self-proclaimed, self-explanatory.

He'd adopted the title in high school. He was tall and dark, dramatic, Leo said, the only black guy in a school of blond surfers. That was when Leo got to know him, doing the play *Guys and Dolls*. Playing the gambler Nathan Detroit, Valiant brought the house down. And when, by happenstance, Leo moved into the Cornell, Valiant took him under his wing, making him his driver and assistant and, in exchange, introducing him to what industry people he knew.

He'd worked then, Valiant had. Then, or before then, worked as a grip on music videos, which made him eligible for a small monthly supplement from the Actor's Fund, for industry people who were sick. She wasn't sure how he managed, but it was what he lived off of. That and a small allowance from his parents.

She'd known him as long as she'd known Leo, or almost. Leo had introduced them at the Los Angeles County Museum of Art, just up the street, in their permanent, contemporary collection, in front of a painting by Rothko called *White Center*. It was the Count's favorite painting. "Like a journey," he had said.

They'd stood across the room from the painting, she and Leo and Valiant. The bands of red—above and below the thick white line at the center of the canvas—reached out, like two arms, and pulled them toward it. The painting had a visceral effect on her. An unexpected heat wave, it had pressed on her skin from the inside out, like desire. At the end of the journey, close enough to touch the canvas, she, *they* were engulfed in the white center: a tunnel of absolution that swallowed them whole. Light without memory.

And then, because the Count wanted to, because he'd been

looking forward to it all month, they'd gone to the museum's theater for a double feature of seventies disaster flicks—*Earthquake* and *The Towering Inferno*. She endured *Earthquake*, endured the ridiculous plot, thanks to Charlton Heston's growl and grit and throbbing muscles. But when *The Towering Inferno* came on and the walls closed in and sweat beaded under her bangs, she knew another three hours was out of the question. She left the theater and Leo followed her, and the Count stayed for the movie and stewed.

She'd had the feeling he'd been jealous of her, of her abrupt appearance in their lives. Before she'd come on the scene, Leo had been his. When she'd asked Leo about the extent of their friendship, he'd been quiet. He'd blushed. "Well," he'd said, "it wasn't for the Count's lack of trying." But when she pressed the question, he insisted that nothing had happened between them, ever. They were friends. It was just—well, he'd said, the Count could be possessive.

After the movie episode, the Count had stayed away for a few weeks. When he'd come down to their apartment, he'd given her flowers he'd picked "midnight gardening" in the neighborhood, and since then, they'd been friends.

She handed him the lit joint.

"I hoped he'd be gone when you came," said the Count. "I've been worried."

"The whole Zero thing," she said, pulling a chair up to his bed.

"He thinks he can heal me. Like he's Jesus or something."

"Christ."

"Exactly." He laughed and his laugh turned to a hacking cough. His whole body shook with it. He reached for an empty glass.

Gwen took it and hurried for water. His kitchen sink was

filled to the brim with dishes stuck with grease and remnants of God knows what. A few weeks' worth, it looked like. And they were crawling with roaches. The Cornell was riddled with them. She held her breath and filled the glass with tap water—all he had—and returned to his bedside. She handed it to him, made certain he had it. He drank it down.

"You look like the Virgin Mary," he said.

"Olivia Hussey?"

"Those cheekbones. Lord."

She held his hand, warmed it in hers.

"I have a favor to ask you," he said.

"Anything."

He brought his other hand out from under the covers and touched her slip. Took the silk between his fingers and rubbed it as though assessing its worth. "Tell me how your mother died," he said. She felt her body tense. "You've told me, I know, but it was so, so lovely how you described her last moment, how you held her. Will you tell me, just one more time?"

"I may need one more hit."

"You don't have to if it's too hard," he said, passing her the joint.

"A bedtime story, huh?"

He nodded, pulled the covers up to his neck and closed his eyes.

He looked peaceful now. The lines in his thin face had smoothed and his body was spent and quiet. Like a child on the verge of sleep, she thought, not looking at the lesion, not thinking about it.

"Okay," she said. She took a deep drag off the joint, held it in and let it go. She would tell him something beautiful. "We were in the car. It was afternoon, a few days before Christmas."

"I love Christmas," he said.

"So did I." She gave him back the joint and said nothing.

"I'm sorry," he said, interrupting the silence.

"You want me to go on?"

"Please."

He'd broken the flow of her story, the one she told people if they asked, but she picked up where she'd left off. "It was a few days before Christmas," she said, and the rest came out in a seamless, practiced rush—this monologue she'd written for herself.

"We were at a stoplight, and we were laughing about something, and I looked up and saw this truck coming for us, fast, down the hill. It swerved around the cars on the other side of the light and veered and it nearly toppled sideways but didn't. Everything was slow motion. The truck was coming through the red light, the huge white truck was barreling toward us, but so slow we should have been able to move. I tried to speak. Time was folding, the world was swallowing itself, it was inside out, slow, and the cement truck with its big headlights was swerving, but not enough. My mother looked up and screamed and her scream made everything white. I reached for her. I pulled her to me, and we held each other. She was mine and I was hers and we wouldn't let go. Not ever. Her eyes were what I saw last."

"*Your* eyes were what *she* saw last."

"It was like some part of her entered me, for safety, and then there was the slow motion shattering of glass. And I put my hands up to block it. That was the only part of me that was hurt. That and my memory. I couldn't remember anything. Not for a very long time."

"God. To be taken like that, in one clean break. The fates snipping your thread without any warning. To go in the arms of your daughter." The Count opened his eyes. They were full of tears. "She knew you'd live, that you'd survive her. And if someone loves you that much, and misses you, it's like you don't really die, not all of you."

The bell rang. Leo had made it back. Valiant wiped his eyes with the sleeve of his robe. "Kid," he said. He gripped her hand and pulled her toward him, whispered in her ear. "You and Leo, you're lucky you have each other."

She kissed his forehead. It felt clammy, and he shivered. "Need anything else?"

He shook his head. "I have Leo."

He let go of her hand, crossed his arms over his chest, closed his eyes. For a moment he seemed not to move, not even to breathe, but then she heard his exhale, followed by a deep breath in. She saw her friend's chest rise and fall, and she forced herself to turn from him.

In the hall, she slowed and time slowed with her. The pot was coming on stronger now and it was good. Like being underwater, thirty feet under the sea, the kelp and the fish deliberate and dreamy.

It was true, what she had said, the part she'd tacked on, just now, to the end of her story. Her mother was with her. Some part of her—of her soul?—she could feel watching her, but from inside her own eyes. Or were they just shards of memory, coloring her vision?

She touched a photo Valiant had framed of himself. In black Ray-Ban sunglasses, a black jacket and a white shirt, his thick hair short and slicked back in the manner of his idols—Dean Martin, Sinatra, Sammy Davis Jr.—he smiled as if he knew something he might tell you if he felt like it. To his hairline he'd added a widow's peak using a black Sharpie. It was a gig poster.

Café Largo, May 10, 1990, two years ago already. *Count Valiant and the Midnight Strangers*, the poster said. *With the Go-Go Dancing Vacarro Sisters*. She had been one of them. Brenda Vacarro. She'd danced to Valiant's campy tune "She-Devil" in a short, tight black dress and black go-go boots, and Leo had played the keyboard. The Peruvian soprano Yma Sumac, so famous in the fifties, had happened to see the show and told him he had a velvet tongue. It was the last time Valiant had performed in public.

Beside it was the beach shot Leo had taken before she'd met them. Valiant in a G-string he'd fashioned of white gauze—Native American–style. The photo was from the front and showed his bare legs and chest. A long piece of gauze wrapped his ankles, his shoulders, and trailed off his outstretched arm toward the ocean behind him. He was looking back over his hand at the horizon, and the long black hair of his wig sent shadows across his face. His other hand was open, palm pressed to his heart. It was a gesture of farewell.

The bell rang again. Leo. She'd all but forgotten about him. She opened the door.

"Just what he needs," he said, taking the cigarettes and the half gallon of cheap vodka from the plastic bag.

"He's worse," she whispered.

"I know." He crumpled the bag in his fist. And then looking at her, really, for the first time tonight, he said, "You look like hell."

"It's been a long night." She stared back at him, hard.

"I miss you, Tink," he said.

It was his name for her, what he'd called her for years now, ever since she'd come home with her long hair gone, with her hair short as a boy's. Tink, as in Tinker Bell. Because she was sprightly, light as air, or stardust, because she was mischievous, devilish, because she had wings and could fly where she liked.

Because he was Peter Pan and they lived in Neverland. Because they belonged together, belonged to each other, but would not lay claim. Because it was the first movie they'd watched together—the play version, with Sandy Duncan as Peter. His all-time favorite.

Leo's bloodshot eyes, Gwen knew, were the same eyes she'd fallen in love with. She wanted to recognize him. The boy who'd said too soon *I love you*, and meant it. The boy with the soft lips and touch. The boy with the little dog, the white fluffy dog who bit. The boy who could play the piano and sing like an angel. The boy she'd believed she could be happy with.

"Did you see the Leave Earth guy?" she said.

"Who?"

"Guess he must have gone home," she said, and left the apartment.

The door opened behind her. "Tink?" Leo leaned into the hallway, and the gold angel on the chain around his neck glinted in the fluorescent light.

"Yes?"

"Dream of flying."

Six

GWEN WOKE TO a tickle on her arm she automatically swatted and smeared. Blood, wings, antennae. The roaches had made it to the bedroom.

She ran to the kitchen, washed her arm and hands with dish soap. The clock on the wall said 8:15. But it always said 8:15. Years ago it had ceased to be of relevance, a dead battery neither one of them had bothered to replace. Below the clock hung a calendar from the year they'd met, 1989. Featuring posters from the twenties and thirties, it was open to December, the image of a naked girl riding a peacock, her champagne glass lifted to the blue-black night and the stars. It was the most recent calendar they owned.

In the bedroom she checked the digital clock by her side of the bed: 9:20. Her alarm hadn't gone off, or else she'd forgotten to set it.

She'd be late for work. Even if she rushed, forty minutes wasn't enough time to get to the club. And there was the test. She could put it off no longer. The test. Thinking of it, her heart beat fast—she could feel it in her throat—and her head became light, and starry. She held the wall, took a deep breath, and got on with it. She could be a person in this world, she told herself. She could face whatever life had to give her.

She pulled on her jeans and the white T-shirt she'd worn the night before and stepped into her flip-flops. She filled her empty plastic bottle with good, cold water, took an apple from the kitchen table, and slipped them both into her purse.

Leo lay asleep on the sofa. He was dressed in his minuteman costume—black knickers, white ruffled shirt, and a black vest with gold buttons. He must have changed sometime during the night. The sign he'd fashioned out of cloth that read SONGS FOR THE ROAD HOME, $5 hung over the arm of the couch. Fifi slept on his chest.

Gwen kissed his forehead and he stirred. He cracked an eye. "You're leaving already?"

"I'm out the door."

"What kind of schedule is that?"

"I'm off tomorrow."

"Drop me?" said Leo, stretching.

On her way to the club, she could get him as far as Pico and Fairfax. From there, he could walk the additional blocks to his Century City street corner—where Pico meets Avenue of the Stars—where he would stand all day with his sign, his bag of tapes, and his smile. Hopeful, always hopeful.

He yawned and sat up, and Fifi rolled off him and onto the carpet. Tail wagging, she licked Gwen's ankles.

He'd have to take her out to pee. This meant ten minutes at the very least.

"I'll get the car and pick you up," Gwen said, purse and keys in hand.

From the top of a nearby stack of books, Leo took his tricor-nered hat and put it on. He tied his ponytail with a red ribbon and packed the bong with fresh dope. "You want some?"

"Ten minutes. Be ready," she said. Fifi at her heels, she opened the door. Taped to the back of it was a yellow *Pay or Quit* notice. She pulled it off, walked back in and stuck it to the bong.

"Shit," said Leo, and struck a match.

Turning too fast, she tripped over Fifi, who snarled, attacked Gwen's toes and, tail wagging, followed her back to the door. Gwen put her leash on. "I'll walk her on my way to the car," she said, and closed the door on the smoke.

Pay or Quit. She knew there had to be a poem in it. If there were ever time to write.

Fifi pulled on the leash to reach the base of an avocado tree, perfumed with what must have been an intricate bouquet of dog piss. Gwen let her sniff. What was another minute? This day would be like the last, and like the next. A blur of dollars and men, marijuana, and lights leaving their flickering spots in her eyes. It would be a day of fastening and unfastening, bending and straightening. At least she got to dance, she reasoned, even if the moves were calculated. Less inspiration than expiration. One long sigh. To say nothing of aspiration—the things she might have wanted. Once. All those dreams. The movies she'd star in before she was eighteen. The countries to which she'd travel. Like her mother, on the sets of films. The life she'd had before Gwen.

The tree in the tiny yard of the Spanish-style building was fruitless. Once, when it was laden with avocados, she and Leo had done some of their own midnight gardening. It had proved quite a harvest. She'd climbed the tree and thrown the green fruit down to him. They'd filled a pillowcase.

She tugged at Fifi and headed to Jin's. The street was quiet, most of the residents having gone off to work, and the day was balmy. The Santa Anas were blowing, and the air was dry and bitter, as if it were tinged with smoke. Maybe houses were burning in the canyons, unless it was the smog.

As she hurried down the sidewalk, she lifted her face to the sun, soaked it in. It made her think of the beach and lying on warm sand. It made her think of her mother, who had loved the ocean like no one else. Her mother had taught her how to bodysurf—how to push off the sand at just the right time, how to ride the wave all the way to shore, head down, arms out and hands fisted like Superman.

Gwen shortened the leash and walked into Jin's with Fifi beside her. Although dogs weren't allowed, she knew he wouldn't mind. He had a little crush on Gwen, and would throw in an extra donut now and then, or a free coffee, if he was careful to keep his distance from Fifi, who had snapped at him once and drawn blood.

"Morning, Jin."

"Miss Griffin." He was watching the news. Denny, the white man from the clip last night who'd had his skull bashed in by a cinder block, had been rushed to the hospital by a few black South Central residents who'd seen what was happening on their TV, got in their car, and picked him up. He was in ICU.

She scanned the pharmaceutical section, and her heart started up again, her stomach churned and her mouth went dry. There it was—First Response—between the Vagisil and the Monistat. One stick for thirteen bucks, or two for seventeen-fifty. Better to be sure.

She filled a large cup with coffee, and grabbed a Hershey's Special Dark bar of chocolate and a bag of almonds to make the purpose of her purchase less glaring. Setting the items on the counter, she felt her cheeks and hands grow hot, as if she were a child and she'd been caught stealing, or telling a lie. She searched her purse for cash.

A man poked his head in from the back room, pulling the thin brown curtain to the side, and she could smell the sweet grease in which donuts were born. He said something to Jin, in Korean she supposed.

"Jin," she said. "Could I have an old-fashioned, too?"

He took a bear claw from the case. She watched him put it in the bakery bag and didn't say anything. She liked bear claws, she told herself. The fried apples and the patches of gooey dough.

"Miss Griffin, my brother, Kim." Kim stepped toward her. He looked like Jin but much younger. She wondered if he was even twenty.

"Good to meet you, Kim," she said, and offered him her hand. He hesitated, but then took it in his, which was slight and limp and a little damp. He seemed gentle, like the boy the night before. He blushed, looking from her to the linoleum floor.

"Good to meet," he said in his thick accent, and went back to his donut making.

Jin rang her up distractedly. There had been looting last night, the news was saying, and other people had been attacked—people driving their cars, people running the stores.

"Why you live here, Miss Griffin?"

"In the Miracle Mile?"

"In this crazy city."

"Why do you?"

"Family."

"Yeah. Me too."

"You have family here?"

"No. I don't have any family here."

"I don't understand."

She slipped the almonds and the chocolate, the donut and the pregnancy test in her purse and sipped the black coffee. A little weak, but it would do. "I couldn't live in the same city with my family, Jin," she told him. She might have said *father* rather than family. They were the same thing.

His eyes lit up. "Oh, I see," he said. And she knew he didn't, not really, and there wasn't time to explain.

"You be careful," he said. And she promised.

In the car, she took a bite of the bear claw. It was good, but it was no old-fashioned. The clock read 9:45, and it was a few minutes slow. She'd be late for sure. She'd do her makeup on the way.

Leo was in front of the Cornell when she pulled up. He ran Fifi inside and jumped into the car, tricornered hat and all.

"We should let her go," he said.

"Let who go?" she said, stepping on the gas.

"Fifi."

"What? It's not like she's our maid or our secretary. We can't just let her go."

"I mean, let her go free. It isn't right. We shouldn't own animals. And decide for them whether or not they can procreate. It's barbaric."

"This isn't Mexico. If you let her go she'll get picked up by Animal Control and either get adopted by someone else or, more likely, since she's a biter, get put down."

Gwen drove fast and blew through two lights as they turned red. She handed him the donut.

"I'm not hungry," he said and took a bite. "God, what possessed you?" He took another bite and gave it back.

"It's your favorite," she said, holding it to his lips. He inhaled it.

"Witch," he muttered, mouth full. "You have water? I just need a sip." He reached into her bag, feeling for the bottle. Her heart lurched.

"On second thought," he said, and reached for her coffee.

He put the bag on the armrest between them. He hadn't seen. But then, he never looked through her purse. He didn't dare. It was a carpetbag affair, terrifying in breadth and density. Like a great mouth complete with teeth—pencils or hairbrushes with thin nylon bristles that pierced you under your fingernails, bare razors. Damn, she thought, she'd forgotten to buy a razor.

"Pick me up on your way home?" he said.

"It'll be six thirty, at least."

"That's fine."

"You have water? Food?"

"No."

"Cash?"

"You know I don't touch the stuff."

"But if someone gave you money for a tape?"

"I'm not an idiot, Gwen."

She searched her purse for a five and pressed it into his hand.

"Honest Abe," he said, and studied the face on the bill before putting it back in her purse.

"Leo—"

"Zero. Please." He tipped the front corner of his hat, grinned, and started singing, a sort of Middle Eastern chant. His voice was liquid, clear undulating blue, lit so you could see to its depths. It made the traffic stop and go rhythmic, made it flow, ebb and slap. The Mediterranean on an afternoon in October. They'd been there once. Made love on a hot smooth rock.

Put the trip on credit cards.

It seemed so long ago, like a dream. Greece and its empty

beaches. Folegandros, the island where she first had Leo in his sleep, took him as a real succubus would, on that cement dock at the beach with the long name, the furthest beach, the one that made the villagers smile when she and Leo had asked. "Livadaki?"

"Ah, Livadaki." They'd nodded knowingly, pointing in its direction, their smiles showing their missing teeth.

Leo was nude when he fell asleep. They'd skinny-dipped in the brisk sea and stretched out on the dock to dry. He was sleeping on his back, and she whispered to him, "Who am I?"

"You?" He'd laughed to himself. She'd touched him, lightly. And when he stiffened, she straddled and rode him.

"You like this, don't you," she teased.

"Yes," he said, under his breath.

"Who am I?" she said again, but he was beyond all talk, this thrust fast and needful. Unconscious of himself, Leo had been, for the first time with her, one with his hunger, his passive, pleasing mode a shadow.

She'd rolled off him, her knees red. He was still sleeping, the hint of a smile on his lips. At the top of the hill, an old Greek woman in a black dress, sidesaddle on her donkey, had stopped and was watching them. How long she'd been there, Gwen hadn't known. She imagined she'd seen everything.

Gwen had smiled and waved at her and dove into the sea. Her hands parted in a breaststroke, her legs kicked and closed. Under the water she opened her eyes, and swimming was like flight in dreams, how it makes you free and limitless. Leo was hers. In that moment—in which he'd trusted her completely, the way a child trusts his mother—she had the power, had that willful, girlish, stamp your foot, dance on the tabletop if you want to power. She had been charged with it.

Now she looked at him, in the passenger seat, lost in his own voice, singing with his eyes closed. She could take him anywhere and he wouldn't know it. She could get on the freeway and head west, till they hit the Pacific, and then veer north, up the coast. She had an aunt up there, in Santa Cruz—her mother's youngest sister, Sam, who lived with Loni, her partner. She'd told Gwen she was welcome anytime. They could stay with them awhile. Get out of the city, have a few days at the sea.

His chant gave way to "The Freedom Song." Her birthday present the first year they were together, it was her favorite of his songs. But the cars were moving too fast. She wanted to hear one verse at least before she let him out. He sang and she joined in, singing higher than him, harmonizing.

> *You gotta roam, darlin', to know you are free.*
> *You gotta roam, darlin', but if you come back to me,*
> *I'll be your new pair of sneakers,*
> *I'll be your old bicycle chain.*
> *I'll be your home, darlin', come back again.*

They were at his stop—the curb before the freeway on-ramp—and she pulled over, watched him open the door, step from her car, tap his hat onto his head so it would stay put in the breeze, and wave good-bye with his fingers—*toodle-do*—one at a time. She had to smile.

Seven

BY DAYLIGHT THE exterior of the club was something Gwen tried not to look at. Like a condom under the pier, or a beggar at a stoplight. It was made of cement blocks and was big and boxy as a warehouse. The white paint was peeling, showing Pepto-Bismol pink beneath. It was ugly—uglier because it aimed at ugliness, because the ugliness was itself an attraction. The club was, simply, ugly as sin.

But then, a club is a weapon. It's all about function. A heavy stick with a thick end. One good whack on the head will do the trick. Boom, down.

Men came to the club to feel the beat of the music in their blood, in their bones. To sit in the dark and watch.

Sometimes, dancing, she'd gaze at the field of men's faces and wonder. How many had planned to go there? How many had tried to drive home? How many had girlfriends, wives? Did they tell them where they'd been? Or did they lie?

These men came to the club to be someone else for an hour, to feel their heart beat in their chest as if they were nameless. To glow with anonymity in a place where anything could happen.

And then there were those men who were single, or at least

interested in more than a mere glimpse of flesh. There were the ones who gave her their cards: coffeehouse kid, artist, real-estate agent, M.D., executive loan officer, V.P. of a film company, attorney. What did these men want? Sex? Or love—a pill for their loneliness. Or were they mining, driven by the desire to bring something found in the dark (as if by feel) into the daylight, to see it sparkle in the sun?

It can't be done.

To make a fantasy real is to lose the fantasy.

"STEVIE," JOE SAID. "You're late."

"I know." She gave him her music—Tom Waits and Louis Armstrong. "Who's managing?"

"I am." He grinned. "You can make it up to me later."

She laughed. He said this to all the girls. Nothing ever came of it.

"You're up next set," he said, "if you can make it."

Brett was onstage—not naked—nude. Like the sign outside said. Stevie paused. To be naked was to be exposed, caught with your pants down. Nude implied awareness and intention. The ownership of one's own body that meant power.

Her legs just parting, her hand rising, she was indrawn, like the tide when it recedes, taking everything with it. Context and content, she asked nothing of anyone. Stevie tried to move, to move on, she had to change, she had to . . . But Brett stole her eyes and gave back beauty, reflected light and shadow—that line beneath her breast described just so when her hand reached high and her head turned toward her shoulder, as if to inhale the smell of powder, perfume, and sweat.

Her smell.

The club no more than the space around her, the scattered

customers, the smoke, a border for her exquisite sex, for her song, Brett looked down at herself, then up, to Stevie. Her eyes held hers, asking, *Do you see?*

Her labia. That smooth, soft cleft.

If labia are lips, then the cunt is a mouth, and a mouth shapes one's voice into words. In the beginning was the word—the word made flesh, in the cave where we each were formed. Even closed, labia sing the mystery of the source.

More than meets the eye. So much more.

The song was fading. Brett closed her legs.

In the dressing room, Stevie threw on the simplest costume she had—a dress, if you could call it that, with a stretchy black lace bodice and a skirt of gauze. Black satin G-string. She buckled her black heels. Pulled on her long black gloves.

Brett was off; Stevie was on.

They passed each other, Brett's hand brushing Stevie's thigh. She caught her breath, looked at Brett, her strong brown back.

There, on her backstage stoop, Devotion was blowing smoke rings in which circle of hell? Limbo, lust, gluttony? "Want some?" she said, angel of the haze.

"Not today," Stevie said, and she walked onto the stage straight.

It was just another dayshift. She could take it. She'd jazz things up with Louis.

She shook her hips and shoulders. She took the pole in hand and spun, the club a blur. Moving in circles, she felt like a kid. Moving to move, to whirl the brain and fall on the grass under the loopy stars.

Slowing, she could see Mr. Cooper in the gloaming, alone at a table, the coal of his cigarette a distant planet. So far off.

How we live and die alone. Vast reaches of lightlessness between us.

Her palms sliding down her thighs as if turning them out, she descended to a squat. Maybe she did need a little something. Just a puff. To fill the void with a bit of fire, of lift, a hot-air balloon to climb inside and ride out, over the sea. To catch the waning morning moon in a net of gauze and bring it back, before it was too late.

"Devotion," she said between songs, "I was wrong." She took the joint and sipped the smoke. She stepped out of her costume. Watching the fumes dance under the bare bulb, she could feel the dream returning. The poetry.

In the light again, she was Matilda waltzing to Waits's scratch and scrape, the song he wrote, so the story went, after drinking a bottle of rye on skid row, on a street corner, with men who were put there, all of them, by women, heartless women—men drinking their bottles of booze in brown paper bags. She liked the story, Waits on the street corner with the down-and-out rabble, and she liked the song—about what couldn't be. Not anymore.

Dancing, she moved as slowly as her body would move. In just her black satin gloves and her heels, she faced Mr. Cooper. She brought her arms up, over her head—her whole body stretching, reaching for what is always just beyond. And there, her hands clasped each other, clasped and pulled, hand from hand, her head back, her back arched—a tensed bow preparing to release. She looked at him, watched him watch her. He was her captive so long as she was lit, so long as the music played.

She wanted to burn herself into his future, wanted his memory of this moment to last him his lifetime—this and the next. She could feel the space between them measured in what time it would take to cross it, and she could feel the instant slipping like a stream, even as it happened, down the mountain.

And where was the camera? To seize the instant, to free it

from the slipstream of time? The lens and the eye on the other side, the eye that wants only to hold. To keep. Each photograph a shrine to the past.

It was how her mother saw things, wanting always to capture.

And her photos from the years before she'd had Gwen, when she'd lived in L.A. and worked in the movies, her photos of Steve McQueen and Jane Fonda, of Warren Beatty and Angie Dickinson, had been for Gwen's whole life boxed in the attic. When Gwen would ask her about it, she'd shrug. It was another life, she'd say. Pouring herself a glass of wine, lighting a cigarette, she'd return to her book, or just stare out the kitchen window at the prickly pear and the creosote, at the sagging power lines and the cool deck and the swimming pool—the prison paradise of her suburban life, what she'd settled for. But once, when Gwen had stayed home sick from school, they'd curled up on the couch and watched old movies together. *Rear Window, Breakfast at Tiffany's.* And her mother had brought down the big black box and dusted off its lid.

The main door of the Century Lounge opened and a flash of the L.A. glare entered the dim showroom along with another customer. *It's a battered old suitcase to a hotel someplace and a wound that will never heal,* Waits croaked. And she watched Mr. Cooper stub out his cigarette.

In the dressing room, Stevie took the test from her locker and tucked it into her moon purse. A few lockers down, in the back corner, Angel and Star whispered and laughed, passing a bottle of Jack between them. Stevie had tried to talk to them once. Hey, she'd said, and smiled. Hey, they'd said back, giggling and turning their backs to her. Since then, she'd held her distance. She figured they were, like her, in their midtwenties, and yet they were all edges, black eyeliner and leather, as if life were a fight. They danced to metal and kept to themselves.

In the opposite corner, near the mirror, Love swiveled on a stool, eating an apple and reading a paperback with the title *You Too, Can Be Prosperous.* Brett was applying lipstick with her fingertip. She cocked her head and assessed its effect. And Devotion was looking at her milkmaid body, brushing her pale Wisconsin hair. It was the golden hair of fairy tales. She could have been Rapunzel or Cinderella or Sleeping Beauty, thought Stevie. All those stories we were raised on, wherein the pluckless maiden is trapped, stuck in her station, until the prince comes along to save her. "I'm twenty-one. I can change," she was saying. "I want to move up north, raise my own crop of Indica, make some real money."

"I love it up north. It's so wild, and clean," Brett said, rubbing lipstick into her cheeks for color. "Santa Cruz is where I'm from. But my fiancé wants to stay here, for the industry. He wants to write movies."

"Santa Cruz? My aunt lives there," Stevie said. "It's beautiful."

Brett looked at her, but Love was talking, about the book she was reading. "Rereading," she said. "It's amazing. You can have anything. Anything you want enough. You have to focus, train your mind. I want to buy a condo, something in Malibu."

Joe poked his head in. "One of you might *want* to get out there."

Devotion bent over; ass to the mirror, she spread herself, checking for the string of her tampon. No green or white in sight, she pulled on a red thong, hooked on a red bra, and hustled out.

Stevie followed her into the showroom, wondering what it was *she* wanted. She knew what she didn't want. She didn't want to be here, at least not today. She didn't want to be pregnant. She didn't want to get old. And like Stevie Smith, she didn't want to marry. Not ever.

She sat down at Mr. Cooper's table.

"You were beautiful," he said, handing her a twenty. "Can I buy you a—?"

"Coffee," she said. "I need to wake up."

He looked as if he hadn't slept. He had deep circles under his eyes and his hands were shaking. "She didn't come home. And with the news last night. It isn't safe out there."

Was it ever? Stevie wondered, but kept the thought to herself. "You must be worried," she said.

The waitress stopped at the table and Mr. Cooper ordered the coffee.

Older, hair in a bun, dressed in a button-down shirt with an apron, she made a note on her pad. "Cream and sugar?" She was looking at Mr. Cooper. She'd worked here at least as long as Stevie, and they didn't know each other's names. That was how it was. The waitresses waited, the dancers danced, and the two didn't mix.

"Black is good. Thanks," Stevie said.

Why had she never bothered to learn her name? The waitress must have been in her fifties. Working in a strip joint by the airport. In her fifties. Stevie hadn't once seen her smile.

She shifted in her seat. She'd stay for the coffee. One cup. And then she'd excuse herself and head for the bathroom, where she'd pee on a stick and wait for her future to appear as if in a crystal ball.

"I wish she'd call," Mr. Cooper said. "Just to say where she is."

She looked toward the bar. The waitress was coming with her coffee.

And there he was. Tony. What was he doing here in the

morning? He was a night customer. She'd never seen him before dark.

She blew on her coffee to cool it. Mr. Cooper had his eyes closed, his chin resting in his hand. He jerked, falling awake.

"Tell me," he said, his dark eyes burning.

"You should go home. I bet she's called by now."

"You think?"

"Not if I can help it," she said and grinned.

He didn't laugh. Didn't even smile.

"The whole Zen thing, you know? Non-thought?" she said. But he was staring at Devotion. Stevie could see her tiny reflection in his glasses. In just her red thong she whipped around the pole, squeezing it with her thighs, her head back, her spill of hair red and lilac in the lights. *Here we are now, entertain us.* She writhed to the beat, her hips making a figure eight, tracing out eternity as she descended to a squat. A purist, she danced exclusively to Nirvana.

Stevie finished the coffee. "Mr. Cooper, good luck." She pushed in her chair.

He squinted at her, as if she were too close, too bright. "Hey. You too. It's not safe out there," he said and turned back to Devotion.

Tony was at his table, drinking his cranberry juice and club soda, waiting.

"I have to pee," she told him without stopping. "I'll be back."

"Good morning to you, too."

Eight

IN THE RESTROOM she ripped the box of the pregnancy test open. Her heart pounded on her rib cage as if trying to escape. She latched the metal door to the stall. Stick in hand, she hovered over the toilet and peed on it.

Three minutes. She had to wait three minutes. The clock on the wall had a second hand—handy at last.

She dried herself with the toilet paper, careful to make a clean swipe. Here at the club, you didn't want to leave even the smallest shred stuck to you. You had to be meticulous.

With her free hand, she pulled up her black G-string and unlatched the stall.

In the mirror, in the white fluorescent light, she was frightful. She frightened herself. She stared at the mask that passed, here, as her face. Under the pancake and the powder, under the wine-red lips and the mascara, was she there? Still?

She looked. Looked for Gwendolyn, the one from so long ago. She could just make her out, the ghost of her, of the girl with the freckles on her nose and the budding breasts, the girl

who had searched her own pupils—those endless black pools—
for clues, wondering what the future might bring.

Never had this come to mind.

And if her mother could see her now?

No, she wouldn't go there. She was too tired. She'd give in to
tremors, fissures. She'd lose her grip and fall. Dissolve into that
ocean that was always below, always inside her. Waiting.

Two minutes left.

She checked the stick. It was dry, but white. Like sand, or
sky, vast with possibility. She could travel the world. She'd save
her money. She'd finish her degree. And then she'd take a year.
Go to Paris, Rome, Lisbon. She'd sit in cafés and write. Maybe
she'd even dance. Why not? What on earth did she have to lose?

She thought of Leo. Out on Pico Boulevard with his tricornered hat and his sign.

It might have been different.

There had been Valiant's contact at Capitol—Frank
Phillips—who'd heard Leo sing one of his songs during Valiant's
show, who'd suggested he record on Valiant's leftover studio
time, who'd thought Capitol might bite. When it didn't, when
his album was shelved, when he waited for months, for years, for
something and for someone, waited like a dry gorge for rain, his
mind changed. They were full of shit. The whole industry—the
suited executives with their BMWs and their twenty-thousand-
dollar paintings on their office walls. Why should he send them
demos for free? Why grovel at their heels? He'd make them come
to him. Those Century City executives. They'd notice him on
their way to work. If he was consistent, he reasoned, eventually
they'd get curious; they'd stop.

One more minute.

The stick was still white. Like that bird. Like its belly and the undersides of its long wings. White with dark tips. What was it called? It was that seabird, the huge one, the one that was so rare—off the coast of California at least.

Albatross. That was it. Albatross. The word was soothing.

She thought of the barge she'd ridden once, the time she saw the albatross. Her father beside her, and her mother snapping the photo from behind. Her father wore a black leather jacket and jeans; his lit pipe held latakia, a spicy tobacco. She remembered the white cable-knit sweater she'd worn, how mysterious she felt, the hood over her head. They were on their way to Sausalito. She must have been eight or nine, because her father had his arm around her shoulders. He was leaning over her as they watched Sausalito take shape in the gray morning mist like some huge mammal coming up for air. And the albatross that had hovered over them for miles, hardly flapping its wings at all, impossibly light, turned and vanished into the fog.

That day her father had bought her a gold ring, her first. Fourteen karat. The thin band fit her ring finger and had at its center the skeleton of a butterfly. He'd slid it onto her finger in the shop and she'd felt grown up.

She liked the feel of it on her tongue, and, holding the butterfly between her teeth, she'd move the ring over her knuckle and back down. It became a habit. Watching *Gilligan's Island,* reading *The Secret Garden,* tucked into a corner of her bedroom writing a poem, she'd move the ring up, then down her finger. As if it would help her to disappear further. By the time she was twelve, she'd bitten off one of the wings.

Twenty seconds.

What do you get when you cross a griffin with an albatross?

Since that day she'd seen it, she, Gwendolyn Griffin, had felt a kinship with the big white marine bird, with its ability to glide and to roam. It was the loner she sometimes felt take her over, the desire to lose herself to the wind. But how did the two fit inside her, and where did they meet—griffin and albatross—her namesake and her urges?

A griffin—killer of horses, guardian of gold—is fierce. With its head and wings of an eagle, with its body of a lion, it is king of air and land. An albatross, on the other hand, is a wanderer, feeding far out at sea. To the ships over which it might hover, it is, according to legend, the harbinger of bad weather, continuous bad weather so long as it stays. Kill an albatross, however, and the bad luck is yours to keep. Her father had told her this, that day the bird had appeared out of the mist and floated like a guardian above them, but Gwen couldn't think of the bird as a dark omen. To her it meant freedom, solitude, beauty.

Still, if there was a moral to the story—the one that was her life and what it had become—it would have to be weather the storm and don't cross a griffin with an albatross. You can't both guard and wander.

Gwendolyn Griffin, in the wide, wide blue, where is your gold?

It was time she looked.

The stick was no longer white. The stick was blushing. There was the pink bar, the test bar, and then, above it, there it was. The second pink line.

She froze. Holding the stick, she was hovering, behind her own shoulder, watching herself hold the stick, watching herself absorb its meaning. She was more, more than herself. According to this stick, she was plus one.

Or was she? These tests weren't infallible. She still had a one percent chance. Maybe her chemistry was funky. She'd try the next stick tomorrow. First thing in the morning.

Who was she kidding?

She pulled the second stick from the box.

Nine

ACROSS FROM TONY her tart red juice and soda was waiting for her. She sipped it through the straw and didn't stop until, at the bottom of the ice, she reached air. She sat back. "I'm pregnant."

He stared at her, set his drink down. "You're sure?" He leaned back in his chair, as if to view her at full length, to take her into consideration holistically, as one might assess the value of a house. Location, lot size, roof, flooring, square footage, plumbing, it all mattered. It all added up.

She sucked an ice cube, chewed it.

She knew when it had happened—the sowing of the seed. Leo had been asleep on the couch in his long red coat, in his vest and white shirt and knickers, his buckle shoes and tricornered hat on the carpet. She'd come home from dancing and found him like that. So she'd played the succubus, unbuttoning his knickers and taking him in his sleep—something she hadn't done in more than a year. Asleep, he was hers. Whispering in his ear, pulling her fingertips over his body, she entered his dream. "Who am I?" she had said, sitting down on him. He laughed. "Don't you know?" In his dreams, she had another face, another body. She was clothed in his fantasies. In that moment, she had loved him without reserve. Inside her and asleep, he was vulnerable and transparent. He was beautiful. And she got carried away. When he tried to lift her from his hips—their routine so ingrained he did it even in his sleep—she stayed on him, one second too long as he came.

Tony's blue eyes were on her. He was waiting for her answer.

"I'm sure," she told him.

"So. What will you do?"

She shrugged. She shouldn't have told him. She wasn't ready to field questions. She had no idea what she'd do.

"You could have whoever you want right now. Think about it. Leo's a musician. How will he support a family? Besides, you're getting your master's and he—does he even have a college degree? You're going up and up and where is he going?"

"You sound like my father."

His eyes narrowed, pinning her down. "Do you even want a family? How will you write with a baby?"

He had a point. And here, he differed from her father, who had never understood her desire to write. When she was a child of five, it was her mother she'd dictated her poems to, and, later, when she could read, her mother had been the one to buy her books. Emily Dickinson and Edna St. Vincent Millay, Elizabeth Browning and Elizabeth Bishop and Stevie Smith—all of them, it occurred to her now, women who hadn't had children.

She put a hand on her navel. "An abortion seems too awful."

"It's nothing. You do it. It's over. You move on."

Brett was dancing again.

The song was Leonard Cohen. His growl speaking just to Stevie. *If you want a father for your child, or only want to walk with me a while across the sand, I'm your man.* She knew Leo wouldn't leave her, not ever. But what sort of father would he make? The opposite of her own father, married, for his whole life, to his law practice. Gone early, home late. His best friend his bottle of Glenlivet.

She watched Brett strut the rim of the stage, watched the five men scoot their chairs in and sit at attention, staring up at her— Lady Brett Ashley—this Aphrodite for the nineties. Her tight curves androgynous. She moved in esses, slow as that hidden snake around her arm might move through hot sand. Brett bent at the waist, hooked her black G-string with her thumbs as if to slide it over her hips and down.

G-string—the lowest string on a violin, which, when struck, would make the whole body of the instrument hum.

One of the men reached into his pocket, put more money on the stage. She strolled his way, let him be the one to take her in. Her G-string over her thighs, over her straight knees, her head between her legs, she watched him stare.

Posing, pausing, she possessed. She stopped time, luminous. And the man with his drum of a heart—in her, the man was caught, his desire the measure of her power, the wall of air and space between them palpable. She was the goddess incarnate, right here in the Century Lounge, more mysterious because he could not touch. Her salt-smell so close, Stevie could feel him lick his lips.

She'd be up next.

"I have to go," she said to Tony.

"Say you're sick. Have lunch with me."

So that was why he had come to the club so early.

He stood when she did. Avuncular Tony. Quiet and kind and

solitary. He looked bewildered, as if, with her being pregnant, he'd lost what had defined him.

She kissed him on the cheek. "I'll think about it."

Behind the red curtain, waiting for her song, Stevie sat in one of the folding metal chairs in front of the mirror, watching Devotion dot cover-up on Love's ass. Love held the back of a chair, her long black hair spilling over it and onto the seat. "We got tired of the L.A. club scene," she was saying in her throaty southern drawl. "There's the Roxy. So fucking pretentious. Or the Whisky with the rockers. It never was my thing, but Linda likes to go out. So we tried Club Fuck. No one makes you do what you don't want to."

Stevie reapplied her lipstick. Wine-dark. Like Homer's sea. She blotted her lips on her hand. The scene in the mirror—Love and Devotion—felt far away. It felt two-dimensional, like a film she was watching—as though this time in her life were already a memory.

"Last night was a body piercing," said Love. "They shaved this girl's head and stuck needles in it."

Devotion took a few steps back, eyeing Love's ass as a makeup artist would. "Were they sterilized?"

"Lord, you'd hope so. Then Linda—she's my husband—she whipped me with a knobby whip. She's the only one I would trust to do that."

"Your husband?" said Devotion, backing up still further to better assess Love's ass.

"When her name was Dan we used to fuck. Now we're just girlfriends. She's on hormones, had her boobs done, but she has to wait a year before they'll lop it off. Lord, she was handsome."

Love arched her back as Devotion brushed her ass with

powder—that final layer, to set the makeup, to catch the light and, thereby, to define the line, the shadow trailing the curve. She dusted off the excess, and the cloud that filled the room was the essence of theater.

Theater, what Stevie had thought she'd wanted. The reason she'd come to this city. To act. To break into the cruelest profession—break into, as if it were glassed in, like a jewel case she wanted to live inside—to be seen, to be valued, to know her worth, to become what her mother had been—a success.

"What do you think, Stevie?" Devotion asked. Love's bruises were the color and size of blackberries, sugared for baking.

"They look all right, but do they hurt?"

Love tossed her head back, filling the room with its just-washed smell. She checked her ass in the mirror. "They look worse than they feel," she said.

Watching her step into the red glow of the showroom, Stevie wished she could, like Love, feel something, anything. She wanted a bruise she could push on, some tender spot to know she was alive. She'd have slapped her own face if Devotion weren't in the room.

Devotion took her Altoids tin from a crack in the wall and rolled a joint. "What's that guy's name? The bald guy you dance for?"

"Tony?" Stevie slipped her shoes off and stretched her feet. She drank from her bottle of water.

"Yeah. Don't you think he's sexy? I love bald men. Do you think they shave or use Nair? You know, to get that smooth, shiny look?" She lit her joint, puffed and contemplated. "Unless Nair would give them brain damage," she said on her exhale.

Stevie laughed, choking and spitting up the water.

"You look like shit," Devotion said.

"Yeah?" Stevie said. "I'm pregnant."

It helped to say it out loud. Pregnant. With one word, the reality of her situation took on a vibration. It resonated in her chest, her throat. Pregnant, pregnant. Its rhythm trochaic. Approaching footfall. The long *a* sound—pray—what she would have to do. And then the *g* and the *n* smack in the middle. The *g* was sexy, as in G-spot, or G-string. *G*, a grand. What Tony would pay her to have lunch with him. And *n* for negative. What she wasn't. She was not *not* pregnant. At the tail end of the word came the *ant*—how small she wished she could become. So she could hide from even herself.

Devotion took a hit. "Pregnant? I didn't know you had a guy."

"I do. Sort of."

"I guess you don't want this." She stubbed out the joint, closed it in the Altoids tin and stashed the tin in the wall.

Brett stepped in from the stage, cash in her fist. She wiped the sweat from her forehead with her wrist.

"Stevie's pregnant," said Devotion, moving for the door, as if her condition were contagious.

She felt her chest constrict. No, she thought. Gwen is the one who's pregnant.

Stevie? Gwen? Who was she? She could feel the walls crumbling, feel her mask slip. She thought she might cry. She hadn't wanted Brett to know, as if her being pregnant would disappoint her somehow.

Brett didn't look at her. Gwen thought she saw her jaw tighten. "No shit," Brett said, and put her feet on the counter and counted her take—ones, a few fives. She added it to the wad of twenties in her purse.

Louis Armstrong was playing and the stage was empty, but Stevie took her time strapping her shoes on. They were alone, and Brett was going to say something. Stevie could tell.

Brett looked at her in the mirror. It was safer that way.

"I was pregnant. A few years ago. It was my boyfriend's baby."

Brett glossed her lips with her finger. Her look hardened.

"You can't write with a baby. And he's a writer. A good one." She swallowed. "You have to starve for a while."

Ten

CENTER STAGE, STEVIE closed her eyes, moved by feel. With Brett's income, they weren't starving, even if he was a full-time writer. Did that mean Brett was supporting him? Waiting for him to sell a novel, a screenplay before she quit? The thought angered her. It was what she'd been doing—supporting Leo. Waiting for something to change. She was used to compromise, she reasoned. But Brett? Brett was too beautiful for that.

Stevie could feel the warmth of the lights on her shoulders, on her face and her chest. The lights were the sun. She was dancing on a beach somewhere. Mexico. Brazil. She could smell the ocean, feel a slow breeze in her hair.

Her eyes opened, and beyond the lights, there was nothing. There was smoke and shadow. She was the show and where she wanted to be was anywhere but here. The four-inch heels, the black lace and gauze didn't fit this dance. She pulled off the costume, pulled her G-string off Brett-style, slow and easy. Holding on to the pole, she slid off her shoes.

She wore nothing, not pearls, not shoes. There was a new thrill in this, a new edge. Her heart in her ears became the rhythm, the pulse of the showroom.

Showrooms are used to sell new cars and boats, new sofas and entertainment systems. What it is we're supposed to want. The lot of us. To go *zoom-zoom*. To lie about in comfort, all we could desire within the reach of our fingertips. Here, it was girl flesh on display—rosy, ripe. Not to take home and call your own, but to watch and to want, so long as the music played. Here, desire itself was for sale.

The stage, she knew, dancing in her bare feet, was just that—a stage one passes through. How long did she have, even without this baby? How long could she play the girl? The breezy, unattainable object of desire.

She watched Tony follow Love to a private dance booth—the corner booth. Their booth, Stevie's and his.

So, Stevie thought, now that she was spoiled goods, he was done with her. She took her breasts in her hands. Her swollen breasts that would continue to swell, that would feed if she let her body have its way, if she let it take her like a tide to some far shore.

Around and around the pole. Such quick revolutions.

In another year, in two, would she still be here? Dancing with abandon? *Abandon*—that pasty, diaphanous partner who would always leave her ample room to give herself to whichever song happened to be on and to whichever eyes happened to be watching, that partner who would never lay claim.

Don't forget our Monday date that you promised me last Tuesday, Armstrong sang. And then there was silence. The room was silent and dark.

"Power's out," she heard Joe say through the open window of his booth.

And Love's voice from behind the curtain of the dance booth where she and Tony were having their time, her southern drawl never so appropriate. "My pussy got so hot it must have blown a fuse."

She could hear Tony's dry laugh. Tony, whose money she didn't need.

Alone in the dark, she laughed at herself. What right did she have to be jealous? He was her customer, her regular. That was the extent of their relationship. She danced for other men, and he was free to watch other girls.

It was a line she'd walked with Leo when she'd first started dancing. Then he'd played her dresser, washing her costumes, her makeup artist, applying the thick white base, the eyeliner at the outer edges of her eyes to make them look big. He'd been her chauffeur, driving her to and from the club, and her cook, with a meal on the table when she was off work, even at two in the morning. For this, she had paid for him to get into the club, and she'd given him money to tip her. It was when he tipped other girls with her money that he crossed the line. Would it have made a difference, she still wondered, if the money had been his rather than hers? His point had been that if she could dance for other men, he could tip other girls. *Yes, but not with my money*, she had insisted. He hadn't seen how, were the money his own, it would have changed anything. *Now you know how it feels*, he had said on their way home that night, giving the words time to sink in, time to sting.

After that, she told him she could drive herself to the club.

She picked her shoes and costume off the floor and slipped through the curtain. No point in being onstage without music and lights.

In the dark hall, Devotion was on the pay phone. "Okay. Okay," she said, and hung up.

She turned to Stevie, her face close and pale. "Riots. There are riots all over the city. We have to get out of here. I promised my mom."

"Riots?" Stevie said, thinking she misheard.

"Riots."

What, exactly, did she mean? Stevie wondered. Riots? What were riots? There had been the Watts Riots. She'd seen photos of them—burning buildings and cars and people flooding the streets, throwing bricks through store windows, looting, and the military with their rifles. But that was so long ago. That was the sixties, when people were fighting for what mattered, for civil rights and getting out of Vietnam. That was before the eighties, before the glam rock bands with their flowing hair and vapid lyrics, before shoulder pads and thick gold chains, before the world turned apathetic and shallow.

No. She couldn't mean riots. Not those kinds of riots.

She saw Devotion throwing her clothes from her locker into her bag.

"You're leaving?" Stevie said.

"Fuck yeah. Aren't you?"

"I guess. Should we tell Joe?"

"Tell him if you want to; I'm splitting this dump."

Stevie opened her locker and put on her jeans, her T-shirt, and her flip-flops. If there really were riots, she'd have to find Leo. He'd be on the streets; he'd need a ride home.

Joe was in his office, messing with the switches, looking for power. "What the hell," he said, making out her street clothes in the dark.

"Devotion's leaving, too. She says there are riots. It isn't safe."

On her way to the dressing room, Tony caught her arm. "Hey," he said. "What's going on?"

"Riots. They're everywhere, I guess. I'm going home."

"You should come with me," said Tony, holding her arm, not letting her go. "It'll be safer in the marina."

"I have to pick up Leo. He's out there without a car."

"Be safe," he said. In the dark, he pulled her close and, before she could turn her head, he pressed his thin lips to hers. She felt a surge, warmth, wetness between her legs. How long since she'd been kissed on the lips by anyone? She and Leo hadn't touched in weeks. Even close-lipped, the kiss felt intimate. And she didn't mind.

"See ya, Tony," she said, turning, feeling his eyes on her as she walked.

Backstage, she grabbed her purse and her almost empty bottle of water.

Brett was dressed. She wore her Derby hat, had her bag over her shoulder. "You coming?" she said. Her arm was akimbo, her head cocked.

In the cool, dim room it was the two of them. Stevie wanted to grab her arm, the way Tony had grabbed hers. She wanted to pull her in and kiss her on her lips. Lightly. Barely. The way girls kiss. If she were a guy, she'd do it. Do it now. She wouldn't just think it. She'd act. But they were walking, too fast. They were almost at the door.

"Brett," she said.

Brett stopped and faced her. "Yes?"

"I'm glad you're back."

Brett smiled at her. A sly smile. Her eyes danced. Stevie felt a wave of heat move through her; she felt her face burn.

They pushed the back door open to greenish, smoke-filled skies. At the gas station across the street, cars were lined up down the block. And the cars that weren't in line were speeding down Century Boulevard. She had, she thought, a fourth of a tank of gas, certainly enough to get her home.

"How far you going?" she asked Brett.

"Silver Lake," Brett said, pulling the front of her hat down, ready for anything. "You?"

"Miracle Mile."

Stevie leaned in to kiss her cheek, and Brett took her in her arms and pressed her tight. Stevie breathed her in—Brett's chest and neck and hair, her smell. In Brett's arms, she felt small and, for that instant, safe. If ever she could stop time, it would be now. This would be the moment she would choose, she thought.

And then Brett let go. And they were in their separate cars. They were moving into the river of traffic, becoming two of many.

Eleven

THE 405 WAS moving—not fast, but it was moving. She passed Arbor, Hillcrest, Manchester. Her window rolled down, she felt the hot breeze messing with her hair. Maybe things weren't as bad as Devotion had thought. Maybe she'd drive straight to Pico and pick Leo up and it'd be just like any other day, only they'd have time at home, together, like in the old days. Time to talk and play music and write. And if they had time, maybe she'd tell him.

The freeway was moving, and then it wasn't.

In their cars, the people looked straight ahead. Sitting ducks, no one would risk interaction, the wrong sort of look that might draw the wrong sort of attention. They had their windows rolled up, air-conditioning on. White noise. And over it, Gwen imagined, their radios issued warnings—which routes not to take. How to play it safe. Sit tight, and everything would be fine. Everything would stay as it had been. No broken jaw and arms and ribs. No bricks bashed into your skull.

South La Cienega was empty to her right, a few cars veering off the freeway down it. If she took it, she'd have further to drive up Pico to find Leo, but if it was moving, it was worth a try. She should check the radio, know what those helicopters flying low over her head knew—where the riots were in full swing, where you didn't want to be. But her car didn't have an antenna so the radio wasn't an option.

As far up the freeway as she could see the cars were inching. And the cloudless sky had darkened from absinthe to a dull gray-green in the time she'd sat in her car, deciding. She was creeping ahead, and in a minute she'd be past the exit. In a minute, she'd be stuck. If cars were taking South La Cienega, it couldn't be that bad. The section of town it traversed wasn't the best. She knew that much. It was run-down, and while prices were a few cents lower at the Arco she passed on a regular basis, she never felt comfortable stopping there for gas. The street—a thorough-fare, a freeway substitute—was a means of getting to and from. And it was open.

Fuck it. It was worth a try.

She pulled into the right-hand lane and put the gas pedal to the floor. She could smell smoke, and as if speed would help her escape it, she drove faster, down South La Cienega, past the hills and the metal oil pumps that always reminded her—with their long, slow necks rising and falling—of dinosaurs drinking water, what were they called, brachiosaurs? She drove past the fields of clover and mustard—fields—as if from another time, so green and yellow, so open. Past the cemetery, through green lights and into the outskirts of neighborhoods, past dollar stores, pawn and gun shops and places for payday loans, to where the river of traffic grew turgid, to where the smoke was thick and then thicker, the black smoke, and she was stopped, trapped, cars in front of her, cars behind her, and on the other side of the street, not two lanes away, the gas station was on fire. The Arco station she'd driven past a hundred times was sending its massive smoke signal to the sky. She could hear what sounded like distant screams.

At first, she wasn't sure what she was seeing. Hundreds of people were on a street where there should have been only cars. People were running across the street, between the stopped cars, *toward* the flames. It took her a moment to understand. Through the smoke, behind the gas station, was a Kmart. And the people running toward it were men—black men—in groups of five, six, seven. On the sidewalk, other men, white men, were walking with their video cameras that read NBC, ABC, CBS. They were recording everything—the looters, the flames, the traffic, the black air. This was news. People across the country—hell, all over the world—would want to watch this; with a bag of potato chips, they'd prop their feet on the coffee table, open a Coke and settle in.

Here she was, in the middle of a full-blown riot. Her attempt to avoid it had landed her a front seat at the spectacle.

She looked in the rearview mirror at the car behind her, an old blue Pontiac. Four black teenagers, looking ready to fight, filled it with the power of youth and rage. They were wearing muscle shirts and had the muscles to go with them. They were sweating, waiting for the perfect moment to jump from the car and join the action. The one in the passenger seat—who looked the youngest, all of sixteen—gripped a baseball bat.

She rolled up her windows and locked her doors. She went to put the inside air on—her car had no air-conditioning, but at least she could keep the smoke out, or try to—and her hand was so shaky she turned the tape deck on, too, and Bing was singing. *Would you rather be a fish? A fish won't do anything but swim in a brook. He can't write his name or read a book. To fool the people is his only thought.* Yes. Without a doubt. She would rather be a fish. A pig. A monkey. Anything but a human.

She turned it off. She had to concentrate.

Where were the police? The fire engines?

The line of cars ahead was backed up as far as she could see and the black smoke from the flaming gas station was a wave, an ocean she was under.

And she'd never felt so white.

Yet she was part Latina. One-fourth, to be exact, from her mother's mother, Carlotta, from Globe, Arizona, a dancer with fire in her blood. But no one would ever guess Gwen's ancestry. Her skin was pale, the majority of her ancestors having come from England, that cold, damp, dismal island, breeder of consumption, of whalers, and of slave traders.

Her right foot shook as it pressed on the brake. Drinking the last from her bottle of water, she spilled most of it down her shirt.

This, she realized, was anger. Manifested, en masse. She was surrounded by it, stuck inside it. Nothing to do but feel the heat, watch the flames spread and rise. Anger. It was the emotion Gwen had the hardest time feeling. Even when she'd acted, it had evaded her, like a memory just beyond her reach. She longed to feel it percolate inside her, to feel it seize her, as it did in her dreams, when it was Leo at whom her anger was aimed. *Get a job. Make it happen—something, anything. Stop smoking so much goddamn pot.* She longed to close her hand into a fist and punch. To bloody a nose, make a mouth swell. If she were angry right now, her leg wouldn't be shaking. And if she were black, she'd be angry all right. She'd be indignant. Out to take the city, to take what had been denied.

She wished her skin were black, and then she realized that not once had she wished this before. She remembered, as a child, having felt somehow fortunate, and also guilty, to have been born white, to have the world open to her, like the door to some invitation-only affair. And that was the seventies. Martin Luther King had triumphed. And there were those who, still alive, had transcended the oppression, the hate, and the fear and were beacons for all. *The Jeffersons* was on nighttime television, and there were the Jackson 5 and Donna Summer and the Pointer Sisters and all of those black ballplayers, but in that north-central section of Phoenix, the African Americans she'd met were waiters at the country club, they were maids or nannies. The kids she'd gone to grade school with were white. And in high school, when there was busing, the races hadn't mixed. The races. As if they were real. As if we all weren't a mix.

She felt like she'd been punched in the gut. She felt sick. She wanted no part of it. America—home of the free. What a joke.

The smoke billowed and, feeding on the gasoline, the flames reached high and wide, and still the traffic hadn't budged. Her gas light blinked on. She'd had less fuel than she thought. She'd forgotten to check and now it was too late. She was sweating. With cars on all sides, she couldn't breathe. The teenagers in the blue Pontiac opened the doors and jumped out. She wished she had a gun. A crowbar. A knife at least. They ran, scattering, and the young one with the bat stopped in front of her car. He looked at her. In his eyes, she recognized her own terror. And then she watched him turn and run past a flaming stream of gasoline.

She had to get away. She nudged her car into the right-hand lane. Careful, so careful. Smiling her pretty-please. Praying not to offend. And then she heard a boom, an explosion. She felt her car shake. And the smoke was so thick she couldn't see anything beyond the windows.

This was it. The way her life ended, hers and the child inside her. In the chaos, she'd forgotten she was pregnant. Now she had two lives to save.

She took to the shoulder of the road. If she hit someone, she hit someone. She had to get out. She had more life to live. What was she doing here anyway, in this city, living so close to so many people, fighting for her share of the air? Pressing down the gas pedal, her foot shook in the flimsy little flip-flop, and she thought of beaches. Boundless stretches of sand without humans. She thought of the ocean, and San Clemente, where she and Leo had driven one early morning last autumn to watch the sunrise, where they swam in icy waves and rode them to the shore, where they'd wrapped themselves in towels and eaten green apples. She wanted more. More dawn skies, more salt air, more apples. She gave the car more gas.

Hell, yes. Thank God. Out of the jam, she could see again. She could breathe.

And here was a street, a side street, the entrance to a neighborhood. She turned right, slowed as she realized: the street was awake. It was eyes and dark, glistening skin, everyone in front of their apartment buildings, their tiny houses with chipped paint, with small, sliding windows guarded by black iron bars. In their patchy, treeless lawns, women held children on their hips. One woman in a dress with pink and blue flowers, strangely vivid in the haze, was crying, screaming after a man as he ran from her, ran with the other men down the street, heading for the thick of it.

She saw men and some women running the other way, too, back to the neighborhood, returning with their arms full of shoes, clothes, toys, with boxes on their shoulders. The big pack of Pampers. A microwave oven. The new TV for the family, the TV they'd never be able to afford. It was Christmas, without interest. A true miracle.

Gwen thought she might turn around, go back where she came from. But what was there to go back to? Smoke and cars? There had to be a way out if she kept on driving.

She drove—not too fast, not too slow—through the neighborhood that was not hers. She could have been driving down a street in any city. This was not the Los Angeles she knew. Though her drive past this neighborhood was routine, she'd always been in that world of her own making—of her own music and her own thoughts—sticking to the thoroughfare and seeing what she chose to see, driving with blinders on, mostly.

She drove, and the people—a woman with a boy's hand in hers, an old man leaning on his cane, a man carrying a box on his head—watched her in her dirty gray Nissan. They watched her and she watched them. *Them.* When had *they* become *them*? When had they gone from subject to object? When had they become the other? The *they* on which one can project one's own darkness, one's shadow. In order to bring it to light?

What she felt was their anger, frightening and beautiful. And what did they see in her? Privilege? A girl who had gone to college on her daddy's dime? A girl who floated over the engine of the city, who flitted where she liked, who lived where there were trees and shopped at boutiques? No, she reminded herself. She wasn't one of *those* people. The rich ones with assistants and nannies and maids. She wasn't driving a Porsche. She wasn't driving a Jag. She was in a dirty, gray, falling-apart Nissan Sentra, for Christ's sake. And anyhow, this was what *she* saw, looking through her interpretation of their view. It was all made up. How could she possibly know what they saw?

They watched her and she watched them and the street was longer than she'd thought. The street curved to the left and then to the right, and now she was driving faster, and she turned left, because she could see a way out of the maze. And here she was, back on South La Cienega, a few blocks from where she had been stuck in the traffic and the smoke.

This time she wasn't going to wait in line. This time she drove on the shoulder, in the lane that wasn't a lane—past one streetlight, past two, past the smoke and the blockade of cars—until she was free. Free on the open road. She rolled down her window, took a deep breath of the burned air.

The rush of it flooded her veins. It filled her with a new kind of high. She was beyond thought, her every cell feeling for her next move. She floored the gas pedal, and her tin can of a car went a hundred in a thirty-five-mile-an-hour zone as she passed a fire on her left, a torched store, another and another. Inside the chaos, she was all animal, all instinct; alive to the pulse of her blood, to the prickling of her armpits; alive to each impression— the bitter smell of the smoke, her burning eyes and nose and throat, the flames and the empty streets. It felt like she was in a war zone, and it looked like what she had seen on the news and in movies. But from inside her car, the city seemed quiet, dream- like and open, as if anything could happen.

And here, inside the slow-motion silence, her stale life was so much ash on the wind. She was light. She was flying through a city of rubble.

In this new space only survival mattered. She reached for the bottle of water. A few drops left. Christ. And she didn't have another. A person could live three days without water, she told herself. At least a normal person could. She swallowed, tried to breathe through her nose.

The gas dial was past empty, as low as she'd ever let it get. And here was a gas station without any line. She pulled up to a pump, looked around. The place was abandoned. She opened the door to the mini-mart: no one. And there were the glass refrigerators, the rows of cold bottled water. She couldn't help herself. She ran and took just one, just what she needed. After all, she thought, shouldn't water be free? Back outside she read the sign PAY BEFORE YOU PUMP, but if there wasn't anyone to take her money, was she stealing? Maybe they'd run out of gas, she reasoned. She'd just see. She untwisted the gas cap, fit the nozzle into her tank and squeezed the handle. Gas poured out. She filled her tank. For survival, she told herself, getting back in her car and locking the door. She untwisted the lid to the water and gulped down half the bottle.

She turned left onto Pico. There wasn't a car in sight. It was an afternoon in spring and ash floated like snow under a dark sky. It was a dream of Los Angeles. A postapocalyptic future. The people were gone—the Los Angelenos with their BMWs and their Mercedeses, with their face-lifts and their silicone breasts and lips and cheeks, with their hair plugs, their hair dyes and gels, with their designer jeans and shoes and jewelry, with their millions of tiny plastic water bottles. The plague of people was finally over.

She slowed down. Something was in the road, crossing the street.

She stopped.

Was it a long, very ugly dog? She didn't recognize the breed. She inched her car closer, squinted at the animal.

There, crossing Pico Boulevard, was a cat, a huge wild cat, a mountain lion, she realized, golden in the sepia light, right in front of her car. Where had it come from? Where was it going? It walked as if it owned the city and had decided to come out of its den and make that clear. And then it turned and looked at her. No, not at her, it looked *through* her. In its huge gold eyes, in *her* eyes—the eyes of the lioness—Gwen disappeared. In her eyes, there was no future and no past. There was only this moment—in which Gwen was awake, alive, her pulse beating now, now, now. The mountain lion stared at her, blessed her with that dismissive gaze in which Gwen was nothing after all, so she could be anything. Anyone. Right now.

The lioness turned her head and walked to the other side of the street, where Gwen watched her disappear into the haze as if she had dreamed her.

She started moving again, dazed, and drove on through the vacant town. If only this *were* the end. How quickly the ivy would take over, snaking up through the concrete, through the pavement, breaking the sidewalks, the streets, and the parking lots into rocks and then into sand. The grass would move back in, along with the hawks and the owls, the foxes and the coyotes. The blue sky.

Up ahead, a building was burning. A corner convenience store. Like Jin's. In front of the store stood an Asian man and woman. He held her in his arms as she shook, her head buried in his shoulder.

Gwen drove around a group of teenage boys running through the smoke, down the center of the street, with backpacks on their backs and in their arms—backpacks overflowing with who knew what stuff. In her rearview mirror she watched them turn into an alley. She drank her stolen water, passed a car going the other way and another burning building. She slowed down, unable to see more than ten feet in front of her.

Through the smoke, Gwen could just make out a figure approaching. Unmistakable. The tricornered hat, the red coat with gold buttons, the knickers. Striding down the sidewalk, his head high, there he was. Revolutionary Man. His face smudged with soot, he was aglow, victorious, walking out of the battle with the British troops, unscathed. Instead of a musket, he held under his arm his shoe box of cassette tapes. And, spanning his chest, there was his *Songs for the Road Home* sign.

She'd found him. Somehow, in the mayhem, here he was—intact, apparently unharmed.

She pulled to the side of the road. He was running toward her and his eyes were teary. He'd been worried, or maybe it was just the smoke. He got in the car. "Tink," he said, touching her face. "Thank God."

She put both hands on his head, as if to make sure he was real, and planted a hard kiss on his lips. "You're alive," she said, amazed at how good it felt to see him.

She hung a U-turn in the middle of the road.

Home. They were going home, she and Leo and—she remembered, again—the baby inside her, the baby he knew nothing about. A baby. How could she even entertain the thought? How did anyone bring a baby into *this* world?

She made a left onto Fairfax and flew down it, past the antique stores and the Jewish delis, past the dry cleaners and the kosher bakeries with wedding cakes in the windows. They flew down the street that was always, at this hour on a weekday, stop and go, but today was deserted. The people had gone home hours ago and were now glued to their televisions, eager to see just how bad things were going to get.

Leo took a joint from his box of cassette tapes and lit it. Right there in broad daylight. "Holy fuck," he said. He rolled the window down and exhaled, adding a little cannabis smoke to the smoke from the burning buildings. "Have you ever felt so *free*? It's *alive*. The city is finally *alive*. The structure is crumbling, Gwen. Every artifice, every wall. Made to keep us all in line, to keep us marching. We could do anything right now. Anything you want."

He took the steering wheel in his hand and spun it to the left. Her car veered across the double yellow lines and into the left lane where oncoming traffic would have been if there were any. "See?" Leo said, looking at her and not the road. "You've got to break the chains. If not now, if not *right* now—"

"Leo! Fuck! We're not in England." Gwen took back the wheel and swerved into the right lane, just missing a car—a pimped-out Cadillac—as it made a right turn toward her.

"Open your mind, babe." He offered her the joint. She kept her hands on the wheel, her eyes on the road.

"What are you," he said, "going Amish on me?"

"Amish?"

"Mormon, then." He put out the joint in her ashtray. "Come on! Wake *up*. This is as wide open as it's ever going to get," he said, and he leaned out the window into the wind and started singing.

She had felt free, had felt the vast wilderness pulsing inside her, until he got in the car and she became the responsible one. Didn't it always happen like this? She'd be at the wheel, making sure they didn't crash, making sure they got where they needed to, while Leo was out the window singing. Were she to call him on it, she knew what his reply would be. I'm a musician, he'd say. As if musicians lived entirely in the ether. As if the title ex- plained everything. And maybe it did. Maybe that's where she'd gone wrong in choosing him. She'd wanted a man who could feel things, who could open himself to her and be vulnerable and present, who'd drop everything and take off with her on grand, impromptu adventures. She'd wanted a playmate—Peter Pan—

and that was just what she'd gotten. But two children couldn't survive on their own. One of them had to be the adult.

Chanting, his mouth was wide:

> *Kali, Kali—*
> *Terrible beauty.*
> *Kali, Kali—*
> *We bow, bow down to Thee.*
> *Kali, Kali.*

Lilting, lifting, his voice was pure, so fucking pure, it made the smoke lyrical, almost holy.

He pulled a small bamboo pan flute from his shoe box and played and sang and played. Here was another fire. She took her foot off the gas and coasted by it, feeling the heat and watching the flames dance.

He was right to call on Kali. To recognize the riots as her work. Hindu goddess of fertility and birth and destruction, her womb a void, an abyss, Kali was the fierce, fiery mother of all. Black-skinned, red-eyed goddess of the night, she wore only a necklace of skulls and a girdle of men's hands. She danced, holding in one hand a sword, in the other a man's severed head. Try me, she'd say, staring you down, drowning you in her deep laugh. Her breasts, so full of milk, of what could give life, were bloody from her kill. She was the great paradox, the destroyer of illusions. Her tongue extended like a flytrap, she tasted the world's flavors free from discretion. Her blackness, since it was all colors combined, embodied the universe, the totality, and since it was the absence of color, it was also the ultimate reality—that which transcends appearances.

Gwen could feel Kali entering her heart. She was a fire consuming all Gwen had ever thought she needed and loved and was. Daughter, lover, student, stripper, poet—all of it, every possible label, was fuel for the flames.

What remained would be scorched and smell of smoke. What remained would burn her eyes. Her open eyes.

Yes. She would keep them open. She would see it through, this cremation of her selves, this work of Kali. She would see what she was left with when morning came; she would see who she really was.

Leo was singing a new wordless tune, one she hadn't heard before. And in a clear patch of air she could make out the Los Angeles County Museum of Art. As they passed its hushed expanse, she wondered if anyone had thought to loot the paintings. There was one she coveted. It was on the third floor, in the American Collection. Granville Redmond, from 1926. *California Poppy Field*. It was so big that if you stood close you could see the dots it was made of, you could lose yourself in pure color, but standing back a little you felt like you were in the field of orange poppies, like you could sit under an oak tree if you wanted to, lie back and watch the clouds move across the far peaks. If she could hang this painting on her wall, look at it when she first woke up and before she went to bed, she was sure all that peace and the sense of quiet distance would change her in ways she couldn't imagine.

She flipped on her blinker to turn right onto Sixth Street, their street. Why on earth was she using her blinker? The habit of courtesy and lawfulness was entrenched. Maybe Leo was right and she should loosen up a little.

Before she could turn, Leo pointed. "Shit," he said. "Look!" She stopped the car. On the next block, in front of the 99 Cents

Only Store, there was shouting, and then gunfire—loud blasts that made Gwen duck behind the steering wheel. People were running, and there was screaming.

"I'll kill you, motherfucker!" someone yelled. More shots thundered and an old Chevy peeled off down the road.

Gwen put her foot on the gas. "Wait," Leo said, craning his neck to keep watching. But she meant to get them home. They'd pass the tar pits and have just a couple blocks to go.

She clamped her teeth, pressed her lips against the shrill, nameless fury that without any warning seemed to be rising inside her. She could scream at him for days, one interminable roar, but what good would come of it? In the confining silence she drank her water. It only made her want more.

She drove fast down Third, straight through a red light, and took a side street to Sixth. Making a right onto South Cochran, she was home. The Cornell was still standing.

"Tink," Leo said, "get out. You'll be safe here. I'll park the car."

She pulled up to the curb. They could see, on top of the Cornell, a few of the residents watching the city burn.

"I'll meet you up there," said Leo, and she was too tired to disagree with him. He took her place behind the wheel. His eyes were the orange of the sky; they were ignited, and she wondered if he would return or if he'd drive off into the heat, into the blazing heart of the city, if he'd join those incendiaries—because fire meant liberation from form, because flames were rapturous, because change was at last upon them.

Twelve

SHE TOOK A long breath and turned toward their brick building—brick, like the house in "The Three Little Pigs," the house that survived the wolf and his tricks, the one that kept the pigs safe. The Cornell had never felt so much like home. She hurried through the courtyard—past the fountain and the flowers and the hazy stone faces—through the lobby and up the four flights of stairs. She climbed the little hatch and walked out onto the roof, abuzz with tenants—Greg the manager and Psycho Barry among the dozens of strangers with whom she lived and had seen, if at all, only in passing.

On all sides of the Cornell the city spread as far as she could see, and it was burning. She counted eleven fires. On all sides helicopters circled and hovered. Below them, the fire trucks and the police cars screamed, their red flashing lights projecting panic onto the low-hung layer of smoke as their sirens called and called down the empty streets.

Alone on the roof's western edge stood the Count in his full rocker getup. He looked the way he had when she'd met him, with the long black wig, the white T-shirt and the vest with the fur and the suede fringe, with the tight black pants, the belt with silver studs and the silver bracelets jangling on his arms. With a grand gesture imbued with the confidence of an explorer, he squared his shoulders and pointed to the west, where the Pacific lay beyond their view, and she saw something new go up in flames. Everyone on the roof saw it, too, and they oohed and aahed, as if they were watching a fireworks show. The flames leaped higher and the smoke blackened and rose.

When Valiant saw her he smiled—an actual toothy grin. It had been years since she'd seen him smile like that. He was boyish, spry, his dark skin glowing. Hell, he almost looked healthy. Like a big brother, or maybe a big sister with the long hair and the bracelets, he took her in his spindly arms and squeezed her tight, picking her up so that her feet came off the roof. She gave him a kiss on the cheek. It was smooth and smelled of Polo aftershave. He'd cleaned himself up for the occasion. She noticed that he'd covered up the lesion on his neck with makeup. He set her down and looked at her as if she'd just come back from a long sea voyage or a trip to outer space.

"The lovely Gwendolyn has returned. Thought you'd never make it."

"Oh, Count," she said, happier than she'd been in a long, long time. "It's good to see you, too."

Her friend was back. It had taken a city on fire to resurrect him, but he was here, standing beside her. His eyes were still sunken, but they had a glow to them, like Leo's. It was the reflection of the sky—the sun through the filter of smoke casting the scene in its eerie, crepuscular, end-of-the-world orange. And it was the light inside him rising, surfacing, the light this disaster had awakened. There was a quickening, a vibrancy Gwen hadn't seen in him since his nights at Café Largo, sitting at the piano, cracking jokes and crooning to the crowds.

To the east now, another building, freshly torched, was adding to the smoke-thick air its dark song.

"La Brea," said Leo, stepping onto the roof. "They're looting the shops."

"You drove down it?" Gwen said.

"Just to see."

"How's Jin's?"

"Still there. He's outside it with his brothers. They have guns. No one's going to mess with them. But La Brea's a fucking madhouse."

"Which stores?" said a boy walking toward them, one of those tenants Gwen hadn't noticed before. There were so many of them living one, two floors up, living their own lives. This was the first time they'd all been in one place—this was the big get-to-know-you roof party.

On the roof of the new building across the street—the building that brought the neighborhood squarely into the nineties with its mauve stucco, its balconies' metal railings painted aqua, and with its name, the Palms—the residents were barbecuing. She could smell the seared meat. It made her stomach growl.

The boy stood between her and Leo. He had cropped blond hair and black eyeliner. He was shirtless and tan and he stood, in his low jeans, drinking his Miller. "They're not looting the Music Store, are they?" he said, flashing his white teeth.

"Are you a musician?" said Leo.

"A guitarist. They have some very pretty guitars."

Greg sauntered over, the gray roots of his brown hair shining despite the smoke. "You know," he said, placing a soft hand on the blond boy's shoulder, "you're not allowed to have alcohol up here."

"Isn't this just dreadful," said the Count. He joined the group and looked down at them all. "Leo, you wouldn't mind leaving your beautiful new friend, would you?" He took his camera from around his neck and gave it to Leo.

"I was just leaving," the boy said, handing his Miller to the Count and grinning. "There's a Les Paul calling my name."

They all watched him go.

"Jesus," said the Count. "That gorgeous ass. Where has he been hiding?"

Gwen smiled. It was good to see him back in action. "You ought to get out more."

"Yes, my dear, you have a point."

"I'll take that," Greg said, and he reached for the beer.

"It'd be a shame to waste it," said Valiant, downing it. Greg glared at him. "What? Isn't beer mostly water anyhow?" Valiant handed him the empty bottle. With a flip of his hair, Greg headed for the trash can.

"Poor guy," said Leo.

"He needs a drink," said the Count.

"Or a boyfriend," said Gwen.

The Count walked to the roof's southwest corner. He straightened his wig, tucked in his T-shirt, and stood tall, shoulders back, chest out. He stood with his hands on his hips, his arms akimbo, looking out at the city so his face was in sharp profile to the camera. Behind him three fires burned, each with its own bleeding heart.

This was one of those war-torn cities in another country, one you had to cross the Atlantic to get to. This was Beirut or Prague or Berlin. This wasn't L.A. At least it wasn't the Los Angeles Gwen believed existed when she was a kid, when she'd visited with her mother and stayed at the Hotel Bel-Air or the Chateau Marmont, when they buzzed around Beverly Hills in her mother's convertible Porsche visiting her old friends—actors and producers—and L.A. was green and flowering, bougainvillea and honeysuckle and hibiscus spilling over the stone walls and into the windy streets, when L.A. was the Malibu coastline, when it was Gladstones for lunch and Chasen's for dinner, when it was so many stars in Gwen's eyes, as if she were dizzy from spinning too long. Her mother had seemed most alive here, most herself. She'd been quick to smile, and so carefree, so beautiful Gwen almost hadn't recognized her.

Leo snapped the Count's photo and handed the camera to her.

"You mind?"

He stood where Valiant had and Gwen pointed the lens at him, got ready to shoot. She knew why her mother had liked being a photographer. There was power in looking through a lens. With a camera over your face, you become a witness. You take yourself out of the scene, and make of its disparate elements a coherence, a meaning.

Valiant's camera was the same kind her mother had used, an old Nikon, and he shot only black-and-white. You had to take your time with the f-stop and the shutter speed. You had to get it right before you clicked. She placed Leo at the edge of the frame, the three fires to his left. She brought the top gold button on his jacket into focus.

"Ready?" Her hair was blowing in the warm wind and she had to hold it back with her hand so it wouldn't block the lens.

Leo's bloodshot eyes were dead serious. He'd felt the city seethe beneath its skin, and now that it was breaking open, breaking out, he was proud, as if it were somehow his creation. His hair in that low ponytail, his black tricornered hat firmly on his head, he faced her. He held her eyes with his. He was all intention—this boy, this man. The father of her child.

She pushed the thought from her head. She'd not decided. There hadn't been time. She needed to walk somewhere alone. She needed to write, to think.

A few sun-streaked wisps of Leo's hair blew across his face and she clicked the shutter.

There.

"It's good?" he said.

"I think so."

"It'll be the cover of my CD, when it gets made. And Gwen," he said, "it'll get made. You'll see. This time next year I'll have a big fat contract."

She watched him walk to the center of the roof and sit down. This was nothing new. She was used to his mood swings around money. One minute he wouldn't have a thing to do with it, and the next he was going to make a million.

He closed his eyes and sang a cappella one of what he called his Songs of Independence, the one with the fallen angel. Surprised, a few tenants snickered. Or had she just thought they snickered? She never had been comfortable with Leo's pot-enhanced eruptions into song, at least not when they were in public. She joined Valiant at the roof's edge and gave him back his camera. He slung it around his neck, aimed it at Leo. Took a picture. "This is history," he said. "And we're here, kid. We're part of it."

People were gathering around Leo now. They were sitting down to listen. The group was largely female, but there was Psycho Barry, sitting closest, hugging his knees and humming along with him.

The ash fell in big white flakes. Los Angeles snow. They leaned on the railing, Gwen and Valiant, as if they were on the prow of a ship looking out at the horizon, that line they could never reach. They watched the fires, listened to Leo's voice.

Angel, angel, fallen, fallen,
angel, my angel girl, fallen girl.
Ashes of what once were wings,
dimes in her cup she sings.
Angel, angel, fallen.

Gwen caught a flake of ash in her hand.

"It's beautiful, isn't it?" Valiant said.

"The city?"

"Spread out below us. Burning."

"It's pure. Or true or something."

"It almost makes it okay."

"The wreckage?"

He nodded. "Dying," he said. The blood left his face. He stooped, leaning harder on the railing.

Gwen put a hand on his back. Even through his vest she could feel his ribs separate with each slow inhale. She rested her other hand on her navel, took a breath and felt her stomach rise and fall. She knew she would remember this moment, the heat and the antique light, like an old black-and-white photograph yellowed from the sun. And Valiant alive beside her. His eyes shining like a night sea, like the great beyond.

"My whole life I've waited for this," he said. "My whole life I didn't know. But this was my dream. This city on fire."

"Bahía de los Fumos."

"You remember."

Years ago, he'd told her the story. The first Europeans to have sailed this coast saw the brown haze over the hills, the haze from the campfires of the Gabrielinos, and called Los Angeles, or what would become Los Angeles, Bahía de los Fumos. Bay of the Smokes. That was three hundred and fifty years ago. And here it was, still home to fires, still hung with smoke.

But now there were buildings for miles; there were red lights and sirens whirring; there were firemen with their long hoses chasing the fires down, and there was the clatter of the helicopters—those giant metal beetles with their hungry hidden eyes, their cameras aimed at the thick of the chaos, hungry for blood, for explosions, for the blackest of smoke.

Leo had finished his song and the people were clapping. "Encore, encore," Psycho Barry chanted. And Leo pulled his pan flute from his coat pocket and launched into another song.

Valiant put a cigarette between his lips. He flicked the lighter with his thumb and the flame flickered and died in the breeze. He tried again and Gwen cupped the flame with her hands to block the wind as he lit the cigarette.

He coughed on the smoke. "Did I ever tell you my house burned down?" He was watching the horizon, and his voice was even, distant. "When I was a kid. Six years old. I don't have any pictures from before that 'cause they all burned in the fire.

"It was electrical. A short. It happened in the night. My dad carried me from my bed, outside, and my mom and brother, we all watched the house burn. And after that, I started lighting things on fire. I lit things on fire just to watch them burn. Ants under a magnifying glass, leaves. And then bigger things. Textbooks and homework. And when I was in high school, I had these friends. We'd go out on weeknights. We'd go to the beach and get drunk, and then we'd torch things. Trash cans, chairs, sofas. Once it was a car. The car was on this hill and my friend set it on fire and released the parking brake. It rolled down the street in a blaze and off a cliff and landed in a canyon.

"The fire could've been worse than it was. It could have been a lot worse."

Gwen took his cigarette, to take just a puff, and then she remembered. "I used to fantasize about fires," she said, giving him back the cigarette without smoking it. "Sometimes I still do. About what it would be like to lose everything except what's on your back. To start over. To know that a memory is really a memory, not because you have a photograph of it."

A few of the fires were out now, and a fresh one had sprung up—a just-born star.

"Will you take one more?" said Valiant, lifting the camera from around his neck. "And then I'm going in. I'm tired."

In the frame he was without pretense. He was the boy whose house was burning. His eyes wide, his face open to the heat and the light—yellow, orange-red, each flame with its blue secret center, its cool, disinterested heart. What had been home would be just a few bones, charred and fallen; but burning, it came to life, monstrous, ravenous. As if the home itself were done being a home, as if it were ready to move on, to lighten its load, to become ash, air, thin memories, thinner over time, until they were mere glimpses of once familiar feelings, triggered by the tone of a stranger's voice, or by the scent of a passing woman's lotion.

She gave the camera back to him.

Leo's song was over and the small audience disbanded, leaving two girls standing, whispering. They were girls Gwen hadn't seen before. One had hair down to her waist, and the other wore cutoffs nearly high enough to dance in. They were stealing glances at Valiant. A guy in a muscle shirt joined them. Gwen couldn't hear what they were saying, but as they looked at Valiant, she knew they were seeing him as someone he wasn't. His black, Brazilian skin, once exotic—adding a splash of color to the Cornell's largely white resident population—made him dangerous now, as if, because of his skin color, he couldn't be trusted. Who knew? He might torch his own building. The group was growing. There were five of them, talking, looking.

Valiant was frozen, watching them. Gwen took his arm and turned him toward the stairs. He was trembling. His face shone with perspiration.

"What is it?" he said. He ran his fingertips over his forehead, his cheek. "Is there something on my face?" He touched the sore on his neck. "Did the makeup come off? Is it showing?"

"No," Gwen said.

"Is the wig too much? Or the bracelets?"

"You look gorgeous."

Leo met Gwen and Valiant at the stairs. He stood before them, wind in his hair like a fan on a movie set and the sky behind him a scrim lit with an orange gel. He looked past them at the city—the city consuming itself, the city in need of redemption. After a dramatic pause, his eyes intense, unblinking, he spoke.

"I've had a vision. I know what I have to do." And he turned from them, and headed down the stairwell and into the Cornell.

"Oh God," said Valiant, happy again. "What now?"

Thirteen

IN THEIR APARTMENT, Gwen watched the news—the fires, the looters, the inferno the City of the Angels had become. The worst the country had seen since the Watts Riots of '65. Tom Bradley, the mayor, had declared a state of emergency. Pete Wilson, the governor, was sending in the National Guard. And Bush insisted that anarchy would not be tolerated. Always the passive politician voice. Would not be tolerated by whom, she wanted to know. And there was a dusk-to-dawn curfew. So long as the sun was down, the citizens of Los Angeles had to stay in their homes.

"There it is. The fire I passed," Gwen said. They were showing it, saying it was the biggest of the fires. The Arco station on La Cienega. And here it was, the fire, three feet by two now; the mass of flames, the thick smoke, the line of cars she'd been stuck in was contained in this small black box, so easy to watch. It had become entertainment. She saw flaming gasoline stream down the gutter and then *ka-boom!* A car exploded. It could have been me, she thought. But it wasn't. She was still flesh and bones, curled up with Fifi on the sofa, drinking water from a mason jar. Cool and clear, glorious water.

"Leo," she said. "Look." For once the news mattered. At least to her it mattered.

At the kitchen table, he sat with his back to her, sketching.

"Hmm?" he said without turning around. He filled the purple water pipe (not bong) with the pot he'd bought that morning. He'd cashed the residual check and spent it on a quarter ounce. Carpe diem, he said when she mentioned the ring for his mother, back rent, and the *Pay or Quit* notice. We're alive today. We still have a roof over our heads. How do we know Los Angeles is even going to be here tomorrow? And besides, he told her, the guy threw in some mushrooms, and hadn't she wanted to take them again?

Communication was out of the question.

She picked up the remote to turn off the TV and found that she couldn't. She was mesmerized. Here was an open gun battle, a Korean shop owner, or two of them, defending their store, their lives, firing at what looked like an all-black mob and people in that mob firing back at them. There were screams. The commentator said the police had fled the scene. She thought of Latasha Harlins, the fifteen-year-old black girl shot and killed by a Korean shop owner, a woman, just last year. The woman had thought she was stealing a bottle of juice, because she'd put it in her backpack, but the girl had died with the cash to pay for it in her hand. The woman claimed self-defense. She'd grabbed the girl's backpack to get the juice and the girl had knocked her down. The woman had swung a stool at her, and the girl tossed the juice onto the counter. As she was leaving, the woman had shot her. Gwen remembered seeing the footage—security cameras showed her shooting the girl in the back of the head as she was trying to leave the store. The woman had gotten off with probation, community service, and a fine of five hundred dollars.

And now this. Gwen pressed the power and the TV went black.

She closed their windows to the sere April twilight, fastening the little metal latches that wouldn't keep anyone out anyway. She left the long kitchen window open, so some of Leo's smoke could escape, so her eyes might stop burning.

Their message machine was flashing. Two new messages. Before she hit play, she knew who had called.

Message one: *Leo. Tesoro. Come va? I turn on the news and that city you live in. Pazzo. Why you don't pick up the phone? Why you don't call your mama? Porco canne. My son the bum.*

Message two: *Gwen. It's your father. You need to call me. I haven't heard from you in weeks. I'm worried. Call me, you hear?*

Gwen pressed erase all.

Her father. Every so often he'd surface from the law practice he lived for and give her a call. How was she, he'd want to know. He was thinking about her. And when she'd try to tell him how she was, she could hear him half listening. Uh-huh, he'd say, and she'd stop talking. She'd ask about him and half listen back. So what, exactly, was the point? Why did they bother?

She knew she wasn't being fair. He cared about her as much, she supposed, as he could care about anyone.

She should be a good daughter. She should call him. Later.

"Leo, did you hear? Your mother's message?"

" 'My son the bum.' Yeah, I heard."

She looked over his shoulder at his sketch. In it, a man was walking down the middle of a street, the buildings on both sides of him burning. She looked closer. The man in the sketch was naked—Leo had drawn in chest hair pointillist-style and doodled a dangling penis—and he held above him what looked to be a flag.

"Hand me the phone, will you?" He took a bong rip and dialed. "*Ciao*, Mama. Yeah, yeah. I'm fine. We're fine. Hey, Mom. You're watching the news? Well, keep watching. Yeah. You'll see. I'm going to be on the TV. Yeah, on the news. Tomorrow."

Gwen couldn't believe what she was hearing.

"Don't worry," he was saying. "Yes. I'll be safe. Aren't I always safe?

"*Va bene, va bene. Anche io te amo*, Mama." He hung up the phone and knocked the ash from the pipe, repacked it.

"What the hell, Leo. What the hell." She wanted to smack his head, knock some sense into his brain. Or else she wanted to punch him, to give him a taste of the world—the one out here, the one she was living in.

A shadow darted across the table and Leo sprang into action. In a single swing of his arm he detached the DustBuster from its holster and vacuumed the roach before it reached the edge. *Va-room.* The great mouth of a god, inhaling. He held it up to the light and peered through the poop-splattered brown plastic at the roaches crawling up the sides and over each other. "Hello, my little friends," he said, tapping the canister. "Don't worry. Soon you will be free, you will be in roach heaven, in the promised land, in the Dumpster of your dreams, climbing mountains of pepperoni and chicken and cheese, spelunking caves of beans and tuna fish and Spam, swimming in oceans of spaghetti and meat sauce. Soon, my little friends, you will feast."

Fifi leaped from the couch and yipped at the door. Gwen heard the knocks through her piercing bark. One, two, three, and four. It was Valiant. He always knocked four times, and besides, he was the only person who came to their door—apart from the Mormons or the Jehovah's Witnesses, whom Leo, depending on how high he was, would invite inside, afternoons, for a captive audience.

She unbolted the lock. He brandished a smile, creasing the thin skin of his cheeks into tiny ripples. In the stark light of their hallway, it seemed to Gwen he had aged ten years. He had swapped the wig for the turban, and he was wearing a red smoking jacket over a pair of faded jeans that, in spite of the cinched belt, hung off his hips like pajama bottoms.

"Thank God," she said, taking his hand. "You have to see."

She led him to the table where Leo was hunched over the paper, sketching. Valiant pulled out a chair and sat down. He plucked the sketch from Leo's hands, leaned back, contemplating, and crossed his legs. Shaking his head, saying nothing, he put the sketch back on the table. Leo took it back, glared at him, and started drawing again, and Valiant took a Camel from the box. In front of him, Gwen set the ashtray she had made of clay in the shape of a V, for Valiant and his visits. He lit the cigarette and she held her breath. More smoke.

Gwen walked the aisle between the stacks of books and videos into the living room, and lay down on the sofa. Isn't that what you did when there was a fire? To avoid inhaling the carbon monoxide, you got close to the ground. She could feel the walls closing in. The ceiling was lower and, like the sky above it, laden with smoke. And on all sides of her there was the city—the city of people like her, hiding in their homes, afraid, which she'd never wanted to be. If something made her heart beat, she did it. That was her pact with herself. Not to back away from life. Not to cower, but to strike out. To go where she needed to, even if it wasn't pretty—that place she needed to go—even if she had to move through its darkness and grit by feel.

Her heart sped. She was trapped, stuck in this apartment,

or, to be exact, the building. She couldn't leave the Cornell until morning.

She could feel her blood pulse in her head, in her hands, in her feet, as if she'd shrunk, as if her body—once her ticket to freedom, her instrument for expression—were now a cell.

If she was the inmate, who was the jailor? The child inside her? Her silence? Her fear?

The cell had a door, open a crack. Leo didn't know yet. If she got an abortion he'd never know.

But then she'd never know either—never know what life her fear had deleted. It would haunt her, that choice, follow her everywhere, a skulking, hungry shadow, the way her mother's abortion had followed her, waiting on those afternoons for her to open the bottle of wine and fall into her melancholia. By sundown there would be the choking sobs. Gwen remembered stroking her mother's hair as she lay on the ground in the garden, between the Mexican primrose and the poppies. It was the only thing that helped, she'd told her. Feeling the earth beneath her. Gwen's father hadn't known about the abortion. It had happened years before they had been together, and her mother hadn't thought it was something he needed to know. And he was at a loss to understand her pain. "Is it like a three-putt in golf?" he'd asked her mother once, confused, and she'd looked at him as if she had no idea who he was.

Her mother had always confided in *her*. That confidence, that trust, had been the cement, the bond between them. She wished she could talk to her now.

Gwen thought of the other option. Not adoption. She couldn't live with that, either. Knowing her child was calling someone else "Mother"? A child she'd never know being raised by a stranger? That was out of the question.

The other option was leaving. She could leave Leo some afternoon when he was on his street corner. Or else she could leave tomorrow. Her heart hopped into her throat. She thought it might leap from her mouth like a toad.

Could she do it? She'd just pack her things into her car—everything she owned would easily fit—and she'd disappear. She'd raise this child on her own.

Some women did that.

"I don't care what you think," said Leo, packing another bowl.

"I haven't said anything," the Count said.

"But you're thinking. You're thinking you know."

"All I know is this sketch looks dumb. A naked guy in the middle of a burning city? Ouch."

"Holding a white flag. I'll be naked, holding a white flag. The message is clear. Isn't the message clear, Gwen?"

"What?" she said from the sofa.

"The message. A man naked with a white flag. What does that image say to you? It says vulnerability. Peace. Innocence. It's Eden, for Christ's sake. Starting over. A second chance at this society thing. This life on earth."

"So that makes you . . . Adam?" the Count said.

"If that's how you want to look at it. I'll walk from here. Barefoot."

"You *would* look kind of odd in only high-tops," Gwen said.

"At dawn, when the curfew lifts. I'm going to walk into East L.A."

"Naked, holding a white flag," said the Count.

"And you're going to walk beside me," Leo told him. "You can photograph the whole thing."

"Really? You know I've always wanted to photograph you naked."

"So you're game?"

"Leo, you're out of your fucking mind." The Count laughed—he was having a good time with this. "You're loaded."

"All the more reason." Leo tugged at the elastic tie in his ponytail, yanking out a few hairs as he freed the dark tangle. "I'm not confined by common sense."

"Leo, you're insane. You've been smoking too much pot."

"Well, isn't that the pot calling the kettle." He lit the bowl, and the chamber filled with smoke. He took his finger off the carburetor and sucked the smoke down.

"Yeah," said the Count. "I drink and smoke, but I don't smoke like you. You don't stop."

Gwen was ready for the Count to leave. She loved him, but the arguing and the cigarette smoke were making her queasy. She turned toward the back of the sofa, closed her eyes, and tried to drift. It was here where she'd first lain beside Leo, where he'd first held her in his arms and told her he didn't know how it was possible—they had just met the day before—but he loved her. It was here she'd looked into his eyes and known she loved him back.

Fifi jumped onto the sofa and turned in a small circle until she settled down on Gwen's feet. Gwen opened her eyes, the smoke making them burn and water. The apartment was bleary. When it had been his and she was a visitor, it was different. Maybe she was romanticizing things, but she thought it was. There weren't the piles of debris to negotiate. The room was clean and the windows were open. Even Fifi had looked presentable. Her hair had been short and white—not the bedraggled, matted gray it was now. She'd even had pink satin bows on her ears. That first afternoon, Leo had been expecting Gwen's visit, and he'd had roses on the coffee table, opera on the phonograph.

And there'd been the painting, the one above the sofa. The one she'd taken her time looking at. There were note cards taped to the wall around it now, but it was still there, in its gilt frame, with its scene, its inkling of a story. Impression of a woman in a white dress, under a broad white hat, heading toward the mottled gray-blue lake in the distance, toward the sky of the same color, impression of a man in a dark suit and a bowler hat coming from that lake, passing her, almost. They were close, the man and the woman, his hat skimmed her parasol, and yet each faced the direction in which they were, respectively, headed, as if their lives would have them meet, and then continue on their separate ways.

Leo had bought the painting just before she'd met him, at an estate sale, when he'd been living off his winnings from the game show *Wheel of Fortune*. "Show business is show business," he explained. With his quick game-show money, he'd moved from San Clemente to Los Angeles, found this apartment, furnished it with a wooden kitchen table and chairs, a plush sofa. As a girl just out of college, Gwen had been impressed. His apartment had a feeling of solidity. And she'd let her guard down and stayed.

She sighed. She was here, might as well make the best of it. Staring through the smoke at the ceiling, at the plaster, the way the lamp lit its raised shapes, she noticed faces there, too—like there were in the shower. But these were the faces of animals. The face of one animal and the body of another. There was a pig-fish—the face of a pig, or else a peccary, and the fins and tail of a trout. Maybe the peccary was becoming the trout, or the trout the peccary. Or maybe she was breathing too much of the ambient pot smoke. And there, with the wings of a bat, was the face of the mountain lion from this afternoon, staring down at her with its huge eyes.

"I saw," she said. "Today when I was driving—" And then she didn't want to go on. To tell her encounter would be like telling a dream. She'd lose it, she knew, in the telling.

"Leo," she said, changing direction. "Sorry. Zero." He looked at her now, and she went on. "Today, when I saw you stepping out of the smoke, you were so American, you were epic, almost. Like you were emerging from a battle with the Brits or something. Why not be Revolutionary Man and walk into East L.A.? Why be naked?"

"You're asking me?"

"Well?"

"So you're the only one who can be naked, then?"

"I'm naked where one expects to find nakedness."

"Where one pays for it."

"And where it isn't illegal."

"How fucked up is that? It's illegal to be in our natural state. To be naked in public. Unless the purpose is to entice, to titillate," he said, emphasizing the *tit* in "titillate."

"At the club, it's nude, not naked."

"Nude, naked," the Count said, crushing his cigarette into the ashtray in a single twist. "Come, my dears, let's put it to use. You're both cordially invited to my lair at two A.M. for a party in which we will wear nothing. Or at least nothing that counts, or nothing that covers where it counts. You get the picture." He stood and opened his box of cigarettes and then closed it. "Fuck. These will have to last me."

Gwen pulled herself off the sofa.

"You're in?" he said, making his way to the door.

"We're in." Gwen kissed his cheek, and the Count opened the door.

"You should speak for yourself," said Leo, slamming the refrigerator shut, and the Count, who could sense drama coming from a mile off and wouldn't miss it for the world, let the door close. He lit another cigarette and, taking a seat on the sofa, settled in for the show.

Gwen refilled her jar with water. She'd never been so thirsty.

"You know what, Leo?" she said. "I think it's a splendid idea—the naked East L.A. thing. A triumph of a plan. The plan to top them all. I think this is one you have to do. For real. In fact . . ." She paused, thinking it through. "I'm going to help you. All you need is a white flag, right? Ought to be easy enough."

She grabbed a wooden spoon. "Too short? Let's see, you want the flag to fly above your head. To flap around in the breeze. Innocence. Peace. Love. You're sure you want it to be white? I know it's the flag of surrender—you ride across the battlefield with a white flag and it means your side surrenders—but in this case the tension is all, well, so black-and-white. Maybe a color would be more neutral? Maybe a green flag? Like Whitman's flag of my disposition, out of hopeful green stuff woven. You know, when he's talking about the grass as a uniform hieroglyphic, growing among black folks as well as among white?"

She caught her breath and looked at him. He sat in the chair and stared at her. This was the most she'd said to him in months. Always she was in a hurry to get to work, or she was spent after a long night. Or she was guarding her space, writing in a fever—annotations, poems—her next deadline for graduate school just around the corner. And when they did have a rare moment together, he was the one with the diatribe and Gwen was in the chair, pretending to listen.

"Are you all right?" Leo said.

"Is she all right?" the Count said. "Are you kidding? The girl is lucid as hell."

"You stay out of it," Leo said.

"He's right," Gwen said. "I'm lucid as hell." She opened the refrigerator. In the drawer she found a cucumber, somehow still crisp. She washed it off in the sink and bit into it. It was perfect. And the smell. She thought she'd never really smelled a cucumber before—so bright and green, like being in a garden on a wet spring morning.

"You're set on white?" she said.

Leo didn't answer.

"It was your vision, right?"

He squinted at her as if trying to bring her into focus. He nodded.

"He isn't saying much, is he?" Valiant said.

"Not so much," said Gwen.

Leo looked from Gwen to the Count and back to Gwen. He clenched his jaw and folded his arms across his chest.

"Well, white it is," Gwen said.

She stood on the kitchen table and took a curtain rod from above the window. The white curtain fell to the floor. "Here's your pole," she said, holding the metal rod.

She took scissors and cut a square from the top of the curtain. She put the rod through the tube of fabric at one end of the square, and with duct tape she wrapped the rod from top to bottom so the fabric would hold.

"Here it is," she said. "Your white flag."

"Very nice," said Valiant, exhaling.

She waved the makeshift flag and did a little dance down the living room aisles and back into the kitchen, where she handed the flag off to Leo as though it were a baton in a relay race.

The Count grinned, applauding gleefully. And she felt herself glow. How she did adore an audience. "Your turn," she said to Leo. "And if you're going to hit the streets at dawn you'll need your rest.

"Count," she said, turning to him, "he's sorry, but he can't make it tonight. There are urgent matters to which he must attend."

She bit into the cucumber, smiled as she munched. "Leo," she said. "I won't wake you when I get home tonight." She kissed his forehead and raised his hand that held the flag so it was straight up.

"Looks good. The news is going to love you. Zero. Our new savior," she said and turned and left him there, holding his flag and without a thing to say.

She glanced back at the Count, who was openmouthed, agog and aghast, but thrilled, as if she'd just thrown him a surprise birthday party.

She walked into the bedroom and closed the door behind her. She latched the French windows to shut out the singed smell of the night, to try to at least. She lay down on the bed. The walls were thin. She could hear arguing, name-calling and expletives, as though they were brothers fighting, and then the door slammed.

At last it was quiet. And she knew Leo was too high to come in and talk to her. He had no intention of being brought down.

Her body was pulsing, still, with adrenaline, as though she would have to run, keep her body in motion to stay alive. It had been too long a day already. She let her body sink into the bed. She was safe, alone. The windows to the courtyard were shut, the curtains drawn.

She watched the dimming twilight as it held each object. This room she had slept in for years was still very much Leo's. His oak headboard and chest of drawers made the room warm and heavy, of another place and time was what she'd thought in the beginning—an apartment in Paris in the fifties, someplace where she could curl up and forget—the strings of auditions and actors, and the callbacks (from both) that hadn't come—forget how tired she was of running, forget all those nights she'd spent in her studio apartment, listening to the classical radio station and reading a book, alone. And now that time was gone; it was long ago when she'd felt saved from herself, when this place felt like somewhere she could stay for a while, safe from the world.

In the corner, Leo's arrangement of old stuff—suitcases and wooden tennis rackets, a violin in its case and a pack of Lucky Strikes—had a kind of hopeful, sad, romantic charm. As if his life had once possessed ease and luck, lighthearted whimsy. Of course they were only props, the old stuff. Set dressings. He'd never played tennis, nor had he smoked or played the violin. At first the arrangement had been fresh, crisp, like newly displayed dried flowers, and it was now covered with dust, now it was *old*, old stuff, and it made the room feel stuffy and crowded, like an attic.

Beside it, the desk loomed. His desk. Wooden, with a fold-down top, he'd cleared it for her when she moved in, so she'd have a place to work. It, too, was neglected, piled high with mail and drafts of poems, journals and books. There wasn't even space to write. And what she wanted more than anything was to write, to sort her mind—the tangle and tumble of thoughts, like kelp and sea stones heaped along a shoreline. There were treasures, she was certain. Beautiful, sea-worn stones having come so far, taken so many years to round. She could hear the roar of the waves, the clattering of the stones, the hiss of the foam. There would be time, she told herself. Soon. Time to search this ocean inside her. Soon, when she wasn't so bloody tired.

Her head throbbed. She took off her jeans and T-shirt and

bra and slipped naked between the cool sheets. She'd sleep a little. And then she'd bathe and wrap herself in a robe—that frayed silk robe of her mother's. She'd wear a high pair of heels and a strand of long, fake Mardi Gras pearls. She'd show her tits and everything else, because that was what you did when there was a curfew and you were pregnant—your body changing fast. That's what you did when your best friend was dying and your boyfriend was planning a stunt that, were he to follow it through, could get him arrested or beaten or killed the very next morning. That's what you did when your city was burning, the city in which you'd lived and dreamed and loved; that's what you did when you had just this night.

Fourteen

VALIANT'S HEAVEN-BLUE LIVING room twinkled with strings of little white Christmas lights he'd draped around the windows and doors, and with the devotional candles on the vanity, which, centered along one of the long walls, was the focal point of the room. Gwen stood before the mirror, looking at herself in the black silk robe, the Mardi Gras pearls, and her high heels. At least twenty candles of Saint Sebastian lined the edge of the vanity with a flickering rim of fire. His wrists bound, his body a pincushion of arrows, he was, she knew, patron saint of both masochists and the dying. His image multiplied made a circle that challenged pain and death itself. Fuck you, the candles said. Bring it on. Without you, there can be no ecstasy, no release from the self, no transcendence. You are wax and wick, the candles said to pain, fuel for liberation, for light.

Below the center of the mirror, a single candle faltered: the Virgin of Guadalupe. The dark Virgin, the one Gwen had always felt most drawn to. It reminded her of her grandmother Carlotta, whose pendant she had, still, somewhere. When had she last seen it? She had found the pendant years ago in Carlotta's gold-leafed antique jewelry box. It was after her funeral and Gwen's mother and aunts were diving in, dividing her treasures—the diamond rings and bracelets and necklaces—among which the Guadalupe pendant on the thin silver chain had stood out. Its tarnished edges and its enamel face had spoken to Gwen of her grandmother's girlhood, of that time before she'd met the man who would be her husband, who'd buy her diamonds and dresses and escort her to charity balls, before she'd exchanged the name Carlotta for the anglicized Carla. Gwen had never seen her wear the Guadalupe pendant. With its red and green and gold, it was too bright. Too Mexican. Gwen had put it on then and there. For a long time after that, all during high school, she never took it off. And now she needed to find it. She wished it hung over her heart, instead of these fake pearls.

The Guadalupe candle was new. It would have to burn awhile before the image would really light up, like sun through stained glass. You could still see, over the rim of the candle's clear glass, the flame—the blue base, the yellow tip, and, between them, the pellucid window, oblong, like those windows in submarines, or in illustrations of submarines, the window from one world into another.

On the vanity, inside the ring of candles, Valiant's wigs framed their mannequin heads. The black rocker wig and the one with the straight bangs—the pageboy he wore when he wanted to look pretty. In a wooden box between them he kept his makeup. Black eyeliner and mascara, eye shadow and blush and translucent powder.

Waiting for the Count to emerge from his bedroom, where he was still engaged in who knew what preparations, Gwen took off her black silk robe and hung it over the vanity chair. Leo was downstairs asleep on the sofa, which meant this party would consist of just the two of them—Valiant and her. They hadn't seen each other naked before, but it seemed natural, a fitting progression of their friendship. In just her heels, she realized she felt clothed, her body a sort of rubbery costume she wore with confidence. She was a little prickly, the hair on her pussy, her legs, and her armpits just starting to poke its way out of her skin. It was a luxury, those days she didn't have to shave, when she could let her body do what it wanted—to bristle as if in defense, to grow its veil of hair. And, yes, there was the razor she still needed to buy.

At Valiant's bar on wheels—the low cart with booze and mixers and a full canister of ice that he called his *rolling bar*—she started to pour herself a vodka and tonic before she remembered. Her body—this suit she wore with such ease—was changing.

It was hard thinking of her body as a machine, busy all by itself. Busy making someone. Someone else. All she had to do was supply the right ingredients—to eat and drink the right things, pure things—avocados and oranges—to breathe pure air, to think pure thoughts. All she had to do was be healthy, good to herself.

She wasn't sure she knew how. And anyway, she'd not decided.

You get an abortion and it's over was what Tony had said. *It's over.* There was such finality to it. There would be no turning back from that. No erasure. When she was forty-five, and her clock with its nonrechargeable battery was nearing the end of its ticking, and the silence was looming, she wouldn't be able to return to this time. She wouldn't be able to choose again.

She left her glass on the bar, untouched, and sat at the vanity, Valiant's shrine to transformation. Above the mirror and to both sides hung his triptych self-portrait. He'd painted his body black and while the paint was wet pressed his flesh against the raw white canvases. To the right was his face in profile, his shoulder and arm, a few ribs. To the left was the canvas with his feet and legs. And in the middle, above Gwen, hung his thighs, his ass, and his hips, the form a dark, open hibiscus from which his cock emerged—the majestic stamen. He'd painted it, Leo had told her, before Gwen had met him, just after he'd tested positive. And she could see why. Here his full-sized body (his cock, she figured, had to be a bit larger than life) was cast in permanent shadow. A perfect negative of himself, the painting was the world without him in it. It was like those cartoons in which the character runs right through the locked door, leaving a hole in their shape punched out of the wood. The painting was an act of bravery—his way of looking things in the face, his refusal to hide.

Gwen dipped his powder brush in the jar of loose powder. It was the color of moonlight, of starlight. She dusted her forehead, the tip of her nose, her collarbones, her aching nipples, her belly with its slight swell. In the candlelight, she almost glowed. She was Tink, still, made of air and shimmer. As if she might lift right off the chair and float on out the window.

These Last Days was playing on the fifties radio. It was Valiant's favorite show, to which he'd tune in religiously for his dose of weekly humor. Veronica Lueken, a white, middle-aged, self-proclaimed prophet from Bayside, New York, saw Mary appear on the fairgrounds near LaGuardia, while devotees flocked to hear her message. The show always started with Veronica's secretary, in her heavy New York accent, giving the update on Veronica's health. This week was no different. "Veronica has not been doing well. Her pancreas has been giving her problems, as well as the medication prescribed for her diverticulitis." And then Veronica herself came on, overwhelmed by what she saw, her voice strangulated with zeal. "I, I can see Mary. It's Mary. She knows me. She's, she's wearing a blue robe and underneath is—ah, ah, ah—a flowing white vestment, and she has sandals on her feet. She sees all her children gathered here and she's happy, she's smiling, she's, she's, she's talking to me now. How lovely you all are, she says. Oh! And now, she's crying. It's the sinners, the homosexuals. They've brought this plague upon us. The AIDS. She says they must repent. She says—"

Valiant entered from the hallway, switched off the radio. "She says they must change their evil ways," he said, imitating her fervent breathlessness. "I've heard this one," he said in his own voice. "It was on a few weeks ago."

"Why do you do that to yourself?"

"Come on, Gwen. It's hilarious."

Ready, apparently, for the riot-night festivities, he stood behind her, wearing his aqua satin robe, its sash in a loose bow at the waist. He took a black scarf from where it hung on the mirror and tied it around her neck. The scarf was almost too tight. Cradling her jaw in one hand, he tilted her face up, toward the Christmas lights. He turned her face to one profile and then the other. Was she a model to him now? Or an old film actress? What part would he ask her to play?

She laughed her high-pitched, nervous laugh, but clamped her mouth shut as soon as she realized. She hated this titter and how it flew from her mouth before she could stop it. It was the same laugh that had come out the time her mother ran over her cat, Mouse, in the driveway. The cat was flapping and splashing in a puddle of its own blood and she, Gwen, was laughing this awful laugh. She'd just won a modeling contest, from a photo her mother had taken. She was going to be in *Teen* magazine, and they were on their way to tell her grandmother the news when they'd backed over the cat. Her mother's tears dripped from her chin, and all Gwen could do was laugh. They'd buried Mouse in the vegetable garden and grown carrots over him the next summer.

The room was too quiet. She could hear the clock on the wall ticking. The antique clock with the brass rim and the big numbers. It said a quarter to three.

"These cheekbones," Valiant said and sighed. "You should have been a movie star, darling."

"You think?"

He turned her face to the mirror. "I *know*." Valiant ran his fingers through her hair, taking his time, unknotting strands. He'd never done this before, and she found herself holding her breath. "You know," he said, looking at her mirror-world eyes, holding them with his. "When I met you, I hated you immediately." He tugged at a knot in her hair until it gave.

Gwen winced. "I know," she said, "I—" And she wasn't sure how to finish her sentence. She'd known he was jealous, but that was then. They'd been friends for years.

"All this blond hair, how in love with you he was. I thought you'd take him away."

"I wouldn't have dreamed of it."

"No, I know that now. And here you are. One of my very, very best friends," he said, pulling through another knot. "I was scared of nothing." He lifted her hair, took the whole of it in his hand and drew it back, tight.

Gwen looked at her face in the mirror and saw—not herself—but Carlotta. (She refused to think of her as Carla.) Yes, it was her grandmother, young, in her red dress with the ruffles along the hem, castanets in her hands. Staring back at her, she saw Carlotta's eyes, their shock of green. This was the Carlotta who would eat a man alive. She recognized her fire—destruction, creation. A world of possibility.

She knew what she'd do. She'd take the risk. After all, the Count was someone she could talk to. He was her friend. She could confide in him.

"I want to tell you something," she said. "You have to promise me you won't tell anyone."

"Oooh. A secret. I promise, *if* . . . if you promise me you'll never leave me. What would I do without you and Leo?" he said, smiling a hopeful smile and twisting her hair until she felt her roots tug on her scalp.

What *would* he do? It was a good question. If she kept the baby and she stayed with Leo, that would mean they'd leave him. Because she wouldn't raise a child in Los Angeles. She wouldn't.

"What is it?" he said. "You're so serious."

"Oh." She was stalling, losing her gumption, thinking of something else she could say. "In the mirror. Have you ever thought about it? How you can't see yourself, ever, the way others see you? It's opposite, in the mirror. It's all reversed."

"You've been smoking, haven't you, kid." With a laugh, he let her hair go, so that it hung bedroom-messy over one of her eyes. "Look at you. A young Ann-Margret—before the car crash and the reconstructive surgery. Ann-Margret in *Kitten with a Whip*. Anyone ever tell you that?"

"Just you."

"Oh, I've been saving something," he said. He put an LP on the turntable and crooned along with Sinatra. *Fly me to the moon, and let me play among the stars.* "One moment, dear," he said. "I'll be back."

Gwen stayed in the chair, looking at herself. She loosened the scarf, took the pageboy wig from its mannequin head and put it on. She tucked her own blond hair up under the wig's mesh cap until she was all brunette. Now she resembled her mother. Her image flickered in the flickering room. Here and gone.

It was déjà vu, a dream she was just remembering. On the bed at dusk, she had closed her eyes. She'd slept deep and long and now the dream she'd had was coming back to her in detail.

She is huge, her belly and her breasts, seven months pregnant at least, and onstage as if by some mistake, unshaven, unprepared. Teetering on her heels, she tries to spin. The men stare at her in horror. They had not come to see this monster of a woman. Her mother sits among them. And then she stands up, a pistol in her hand. She aims the gun at Gwen's womb, fires and misses. And Gwen, in all her bloated glory, flies through an open window. And she is safe. With the baby inside her—the girl—she flies over hills, and can see the moon, and stars. And then the scene shifts.

Her mother is a model, on a sofa beside another model, in a green room, backstage, behind the runway, sipping tea, laughing and holding the woman's hands. It is her mother before she was a mother, her hair spilling like dark wine.

Seeing her like that, in the dream, Gwen is lit. She is filled. Her heart is a tended hearth.

And now, at the vanity, Gwen took from Valiant's wooden box a container of eye shadow. Shades of shimmering blue. She touched her finger to the lightest of the blues and ran it over her upper eyelid, just under her brow. Right, then left. And the darker blue lower, above her lashes. Like the wings of a butterfly. One of Nabokov's blues.

Her mother's eyelids are gold-white in the dream. Opalescent. Her eyelids glint, as if reflecting some other world in which the colors have a smell, a taste. Semen and citrus blossom, creosote after a summer rain.

"Angel dust," her mother says of her glimmering eyelids. "You want some?"

"I'm all right. I'm doing fine," Gwen says, and as she speaks the words, she knows it is a lie.

"No," her mother says, looking through her. "You need this." She flutters her lashes, and the angel dust fills the air with glints of light that settle in Gwen's open eyes. The world is changed. The world is made of petals. Of pastel-colored petals. Everything. The coffee table, the sofa, the teacups and the saucers. Her mother and her mother's friends, the chandeliers and the walls. And when Gwen sees her own reflection in the dream she is made of petals, too—green and yellow and blue and pink—as if she were looking through the facets of a crystal.

The world is magic. The world is just-born and full-blown—honeysuckle, sunflowers, roses and bees. And her mother takes her in her arms and they waltz. She kisses Gwen—on her eyelids, on her nose—the way she did when Gwen was little. Time is gone. It is a watchful silence, an iridescence, like a soap bubble in sunlight, a soap bubble they are inside, floating and waltzing, and when Gwen looks at her mother again she is Brett.

They stop dancing and the room swirls around them. Brett leans close. Their lips touch and open, and their tongues are fruit flesh, peeled apricots and peaches. Plums.

Gwen pulls back, comes up for a breath. The bubble pops.

The air is clear, but Brett lingers a second longer. Exquisite, untouchable Brett. An enigmatic smile on her lips.

Thinking of the kiss, Gwen felt her face warm. She was here, in Valiant's living room, with the Christmas lights and the candles and Sinatra singing *fly me to the moon.* The clock on the wall said ten to three. The wooden seat of the chair was beneath her and Valiant's rectangle of a mirror was watching her with his eyes.

Valiant was standing behind her. How long had he been standing there? He wore only a tiara, and held in one hand a grapefruit and in the other a vase of flowers. Without his clothes on, he looked so thin, so sallow. Gwen smiled to hide her shock and her sudden tears. His collarbones and his ribs caught the candlelight so that he looked, really, like a live skeleton. Like more of a ghost than a person—as if, were she to try to hug him, he'd turn out to be made of smoke. His cock hung soft and a bit shrunken, nothing like the majestic stamen of his painting, more like the clapper of a small bronze bell. And there was another lesion, this one a little larger, on the side of his shrunken waist.

"For you, my dear," he said, handing her the grapefruit. "I picked it a few nights ago."

"You're still midnight gardening?"

"Only when I can't sleep and the sun is coming up."

It made her happy to think of him stealing through the neighborhood gardens by moonlight, clad all in black, clippers in hand, snipping instances of beauty where he found them—a rose here, birds of paradise there—gathering them in his arms and bringing them home to fill his living room, his kitchen, and his bedroom with life.

He set the vase on the vanity and the room swam in the smell of the roses.

God, the smells. She was high on them. She put the grape-fruit to her nose and she was back in her grandparents' garden, her mother and her aunts in their bare feet and their white dresses, and she slipped off her heels and Valiant took her hand in his and they danced—Valiant, the yellow, fragrant orb, Gwen and the new life inside her.

Too bad Leo was at home, three floors below, passed out on the sofa.

"Tomorrow morning, do we let him?" she said.

"Go through with it?" He laughed. "You know Leo."

"I do. It just seems like this time he really might, with all the riot energy goading him on."

"You want to know what I say? I say we take him seriously. I say we have a little fun."

"Tell me," she said. "What do you have in mind?"

Fifteen

THE HANDCUFFS WERE easy to find. They were just where Valiant said they'd be, in the top left drawer of his bureau, under the Super Shaper Briefs with the snap-on endowment and the butt-enhancer pads, the briefs that were black and silky and spongy, like a padded bra, and which Gwen couldn't help but give a little pinch before pulling the handcuffs and the key from the drawer.

"Now where to find rope?" she said, walking into the living room.

Valiant straightened his black rocker wig and fitted the tiara over it. He poured himself a tall vodka tonic, lit a cigarette, and lay back on his gold velvet fainting couch. He inhaled, breathing the smoke, drawing it deep into his cells. Exhaling, he seemed to relax as the nicotine hit. "Three left," he said, closing the box. "I don't know if our escapade can wait till morning."

Gwen stood away from the smoke at the open window. Fiddling with the handcuffs, she closed one cuff around her wrist. At its last notch, it was just small enough to hold her hand. She felt the cold metal around her wrist and wondered whom Valiant had used these on or, as seemed more likely the case, who had used them on him. He hadn't had a lover since she'd known him. Before that, she knew, there had been both women and men.

The handcuffs made her think of the video the three of them had watched once—Leo, the Count, and her. One the Count owned—a gay prison porno. The jailor and the jailed, the guard and his prisoner—the one with no choice but to submit. She turned the cuff around her wrist. She had found the video fascinating. She could only half look and yet it had turned her on. It was ridiculous, blatant and corny, but she'd never seen men with men. There had been no pretense of tenderness. It was all about ass-fucking.

Right now Leo was sleeping on the sofa and she wanted to go home and rouse him. She wanted him to wake up strong and hungry, alive. She wanted him to handcuff her to the bedposts and take her in every way he wanted. She wanted him to want. To speak to her in Italian and order her into position. She wanted to be made to open, to let go, to submit. It had been years since he'd taken her in this way. They'd played their parts, and she'd turned off her mind and been wild about him. But why did she need him to pretend to be someone else in order for her to desire him?

"Anything happening out there?" the Count said.

"Oh," she said. She felt her cheeks burning, and had to remind herself that he didn't know what she was thinking. She put the key in the lock of the cuff and let herself out. She laid the handcuffs on the windowsill. From his window she could see the alley with the trash bin and the tree that hung over it, a jacaranda, with its canopy of purple blossoms. She could also see the sky and in it the orange glow of what had to be the moon behind the brownish blanket of smoke and cloud. "Just the moon," she said, and turned to him.

Valiant—bony and pallid, tapping his cigarette ash into the black art deco ashtray—flickered with the candlelight. It was as if she were seeing him projected. Like an old film at the end of a reel.

"You can see it, can't you? Leo doesn't, but you do."

She watched him bring the cigarette to his lips in one slow, fluid gesture. "See what?" she said, pretending.

"That I'm going. Any day now."

She wanted to play dumb and ask him where, or to disagree, as though that could hold him here, with them. But she said nothing.

His cigarette lay in the ashtray, turning to ash without his help, and its smoke blossoming in the air between them. "I have to tell you," he said. He seemed to be reclining on the chemical cloud, at once remote and closer than ever. He could tell her anything. So she leaned on the wall to hear what she had always known.

"It's been since high school, since *Guys and Dolls,* a million years ago. He was just a freshman, so young, and he played this Cuban nightclub singer. It was his voice, even then. His voice and his face. I couldn't help myself, I . . . When he first moved here, I told him what I—felt—but it was too much, maybe. He stayed away for a while. And then, well, I found out I was sick, and that was that."

He was quiet and still, as faint as an apparition. "You know," she said. "I think I knew. And it was okay, so long as you were okay with me. And you have been, right?"

"If it can't be me in his arms, you're the next best thing." He coughed, too hard, and the smoke churned and lifted. She stayed by the open window, where the air was clearest.

"So," she said, looking to change the subject, "where should we take him?" She wanted to get as far from this city as possible. She wanted to go where the sky would be blue.

He gazed into a cloud of cobwebs in a corner of the room. She looked at it, too, but couldn't see their destination, just a fly buzzing, straining against the sticky net.

"Tijuana," Valiant said at last. "We'll go to Tijuana."

Mexico sounded good. But Tijuana? "Talk about seedy," she said.

"Yes-sir-ee. Just what the doctor ordered. We'll stay in some cheap motel and drink ourselves some margaritas. Sit down, dear." He gestured to the chair beside him. "Grab your drink. You haven't touched it."

Gwen took the drink in her hand. The ice had melted and the glass was sweating. She put it to her neck. She was hot, she realized, and the cool glass felt good. She pressed it to her eyelids. It was like her mother's kisses from her dream, damp. And for a second, standing there in the middle of his living room, naked and sleepy, Gwen forgot herself.

She came to, came back and sat beside the Count in his green upholstered Venetian chair. She let it hold her, let her body feel heavy as she rested her arms on its worn silk arms, as she sat back, crossing her ankles. Why was it so hard to let go? She wanted to relax every single muscle, to let the chair absorb and absolve her. She wanted to become the chair.

Because if she were a chair, she'd have no decisions to make. If she were a chair, she'd hold anyone who sat upon her three feet off the floor. If she were a chair, she'd give herself to the purpose for which she was fashioned until she snapped beneath the weight she had held. If she were a chair, she'd be a chair until she became firewood. And then she would provide heat and light. A chair didn't long to be a fainting couch or a lampshade or a rolling bar; a chair was happy, she thought, being a chair. Like Prufrock, a chair was glad to be of use.

But what of the French *la chair*, meaning flesh? She was that right now. And was she glad to be of use? On the one hand, yes. On the other, no. Where the exchange was tit for tat, it was easy being flesh. But where flesh met mystery, where flesh doubled and split, with an action all its own . . .

She sipped her vodka tonic, kept the drink in her mouth and, bringing the glass again to her lips, spit the drink back into it. She looked at Valiant. He hadn't noticed. She took another sip, spit it into the glass.

This was ridiculous. How long could she pretend?

Valiant draped a throw over his crotch and thighs. His calves were showing, and Gwen saw they were covered with scabs. Big, oval scabs, the size of the scarabs he'd made. He moved the throw so it covered the length of his legs and she turned her eyes.

She blushed. "I'm sorry," she said. "I didn't know."

"No one does. Just my doctor, and Leo. Leo knows. It was what he was doing last night. Putting his hands on me. Like he was Jesus or something."

"Did it help?"

He looked away. "Suppose I felt like less of a leper."

She touched his arm. She couldn't wait any longer. She needed his help thinking things through. "Listen—"

"Why?" He jerked his arm from her and sat up, jabbed his cigarette into the ashtray. "You want to tell me I'm made of light? That I can heal myself if I think the right things? That we don't ever die, really, so why do I need the AZT and the ddI and the steroids and God knows what else I take every day? And these," he said, touching the dark, raised spot above his collarbone and the one on his waist. "Kaposi's sarcoma, fucking death star."

She froze. She didn't know what to say.

He was softer when he spoke again. "I thought you were on my side. I thought we both thought Leo was out of his mind."

"Yes," she said, and knew she should dive in, tell him now. Yet she hesitated. She was outside herself, looking on. As if she'd need it for a scene she'd act in someday. The woman telling the man—the man who was her best friend and in love with her lover and dying—that she had a life inside her, a person who would come between them, who would change things. She took her time. She put her glass down and looked at him. She wanted him to hear her when she spoke.

"Valiant," she said. "I'm pregnant."

At this, he relaxed and lay back down. She thought she saw a smile cross his lips. Not the happy-for-her sort of smile, but more of a smirk that said, Ah, yes, so this is how it will end. Of *course*. I should have known.

"You've told Leo?"

"No. A few girls at the club know. And you."

He lit another cigarette, sucked on it and aimed the noxious plume at the ceiling, waved the stray fumes from her face. "You're going to tell him. I mean, you have to. It's his kid, right?"

She looked at him. The question didn't deserve an answer. She pushed herself out of the chair. "He's been stoned nonstop since I found out. Today of all days. He'd get all grandiose on me."

"Okay, here's the deal. It's perfect. You'll tell him in Tijuana. He won't be able to bring any weed there. We'll make sure he doesn't try. And then you'll tell him. You've got to give him a chance, Gwen."

"Do I? Why?" She wanted her clothes on. She felt exposed,

with her breasts that were too big already and would only grow bigger. She felt messy and too female. She crossed her arms against her chest.

"This is different. Don't you see?" He sipped his drink. "There's someone else now. It's not about you and me and Leo. It's about him, or her. The person who is going to be here, here on this planet, after I'm gone."

She cringed. Her gut tightened and turned. She felt a tingling move down her arms, felt her hands ball into fists. It wasn't about the baby at all. It wasn't about what was best for the *girl* inside her. This was about Valiant.

She took her robe from the back of the chair and put it on.

"Gwendolyn, darling," he said, rising from the fainting couch. "You're overreacting. It's your hormones."

She picked up her full vodka tonic. She wanted to douse him with it. Or drink it all down just to spite him. Instead, she brought it to the kitchen and poured it down the sink—the clean, empty sink. The dirty dishes that had filled it the night before were washed and stacked on the counter. Leo must have stayed up for hours doing them. Even the counters and the cupboards were shiny white.

She could hear fresh ice clink into Valiant's glass. He was making himself another.

"I'm going to find rope," she said. She took her grapefruit and walked to the door. "I'll be back."

"Darling," he said. She turned, waiting in the open door for his apology. She would accept it, graciously, or at least she would try. "You have to stop thinking of just yourself. You've been really, well, *absorbed* lately."

"I'm going," she said, and let the door slam shut behind her.

She'd been absorbed? Unbelievable. Even for him. She walked fast down the hall. Behind one door, a TV blasted the news, behind another there was laughter, a whole gaggle of voices. Four in the morning, and people were up. She slowed, listening. At the end of the hall a guitar rang out through an amp—C, F, G, D minor, C. The blond boy got his Les Paul. Maybe it *was* Christmas.

Ash had settled over the city like snow and made them all one family. They were children, too excited to sleep. After all, the world was watching. And they were here, alive now. April 30, 1992, the day they'd all seen to its end, was a day that would go down in history. It was a day they'd talk about for decades.

She could sense the energy, the awakened camaraderie. The walls were thinning, softening. She could knock on the boy's door and he'd open it and invite her in, give her a tall glass of something cool, play her a song. The apartment house had become a home, but socializing was the last thing she wanted.

She walked to the stairwell, where a bare bulb buzzed and dimmed.

She thought she'd never felt so alone. And then she laughed. She knew it was a lie. She'd felt alone most of her life. And it wasn't a bad thing. An only child, she'd entertained herself for hours in her room, sitting at her desk with the wide window in front of it, looking out at the cactus and the swimming pool and writing stories into the books she'd bind herself, or making trinkets out of drawings coated with layers of glue for shine and heft. The one time her mother had thrown her a birthday party, she'd lost all the games—pin the tail on the donkey, musical chairs—and she'd known that none of the kids were really her friends, they were just her kindergarten classmates. They were acquaintances. So she ran from the party. She'd climbed one of those grapefruit trees in her grandparents' backyard and she'd hid. She'd not come out until the kids had gone home.

The grapefruit in her hand filled the stairwell with its smell. She breathed it in. The lightbulb flickered and brightened. One more flight of stairs and she'd be up on the roof with the night sky and the cool air.

Soon Valiant would be drunk. But when had she ever been able to stop him? What were a few more drinks once he'd set his course? By morning, he'd polish off the vodka. She'd find some rope. They had the handcuffs. They'd tie Leo up, let him have some water, a token bong rip or two, and maybe an apple, and then they'd walk him to her car. *Escort* it was called in the movies, as though the promise of sex were part and parcel of captivity. They'd snap some photos of Leo tied up in the car, and Gwen would drive the three of them south, into the new day.

But now it was night. It was night and somewhere there were stars.

Sixteen

NOT HERE, SHE thought climbing the stairs. Even without the moon and the smoke there wouldn't be stars. There were never stars in L.A. Not those sort of stars. Here the stars were people on billboards for movies, they were people you might glimpse at a deli with a baseball cap pulled low over their foreheads, hiding their eyes. The stars were the ones who most wanted to not be noticed. They were the ones trying to blend into the ambient light.

She stepped onto the roof, walking across the torch-down to the edge, to the brick wall that came to her knees.

Something was strange, unsettling. The smoke-smell on the air, and the city too quiet for its own good, as if it were up to something. She took a breath, and another, to sink into the stillness, to get to the bottom of things. Not one car zoomed down Sixth Street. Not one helicopter circled. Not one car alarm screamed. The city was spread out below her like a beast sated by a kill, sleeping off its stupor, dreaming of more meat.

This was the hungriest city she could imagine. There was New York City, of course, but there one expected hardship. What it looked like was what it was. There were no palm trees in New York City. There wasn't any ocean you'd want to swim in. Los Angeles, on the other hand, was breezy and warm, and you forgot it was really a beast until its stomach growled and the whole city shook—the people like fleas on its trembling skin. Its mouth salivated and drooled and the streets ran like rivers taking cars and homes and whole hillsides with them down to the sea. And when it was especially famished, Los Angeles became a dragon, the Santa Ana winds breathing fire into the canyons.

The city ate them up, and yet they flocked here, the boys and the girls. Though not for sacrifice. Not so they'd be whittled down to gristle, down to bone. They came here for the same reason she'd come—because they, too, were hungry, hungry to step into the light and to shine. They came here to rise beyond mortality. They came to trick death itself. One's face on celluloid is forever young, forever alive.

A breeze came from behind her, nudging her forward. She teetered on her heels, looking down at the sidewalk. So far down. The cement would catch her like a slap from God, a fly on his swift palm. How easy it would be, she thought, to let gravity have its way with her. She could feel it, gravity, as though it were desire, or love. She could hear it calling.

Gravity made matter possible. She knew this. And the urge to be done with both? To leap into the unknown and let go of this thing—this body, this mind, this person with memories—she thought of as herself. It wasn't the same as being brave. Anyone could tell you that. But the breeze persisted, pulling at her silk robe and her hair, toying with her.

It was like her dream tonight. The dance with her mother in the world made of petals and pastels had felt like a kind of communion and confirmation all in one. The twirling world, Brett's tongue in her mouth, the heat of her own flushed face. She re-

membered that part. It was the part she didn't remember, trans-
lated, now, to a sudden awareness in her body, a shape moving
just below the surface of her consciousness, it was this shadow
that intrigued her, and to which she stopped to listen.

To the east, a few blocks away, neon flashed alien green. The
sign was new—at least she didn't remember it. *Kool*, it said, its *o*'s
overlapping. Her mother had smoked Kool, the menthols. And
the *o*'s reminded Gwen of the snake around Brett's arm, the Ouroboros doubled and linked, a chain of creation and transformation. Or was it two tongues touching? Or else a single eye, the
oval where the *o*'s met its pupil? And now she read the sign backward, the way she'd see it in the mirror-world.

Look, it told her. *Look*.

At what? What was right in front of her that she wasn't
seeing?

"Gwendo-line," a voice said. "Gwendo-line, lookin' fine."

The voice was below her, turning a corner. The voice was
Barry's. "Hey, Barry," she called. He was walking down the sidewalk with something in his hand. A sign, it looked like. Was he
picketing? "Barry," she called again.

He didn't look up. Instead, he waved the sign in front of
him as though it were a flag and he were leading a parade. She
thought of Leo and his flag. Maybe he'd start a peace parade.
Naked people playing tubas and clarinets and drums, playing
Lennon's "Imagine." She could see him, leading them down the
streets, singing. It was the type of thing that would make the
evening news, a side note, an oddity.

Barry rounded another corner and Gwen followed him from
the edge of the roof. He was wearing an old pair of trousers. No
shirt, no shoes. He was shaking his head, deep in conversation.
"A castle is a home. A man's castle. Home of the man. The man.

Instrument of the machine," he said. "Of nothing. The hole. Black, black hole. The whole thing. Your life. Your whole life."

Your whole life. He'd said it. The words from her dream, the part she'd forgotten. Her mother's words. *Your whole life*, she had said. In the dream, before she pulled the trigger, her gun pointed at Gwen's belly. How could she not have remembered? They were her mother's words, their last conversation, what she'd said in the car that day driving Gwen home from her acting class. Gwen had wanted to quit. And what her mother had said was *Not now. You can't quit now. You have your whole life ahead of you. Don't you want something more? More than this?*

It was dusk. Some cars had their headlights on and some didn't. They were passing a Christmas tree lot and she wanted to stop, because they hadn't bought a tree yet. She wanted to go home and decorate the house and forget about becoming anyone. She wanted to be herself, fifteen, on the cusp of everything, the world bursting with possibility. She wanted her mother to love her for who she was.

Gwendolyn. She remembered her mother's choked voice and her too-quick tears from which Gwen had turned, determined to not be moved. Not by her tears and not by the silence that filled the car like Jell-O, red Jell-O, cloying, artificial cherry, in which they were both wedged and sealed. They were at a stoplight, waiting to turn left.

No, Gwen had said, her voice sharper than she'd meant, *I don't want anything.* Of course it was a lie. She had known then that she wanted to dance—ballet. She wanted to pursue it seriously. But she knew what her mother had to say about that. *A dancer's career is short-lived. You'll be finished by the time you're twenty-five. Do you want to spend your life teaching dance class, or choreographing? I mean really, Gwen, think about it. You have so much potential.*

Potential. She hated that word. It meant she wasn't enough.

At the edge of the roof, she closed her eyes and felt herself lean forward, into the nothingness she'd pretended to want. The wind was gone, the night still. Offering itself up. Like a prayer. And then, inside the silence, she heard it—the thumping, the pounding. She could hear them beating, the hearts in the Cornell, in the Miracle Mile; they were the pulse in her head, the hearts of Los Angeles. Thumping. It was just a song and a dance, but she was part of it. She was on this earth. She was here, in this place of gravity and matter and hearts that could feel so damn much.

She set the grapefruit on the torch-down, lay back, and closed her eyes.

She saw Jin, keeping watch over his family, his wife and his two small kids, his parents and his brothers and sisters as they dreamed of green, of forests dripping with rain. She saw Brett, snoring a little, asleep on her back, her arms by her sides, flying in her dream over the empty freeways, through the smoke. She saw Brett's fiancé at his desk, accompanied by his own reflection in the window as he wrote into the night. She could hear the clicking of his typewriter's keys. She saw Love and her husband who was more of a girlfriend now; they were spooning, dreaming of whips and piercings, of dark welts and fissures of pleasure. She saw Devotion and her mother sharing a double bed, their heads cradled in their nests of blond hair. They were dreaming of Wisconsin, a field of moonlit, sleeping cows. She saw Mr. Cooper holding his wife tight, forgiving her her wanderings, inhaling the musk of her armpit, of the nape of her neck as she slept in his arms. And all those men who were alone, alone and awake, drinking away the night—she saw them, too. There was Tony on the porch of his condo, looking out at the dark ocean, smoking and sipping his Cuba Libre. And Valiant, on his fifth vodka tonic and his last cigarette, looking out the window at the orange blur of moon. She saw her father, drinking his Glenlivet in the sparse, dim living room, staring at the flame in the fireplace, no matter that it was gas and a fake log. She'd call him in the morning, tell him she was fine. She saw Leo sleeping on the sofa with Fifi curled up at his feet, and she wanted to climb into his arms. She wanted him to hold her and to never let her go.

They used to come up here, she and Leo. They'd come with a bottle of sambuca, the Italian licorice liquor that he loved. You couldn't drink much, but a few sips numbed your tongue and made everything a little looser, a little more flexible. Summer nights, they'd sit up here and look out at the city and talk and laugh into the early morning. They had been different then. They'd been friends, confidants, lovers. She'd let herself dream with him—a villa in Tuscany with a vineyard and olive trees and white peacocks. The children they'd have. They'd name the boy Pane, meaning bread. And the girl they'd call Sophia.

She sat up, took the grapefruit in her hands and tore into it with her thumbs. It sprayed her face with its juice, its smell clean and new, and sour-sweet—as if the two tastes had been born from this one source. She peeled the grapefruit in a single corkscrew, like she'd done as a kid, up in a tree—all the hours she'd spent, safe among the fruit and the leaves. Disappearing was something she'd been good at all her life. But it was harder now. Under a spotlight, where could she hide, except inside her own body?

She pulled off a section and juice dripped down her arms and onto her robe. She licked her arms, put the fruit in her mouth. Its bright yellow-green taste filled her. She swallowed, and thought she could feel it in her cells, waking her up, bringing her to life. Eating made her hungry, famished.

She could hear Barry singing. *If I had a hammer, I'd hammer in the mornin', I'd hammer in the evenin'.* Thank God he only had a sign. She walked to the edge of the roof. He was under a street-light, and now she recognized his sign. It said NO LOITERING and had been stuck in the grass in front of their living room window for as long as she could remember. Barry was not only a protector, but a liberator.

Let the loitering begin.

She fastened her robe. She'd go home to Leo. She'd curl up with him and dream again.

She ran down the stairs, the clicking of her heels on the cement steps echoing in the stairwell. She'd play *La Bohème.* She'd resurrect the old Leo, the old Gwen. They'd fall back in love. And she'd tell him.

Seventeen

THEIR APARTMENT SMELLED of old bong water and dog shit. Fifi had pooped on the living room carpet and was now just where Gwen had known she'd be, curled up at Leo's feet on the sofa, their snores harmonizing. Gwen choked on the stale air. In these small, crowded, stinking rooms she couldn't breathe. All the windows were closed, and she opened them latch by latch. In the kitchen, the roaches crawled on the wall from the cupboard to where they clustered around scraps of wet, moldy bread in the sink. Gwen picked up the DustBuster and vacuumed what roaches she could while the others ran for cover.

The DustBuster stank, too, its smell musty and strangely sweet. She held it up to the kitchen light. The roaches were crawling over and over each other, sticky with their own shit. She couldn't take it any longer. For once she, rather than Leo, would be their savior. She tightened and knotted the sash of her robe, picked up the dog poop with an old newspaper, and carried the DustBuster and the poop down the hall and out the back of the building to the trash bin. Poor dog, thought Gwen, she hadn't been walked since the morning. And if they couldn't leave the building, what was she supposed to do?

She pushed open the lid of the big black bin and tossed the poop in. The smell of the trash was pungent, and nearly knocked her over. She held her breath and unhooked the DustBuster's plastic container from the holster, smacked it against the edge of the bin and watched the roaches fall in clumps into the garbage. She watched them scurry over the meat bones writhing with maggots, over the empty plastic water bottles and into the tin cans with their remnants of beans and tomatoes, into the jars lined with peanut butter and mayonnaise and pasteurized cheese spread.

They were joyous. They were thriving. She closed the lid of the trash bin, closed the lid on the fetid underbelly of life, the promised land, as Leo had called it. She snapped the DustBuster back together.

Among the purple blossoms of the tree, a swatch of white made her stop. Was it a piece of clothing, maybe a T-shirt or a sweater? She pulled back a branch. It was a rope, weathered and soft, tied in a loop knot over a low branch, as though this tree were once lakeside and a child had tied the rope for a swing, to launch off from the bank, swing out into the middle of the lake and let go.

She loosened the slip knot, pulled the rope through it and brought it back with her, into the quiet Cornell. The rope was made of cotton, and it was a few yards long. She looped it around her wrist, then the other, and pulled it taut. It would do.

Walking the halls she found she was singing his freedom song.

I'll be your new book of matches,
I'll be your full bucket of rain,
I'll be your home, darlin',
Come back again.

She opened the door, careful to close it without a sound.

Was this home? Was Leo?

He let out a loud, openmouthed snore, woke up a little, and, turning on his side, murmured something she couldn't make out and then laughed at himself. He was deep in his dream, and as much as she'd wanted, before, to curl up with him and seduce him in his sleep, she found she couldn't. She needed distance, she needed to think. She sat on the piano bench and looked at him.

If she'd met him today, there wouldn't be a chance she'd fall for him. The realization lodged in her throat like a too-big bite of something she hadn't chewed and now couldn't swallow. She tried to breathe. She looked closer. He slept without a shirt on, in just his knickers, and his arms and chest and stomach were lean and tan. The loose curls, the pink cheeks, the long, dark eyelashes, the beard, all that was fine—lovely, actually. So what was it?

His left hand hung off the sofa. There was something about his hand. Soft and rather small, it was the size of hers. The fingers had a tender roundness to them, as though his hand were the hand of a big child. She'd once felt happy to have this hand hold hers. It had meant they were setting out on an adventure—free day at the museum or a walk along a beach. It hadn't mattered where they went, so long as he was at her side. She tried to imagine this hand building a house, a tree house or even a fort, or hammering up a safety gate. Her own hands were sinuous and rough. They were strong. She'd be the one to put hammer to nail.

What would a life with Leo be—really? She tried to see them in Italy, but found she couldn't see past this apartment. This apartment or another apartment in another town—they'd all end up the same. Cluttered with books he didn't read, stinking of old bong water. But now she was just being mean. The truth was that none of it mattered when they were creating, smoking pot and creating, when he was writing a song and she was writing a poem. At those times, the apartment became a wonderland of wealth, treasures around every corner.

She fit the DustBuster back in its charger and poured the bong water down the drain. The smell made her gag, and she ran to the toilet and dry heaved. She wasn't being fair, watching him while he slept. Judging. She'd been sober for less than twenty-four hours and she was judging. She should give him a chance. After all, she told herself, people change.

In the hall—the hall of fame, as Leo called it—she paused. On the wall hung the cover of Valiant's 1989 LP, *Strange*, featuring his song that had become a kind of cult classic, "I Want Me." In his black leather jacket, his face in profile, his hand in his thick black hair, he leaned on a crumbling brick wall. "A modern Sinatra with teeth," said Jason Jones of *Spin* magazine. "A stunning debut," said another reviewer, but no other albums had followed.

And here were their head shots, signed and framed, Valiant's, Leo's, hers. Leo had insisted she sign hers, to act as if. *Act as if and it will happen*, he'd said. *You'll see.* That was nearly three years ago. In all her time living here she hadn't acted. Not unless stripping was acting. The acting she'd done was before Leo. She'd played a few bit parts on TV, and Slut #2 in a Coke commercial, applying lipstick and whispering to Slut #1 in the pretend college lecture hall. At the time she'd thought the parts would lead to something more, a movie maybe, something with substance and depth that would mean she was a true actress. And then she met Leo and they went to Europe and her agent dropped her and she didn't care. But here the head shot hung, acting as if. And here she was still, living in the tomb of a dream she knew had never really been hers.

She put the rope on the bed and lay down.

Her mind buzzed, her body hovered. There was no way she was going to sleep. She might as well get ready.

She pulled Stevie Smith's *Collected Poems* out of her bookcase. It was where she kept her cash until she deposited or spent it, and here was a week's worth. She'd stuck it in at the poem "Not Waving but Drowning," which, being all of three quatrains, she read in a whisper to the empty room, to the still night, to the wan courtyard light through the curtains.

> *Nobody heard him, the dead man,*
> *But still he lay moaning:*
> *I was much further out than you thought*
> *And not waving but drowning.*

> *Poor chap, he always loved larking*
> *And now he's dead*
> *It must have been too cold for him his heart gave way,*
> *They said.*

> *Oh, no no no, it was too cold always*
> *(Still the dead one lay moaning)*
> *I was much too far out all my life*
> *And not waving but drowning.*

The lines were somehow soothing. Weren't we all dead men? Weren't we all drowning? The question was how to spend the time that remained.

She counted the Franklins, the Grants, and the Jacksons—all

the faces upright, facing front, the bills smallest to largest, the way she'd learned to stack her cash at the club. The order suited her. It gave her a small thrill and made her feel her life was in fact hers to arrange as she pleased. There was a little more than a thousand. Too much for Mexico. She took just the Franklins— founding father with his long hair and his pursed smile, wild Franklin of the naked baths in the wind and the kite flying to catch the lightning—and tucked the wad of five bills into the front pocket of a pair of jeans. She'd wear the jeans to Mexico and keep the money on her. The rest she closed in the book she slid back in the shelf.

Fifi's shock collar was on the dresser. She'd need it, too, in case they had to leave her in a hotel room. It resembled a medieval torture device, with its two metal prongs strapped against her throat, but it worked. It kept her quiet and calm. The double-A batteries were old and most likely dead, but so long as the collar was on her, she wouldn't dare bark. Gwen put it on the bed.

What else would she need? It was warm in Mexico, wasn't it? She found a bathing suit, a sundress, a clean towel, flip-flops, her notebook and her pens—if there was a beach nearby she would be ready. And water, as always she would need plenty of water. Baja was a desert. The thought of the dust and the crowded streets of Tijuana made her thirsty already.

There was one more thing she wanted with her, in case the place got torched.

She searched under clothes in the closet. She looked under her bed, in her dresser and bedside table, between her sweaters. The cigar box, the one that had been her grandfather's and then her mother's—it had to be here, here in this room. She glanced at the desk. The piles of rejection slips, of poems returned, the drafts she'd abandoned. She didn't care if they went up in flames. In fact, she had an urge to burn them herself, all the pages. Even the poems that had come to her quick, like small gifts, the poems she almost liked. She wanted to start fresh. A clean desk, a clean mind. She swept off the papers, sending Leo's arrangement of old stuff tumbling. The tennis racket and the violin case clattered to the floor, where she let them lie beside the empty suitcases.

There was the cigar box, tucked into a corner of the desk, behind the Underwood typewriter that had been her grandfather's, too, had come from his warehouse—the oldest in Phoenix—come home with him when he sold the business. It was hers because she'd asked for it when her grandfather died, because, at eighteen, she knew she wanted to write, knew a writer needed a cool-looking typewriter. When she was small, at her grandparents' house, so small the Underwood on the kitchen table was at eye level, the smooth, round black keys with the faded letters, up so close to her face, seemed big, big and mysterious, and she'd run her fingers over them when no one else was in the room. It had sent a ripple of excitement through her, as though she were stealing something.

She blew the dust from the keys, moved the typewriter over, and picked up the cigar box, blowing the dust from it, too, brushing off the final layer with her fingertips.

Partagas, the wooden box said. *1845, Regale.* She unsnapped the little gold latch. Inside were the tokens her mother, and later she, had saved, remnants that meant Gwen had been a child once. There was a clipping of her soft blond baby hair, tied with a pink satin ribbon. A pastille tin holding her baby teeth, which rattled when she shook it. There was that ring her father had given her, the gold one with the butterfly missing its wing. There was the strand of real pearls. And there were the photographs. The photos of the years.

She took out the stack and flipped through them. It'd been a long time since she'd looked. There was the one of just her head from the day she was born. Plump and rubbery as a beach ball, damp black hair, a double chin, and her eyes swollen shut like the eyes of a boxer. There was one of her mother holding her just after she was born, her mother, looking weak, puffy, and splotchy, but with love in her eyes, so much love, gazing down at her baby girl, at Gwen, as if she weren't a mistake at all, but a marvel, an answer to a forgotten prayer. There was her dad, with all his hair still, squeezing her mother to his side. Both of them flushed and smiling, holding Gwen high, up to the white backdrop of sky.

And there was the photo that was after, maybe a year after her mother had gone. The one she'd taken on her own, setting the timer, waiting for the click. The girl here doesn't smile. Her eyes are the gray eyes of Athena. I'll take you on, she says. Go ahead and look. See these cheekbones? These collarbones? The darkness under my eyes? I don't need food. I don't need sleep. Why, then, should I need you? You or anyone.

She'd made the photo on her own, in the dark room her father hadn't touched, the one room he'd let be. She'd developed the film herself by the glow of the red light and used the enlarger the way her mother had taught her, dodging the edges of the photo to lighten them, for contrast. After she'd developed the paper, dipping it in the baths of chemicals, timing it to the second, she'd hung it on the line to dry beside her mother's last prints, black-and-whites of a prepubescent Gwen and their old French bulldog, Winston, in a pile of fallen pecan leaves. It was the photo that came next in her stack—Winston licking her cheek, a fat smile on her face.

Think of peanut butter, think of whales.

That was the moment, there in her dark room, that she'd known her mother was gone—gone and not coming back. She'd been waiting, she saw now, to walk into their backyard and find her mother clipping the gardenias to float in bowls of cool water to fill the house with fragrance. She'd been waiting to come home late and find her curled into the stuffed leather chair by the lamp in the study, reading and drinking her good red wine and smoking into the night.

She put the stack of photographs on the desk, facedown.

What was left in the cigar box was the old black velvet pouch. Her heartbeat quickened. She loosened the drawstring. The smell of vanilla hung in the open mouth of the pouch, or maybe she was imagining it. She pulled out Carlotta's Guadalupe pendant, drew back the curtain and held it to the light. The Virgin's face was darker than she'd remembered, as were her robes of green and red, as if, during those black velvet years of isolation, the colors had intensified, becoming truer, more themselves. She opened the clasp of the silver chain and fastened it around her neck. The pendant was cold and she pressed it to her chest to warm it.

It occurred to her, as she set the photos back in the box, that she'd show these to her daughter, someday. And her daughter would see them as impossibly old. The thought struck in her a chord at once wistful and shrill. Who would this girl be? What sort of baby, toddler, first grader? Someday she'd be a teenager. This thought, in particular, was terrifying to Gwen, given the recklessness with which she'd lived her own teenage years—the sneaking out her window at night, the pot smoking, the drinking, the raging desert parties. And then there had been the anorexia, the bulimia. It sucked to be a teenager. She'd need her mother. Even if she didn't think she did, she'd need her. And Gwen would be there. She wouldn't check out early. She'd see her through. And this girl someday would be a woman, maybe even a mother.

Dizzy, she sat on the bed.

World without end, Amen. Wasn't that the prayer? Glory to the Father and the Son and the Holy Spirit? Well, she wasn't so sure about those three, but she knew the answer to the prayer was inside her. She was the world without end, here, on the edge of this bed, unsure of her next move, alone, in a city still smoking, waiting to explode all over again.

She lifted one of the old dusty wicker suitcases onto the bed and flipped the latches. Its hinges creaked in protest, but the suitcase opened all right, and seemed as if it would hold. She tucked her things inside, pulled on the jeans and slipped into her heels. She'd head back up to Valiant's, get him off the booze and get some water and maybe some food in him before morning. She fastened the suitcase shut and heard screeching—high-pitched, like an owl's screech.

And then there were two—two screams echoing in the courtyard.

Eighteen

THROUGH THE WINDOW screen she saw Valiant on the ground, his head wrapped in a black bandanna, his aqua robe splayed and his body dull, skeletal under the yellow light. Barry stood above him, holding the sign high, ready to strike him. They weren't ten feet away, separated from her by just the screen.

"Barry, stop!" she yelled. Barry didn't move.

"Barry, goddamn it, it's me. What the fuck?" she heard Valiant say. She opened the French window wide, pressed the side of the screen until the metal bent and threw the screen into the courtyard, stepping with care around it, between a lanky rosebush and a hydrangea.

Valiant held his hand to his jaw. "Crazy motherfucker." Blood ran down his hand and he brought it into the light to see.

Gwen stood back, frozen, like a dream when you can't move. Can't scramble up the wall, can't run fast enough. Can't call out for help. Barry still held the sign aloft. He was frozen, too, staring at Valiant. Transfixed.

"For God's sake, Barry." She said it under her breath, but he dropped the sign.

"Count?" he said, bending over him.

"Who the fuck did you think?" The Count was slurring his words and his motions were slow and broad. "Fuck," he said, touching his hand to his chin again, looking at the blood.

"Barry." Gwen approached so that he could see her. "Give me a hand?"

They each took an arm and pulled Valiant to his feet. She folded his robe closed and cinched the sash. His feet were bare. She searched the courtyard and found his black velvet slippers—one on the edge of the fountain and one under the rosebush—and helped him into them. His blood was still wet on his hand and she was careful not to touch it, not to let it touch her. His arms around their necks, steadying himself with their shoulders, he took a few sloppy steps down the sidewalk, toward Jin's. Gwen spun him around, back toward the Cornell. "You need to go home," she said.

"What are you," Valiant said, "my mother?" He laughed as though he'd said something funny and swung back around. "Not *my* mother. Not mine, but someone's." He giggled. And then he was serious, angry. "I'm going," he said, lifting his arms off them and lurching forward. "I'm not a fucking invalid. I'm going for cigarettes."

Barry picked up his sign and resumed his route. "I'm gonna keep on, then. Keep on keeping on." He was walking away from them, rounding the corner. "You never know. You just don't know."

"I'm going for cigarettes," Valiant said again, stumbling toward the street.

"No one's open," she said. Holding his elbow, she steadied him. Blood from a gash on his chin dripped down his neck. "Come on. We got to clean you up," she said, walking him toward the door.

"Oh, this?" He smeared the blood across his face with the

palm of his hand. He looked tribal, like a warrior off to battle, ready to trade his life for the good of his people, or like a modern survivalist, just come from the wilderness, where he'd killed deer and elk with arrows and lived off raw meat.

She let him go and he wobbled, but fixed his gaze on her. "My blood freak you out? My contaminated blood?"

"Stop it."

He laughed. "You're just pregnant. I guess. Pregnant." He was talking at full volume, his words bouncing off the brick walls. "Hear that, Leo, you fucking lazy-ass wop! Your girlfriend is—" Gwen would have put her hand over his mouth if he hadn't been bleeding, but as it happened all she could do was watch him say the word, and hear it echoing. "Pregnant-nant-ant."

"Come on," she said. "Let's go see Jin."

He grinned and she held his arm and together they entered the empty neighborhood, crossing Sixth Street against the red light. There was a slight breeze and the residue of smoke. Her shoes pinched her toes and she stopped midstreet and took them off and held them as she walked beside Valiant, who shuffled in his slippers, as if down a hospital corridor.

"Hey," she said. "That was a secret, you know. I'd told you in confidence. Because I thought you could keep it to yourself."

"What are you talking about," he said. "I'm dying, and you're accusing me?"

"Just don't tell him."

"About your being knocked up? On the nest? With child?"

"About that."

"You gonna tell him?"

"That's the plan."

"When?" He stopped to let a lamppost hold him up.

"In Mexico," she said. "Remember?"

"Mexico," he said, and she watched the word sink in, watched his body relax into it. "We need rope, yes?"

"I have it."

"Because we're tying him up."

"We are."

"Because he's crazy."

"Well," she said, taking his arm and coaxing him off the post and down the sidewalk. "If truth be told, we're all a little crazy. The point is, don't say anything."

"About your delicate—"

"Right."

"Cross my heart, hope to die, Gwendolyn."

They'd reached Third Street and stood silent a moment, taking in the quiet. The city was only sleeping, but it felt to Gwen as if it had stopped breathing and died in its sleep. Everything looked smaller. Where were the come-along beater cars and their lonely radios bleating love songs into the night? Where were the solitary people out for a predawn stroll? Even the Leave Earth man must have found a box to call home until morning. There wasn't any fried vanilla on the air, no just-made old-fashioneds. In fact, Jin's was dark.

Valiant lumbered to the window and pressed his nose against it, peering in.

"Anyone there?" Gwen said, sticking to the curb.

"Gotta be." Valiant knocked on the window. One, two, three, four—his signature knock, as though Jin would know it was him and would unlock the door. Only how would Jin know his knock? Valiant wasn't thinking—he was desperate, and drunk. He knocked again.

Nothing.

Valiant began to sing, an impromptu jingle.

Jin, oh, Jin, crazy Jin,
Be a darlin', let me in.
See how fine it would be,
give a pack of cigarettes to me.

He danced a little as he sang, hopping from one foot to the other and turning around. They waited for a light to come on, for Jin to stumble in from the back room, a sleepy smile on his face, shaking his head at Valiant's antics, but Jin's Joint stayed dark.

Valiant knocked again, this time harder on the window. One, two, three, four. Five, six, seven, eight. Double trouble.

"Come on," she said. "He's not here. Let's go."

"Oh, he's here. Hey, Jin," Valiant shouted. "You goddamn Chink." Then, "No," he said, in a low voice to himself. "That's wrong." Then he smiled and hollered, cupping his hands to his mouth and pressing them to the store window, "Nip! Gook! Open up!"

"What the hell are you doing?"

"What? It's just a joke," he said. Gwen tugged at his arm and he shook her off and pounded with both fists on the window. "Jin! Cig-a-rettes!"

"I'm going home," she said. Walking to the curb, she heard the latch click behind her, the door squeak open.

"Thank God," Valiant said. "Jin!"

She saw the silhouette of a man in a T-shirt and jeans, his back to her, his legs spread. "Motherfucking nigger." Even with his heavy Korean accent his words were clear. *Motherfucking nigger.* Did he mean Valiant?

The Count had his hands in the air. "Hey, man," he said. A smile showed his white teeth and made his face look like a cartoon.

Gwen came closer. She realized she was walking soundlessly, on her toes.

The man turned. The pistol pointed at her stomach shook in his hands. She held her breath. Her face, her ears were hot, the palms of her hands tingled and pulsed. This was like her dream. The gun at her stomach—did it mean her dream had been a premonition? She wished she could fly. She dropped her shoes. And then she laughed, that ridiculous trill of a laugh that meant things were beyond her comprehension, beyond her control. It was a laugh that should have been a scream.

"Oh God, God, please," she heard Valiant say.

She stopped laughing as abruptly as she'd started. The scene had gone slow-motion, so she knew it was real—a real gun, a real man with his finger on the trigger. This moment was her life. She looked from the O of the gun's barrel into the man's face. She recognized him. It was Jin's brother. The man's eyes darted from her to Valiant and he aimed the gun back at him.

"Kim?" she said. "It's Gwen. Remember? I met you this morning. We're your brother's friends."

He looked at her again, his unseeing eyes flat and frightened, and then shifted his focus to Valiant—Valiant with the smeared dried blood across his hollow cheek. The blood didn't help things. Still, in his aqua satin robe and his black slippers, he was hardly capable of concealing a gun, let alone of beating anyone up. Yet Kim walked toward him, his gun on him, his hand trembling. Valiant backed up until he was against a brick wall. "*Mae de Deus*," he muttered, and closed his eyes.

Inside the store a light came on. In a crumpled, unbuttoned

shirt and jeans, Jin crept out from the back room. She'd never seen him so scared, so tense and humorless. His arms were at his sides, in one hand he held a pistol. She smiled and waved both hands in a frenzied gesture above her head.

Jin didn't smile. Had he seen her? No. The window was a mirror. He saw just himself.

Valiant was saying a prayer in Portuguese. She recognized the prayer, the insistent rhythm of it. Her grandmother used to say it in Spanish, over and over, her fingers rubbing the beads of her rosary. *Dios te salve, Maria, llena eres de gracia.*

She knocked on the window. Jin ducked behind the counter, peered out from the side and from his crouched position pointed the gun. Like he'd seen in all those American Westerns, Gwen thought. *True Grit. Butch Cassidy and the Sundance Kid.*

Kim had his gun on her, too. She put her hands up. She'd be just another riot death. One that could have been avoided had they played by the rules and obeyed the curfew. Cigarettes. They'd gone out for cigarettes. What had they been thinking?

Jin crept forward and opened the door. "Miss Griffin?" he said, and lowered his gun. He shouted at his brother in Korean, and Kim's hand fell to his side. Still holding the pistol, it dangled there like a dead fish.

"Count?" Jin said.

Valiant slid down the wall to the cement and broke into sobs. "Sorry," he said, choking and swallowing. "I needed . . ." he wheezed, "cigarettes."

Jin spat an order at his brother. Looking down at his tennis shoes, Kim walked inside.

"I am sorry one, Count," Jin said and offered him a hand. Valiant took it and stood. "Miss Griffin," he said, "I—"

"It's not your fault, Jin," she said. She picked up her shoes off the curb and went to Valiant's side and steadied him.

His head hanging low, Kim brought out a pack of Camels and a six-pack of Budweiser and handed them to Valiant. Jin barked another command at his brother, and Kim with his dog eyes wet and red looked up at Gwen and Valiant. "Sorry," he said, and plodded inside.

The Count took a twenty from his pocket and offered it to Jin.

Jin shook his head. "Is a gift," he said.

Nineteen

THEY WERE HALFWAY to the Cornell before the Count opened the pack of cigarettes. He pulled the plastic tab with his teeth and spit it into the gutter. He hadn't said a word, and his whole body quivered as if with cold. He stopped, striking a tenuous stance, as he flicked and reflicked the lighter. Nothing. Gwen gave it a try. Her hand shook, and she used her other hand to hold it steady. A flame sprang from the plastic casing—fire where there had been only air. He sucked at the cigarette, inhaled long and exhaled slow. He cracked a can of beer and drank a good bit of it down.

Slogging on down the street, he leaned on her all the walk home, but she didn't feel the weight. The sky was lightening, so reluctantly at first that she thought she was imagining it. One by one, the trees emerged from the shadows. Their leaves began to glow, and then the windows in the apartment buildings. The world was taking form, catching the predawn light. And she had a lightness to her, too. A rush of anticipation. Twice in a single day she'd been reborn. She was alive when she might not have been. The possible was perceptible.

She thought of another sunrise, just after she'd graduated

from high school. She'd walked home from her girlfriend's house through the still neighborhood of her youth, past the dark, dreaming houses. She wore a black dress and walked in her bare feet, holding her shoes, as she did now. At home, she'd stood in the door of her father's bedroom, the room that had been *theirs*, his and her mother's, and she'd watched him sleep. Gwen had grown, changed into someone else without his noticing. She had wondered how he could sleep when she was so awake. Her mother would have noticed. She would have sensed her restlessness, her newfound vibrancy. And Gwen, standing on that threshold, felt her mother's absence carve itself like a canyon through her, a passage made of water and time. She had closed the door on her sleeping father and gone out to the swimming pool where she took off her dress and dove naked into the cold water. Holding her breath from one end of the pool to the other, she knew then that her childhood was over.

She wished she could get in a pool now, could spread her arms and kick and fly through the water—sleek and free and on to a new chapter. "Mexico," she said, because the word itself was a warm embarkation, a flight of the mind.

"*O meu Deus!* Yes." Valiant sighed. "Darling, take me away from this monstrous city. Save me."

They crossed Sixth Street, disregarding the constant red light. Still no cars, but the sky was a pale blue-white, like the film on a blind eye.

The curfew was lifted. Morning had come at last.

She stepped onto the flower bed, the soil cool and soft under her feet, and boosted Valiant through her open bedroom window. He tumbled into the bedroom. "Ow!" he cried, and Fifi trotted in, barking her high-pitched alarm of a bark. Gwen followed him through their apartment. He was moaning, dragging his shoulder along the wall, disrupting the hall of fame. In his wake, their framed photos clattered to the floor. Gwen picked hers up. The glass was cracked, and she took out the photo, glad to have it off the wall.

Still on the sofa, Leo rubbed open his eyes. "What the hell happened to you?" he said, looking at them both.

"We nearly died," the Count said. The gash on his chin, Gwen saw now, was open and bleeding. He collapsed onto the sofa as Leo moved his legs. "We nearly died and you, what did you do? Savior of the whole goddamn city? You slept. Hope you had fan-fucking-tastic dreams while we had guns pointed at our goddamn foreheads."

Disregarding his drunken tirade, Leo got up and put a pillow under the Count's head. His flag was right there on the coffee table and he didn't hesitate. He brought it to the Count's chin, used it like a handkerchief to wipe the blood. "Hold it there," he said, pressing the Count's hand to the fabric.

"Leo," said Gwen. "Your flag." Or was it her flag? She'd been the one to fashion it, to thrust it into his hands.

"Good use for a white flag, don't you think?" he said.

"So you're not marching?"

Leo was in the bathroom, the water was running. "There's time. There's more fabric," he said, coming out with a wet wash-cloth in his hand.

He knelt beside Valiant. With the washcloth he cleaned off the dried blood. He seemed to be careful, folding the washcloth so the blood didn't touch his hand. But what if it did? And what if he had a small cut on his finger? It was hard for her to watch. She turned, hating herself for thinking this way, for not being more generous, more brave.

Now Leo's open hands hovered over Valiant's chin. Leo had

his eyes closed and was moving his hands back and forth in a slow, waving motion, as though he were performing a magic trick. Voilà, she half expected him to say, pulling a rose from Valiant's mouth.

"What are you doing?" she said.

"Shhhh. I'm healing his chin."

"Oh. Well, I'm going to his apartment. Valiant, you need anything?"

"Handcuffs," Valiant said.

"I'm sorry." Leo's hands fell to his side. "Handcuffs?"

"Love," said Valiant, gazing up at Leo, "means never having to say you're sorry."

"I'll be back," she said, and laughed. It was an easy laugh, deep and true. It had been so long she hardly recognized the sound.

In Valiant's bedroom, the outfit he'd worn on the roof when the city was burning was in a heap on the floor. She grabbed the clothes with their reek of stale smoke and his pair of worn black cowboy boots.

She took his camera from the kitchen table. Half the roll was left. She slung it over her shoulder. In the living room, she took the handcuffs from the windowsill. Behind the buildings, the haze was brightening. She blew out the candles—Saint Sebastian and his semicircle of clones—and stood before the Virgin, her face aglow. Gwen closed her eyes and wished—though not for any*thing*. She wanted to glow the way the Virgin glowed, as though she housed a flame, a single, slender tongue of a flame, with its numinous blue window into another world. She opened her eyes and with a small breath blew her out.

On her way to the door she turned. There was something about the room. Something odd. The center canvas of Valiant's triptych—the image of his cock in black paint—was missing from the wall. She saw it then, in the corner, on the floor. The canvas had been stabbed to shreds and the boards that had stretched it were broken. He'd had an even harder night than she'd thought.

She ran back down the stairs. She was racing the sun. It was called daybreak for a reason. They were getting out; they were leaving. The riots could go on without them.

Inside her apartment, Valiant lay on the sofa, groaning, the flag still pressed to his chin. She handed him the clothes, and told him to put them on.

The teakettle whistled. Leo was making his morning English breakfast tea. Ever since he'd started dressing as a revolutionary he preferred tea to coffee. It makes no sense, she'd told him one morning. The revolutionaries threw the tea in the harbor. Exactly, he'd said. But I have to really miss it when I give it up. Otherwise, what kind of revolutionary would I be?

She wanted coffee. It was time for this revolution to progress, full speed ahead. Before she tied Leo up, she'd make a quick espresso. She brought the handcuffs into the bedroom. She'd have to rely on herself to pull this off, now that the Count was indisposed. She'd bring them out when all was ready.

She threw off her robe and fastened a bra, which was tight, the lace just covering her nipples. And the plain white T-shirt— she realized when she stared at herself in the mirror—had never looked quite so much like, well, an invitation. Was it possible to grow a whole size in one night? Or had the ballooning been gradual, something she had chosen not to see?

She knew her body was making a body, knew she wasn't just getting fat. But she cringed at the sight of herself. And it was her father's voice she heard. Her father's stiff, omniscient commentary. She'd been all of twelve, settling in beside him on the sofa one Saturday night to watch *The Love Boat*, a plate of s'mores on her lap. Before she could bite into one of the gooey, sweet graham cracker sandwiches, he'd said, his eyes still on the TV, "Eat it now, honey. Enjoy every bite. In another year, you eat something like that and wham, it'll turn straight to fat." He paused as if for effect. "And I can't imagine you fat," he'd said, patting her thigh to reassure her.

He had no idea she'd take that bit of advice and run with it. That she'd live on a hard-boiled egg and a cracker a day. No idea that she'd take it as a challenge. She could watch what she ate all right, and there wasn't a thing he could do about it. Another three years and he was spoon-feeding her ice cream on that same sofa. Her favorite—rocky road. At first she refused, and then, she swallowed. And this was the gateway to a whole new obsession. She'd polish off cartons—mint chip, butter pecan, black cherry—and then she'd barf them down the drain. He couldn't understand it. The ice cream vanished, the cookies, the chocolate. Anything sweet. She'd hated herself for it. And she'd put on weight in spite of the purging. Enough so that he'd stopped worrying, stopped noticing her altogether.

Since she'd started stripping his only comments had been compliments. "Wow, honey," he'd said when she swam in the heated pool at Christmas in her bikini. "You look like a million bucks." Had he known the cause of her body's full, taut shape, the cause of the new acceptance she'd gained for her own curves, she knew he'd have had other things to say. She could hear him now. Why hadn't she asked him for the money for her school? Or why hadn't she gotten a real job—using her mind rather than her body? After all, didn't she have a college degree?

Someday, when her life was different, she'd tell him the truth. Even the thought made her stomach flip.

She stretched out her T-shirt as best she could and stepped into her black combat boots, a pair she'd bought years back at the Army Surplus Store. She laced them up tight. Like Barry said, you don't know, you just don't know.

The piano filled the apartment with music. It was Leo, improvising. The thin notes shimmered, and she felt she was animating them, moving to their rhythm, unable not to move to it. Life and time was this river of piano set in motion by the tips of his fingers, and here she was bobbing along on it. And she was happy for now, this very moment; and she knew that what would happen would happen, and she'd be glad in that future moment, too, because it would mean she was living her life—this life that belonged to her alone and not to anyone else.

She carried her suitcase into the living room. Leo quit playing and studied her. "Going somewhere?" She smiled and looked to Valiant for support. He had draped the washcloth over his face, and his body lay so still it made her heart stop. She stepped closer, watched his chest rise and fall to be sure he was alive.

She saw the telephone on the arm of the sofa and remembered.

She dialed his number. His machine answered after the first ring.

"Dad," she said to the tape recorder, "I got your call. Just wanted you to know I'm fine. And we're leaving. We're getting out of the city, so don't worry. I'll call you soon." She hesitated. What the hell. "I love you, Dad," she said, and hung up the phone.

Leo sipped his tea at the kitchen table. "So we're leaving, are we?"

She opened the refrigerator and filled a few empty plastic bottles with the cold filtered water. "Morning," she replied, as if she hadn't heard the question. She was aiming at cheery, but she felt sick to her stomach. The refrigerator reeked. Old garlic? Onions? Tuna—maybe that was it. She swallowed, turned from him so he couldn't see. She wasn't going to run to the bathroom. Too obvious. What she needed were crackers. It was her mother's standby remedy for nausea. Saltines—the kind with actual salt—and soda water. She remembered there being Saltines in a cupboard. On her tiptoes, she opened the cupboard door.

Running from the light, the roaches scattered. She was sure these were the same roaches she'd relocated to the trash bin only hours before. She thought she could hear them cheering for Leo. *Hey! Hey, it's Leo! Friend to all! We salute you! Hey, Leo, brother, what's for breakfast?* They'd never leave. So long as Leo lived here, the roaches would, too. She saw the box of Saltines in the far back and extracted it. Inside was one sealed sleeve of crackers.

She tore it open and ate one, washed it down with water. She felt better.

Leo was still drinking his tea, observing her as if from a distance. Behind him, just to the right of his head, hung the crucifix, *his* crucifix. It framed him strangely. If he were in a comic strip, it was where his thought bubble would be. The brass Jesus, darkened with age, nailed to the wooden cross—what his mother had given him when he was twelve and he'd wanted more than anything to be a priest. My little saint, she'd called him. *Il mio salvatore.* How could she have known he'd end up thinking he *was* Jesus. It had hung on this wall since Gwen had known him. Odd place for it, she'd always thought, there by the kitchen table. Christ looking down at them as they ate, smoked, drank, and talked. His head drooping like a heavy flower. His body wounded and anchored, bound to the earth, and the spirit—up and gone. Free.

"You're making another flag, then?" she said.

"I suppose."

"Don't you know?"

"Gwen—"

"You're not backing out now, are you? Covering your tracks?" She knew he wouldn't get past the door, not if he were naked, and yet, she realized now, she wanted him to reach the threshold, maybe even put his hand on the doorknob, give it a turn. She wanted the chance to pull him from the brink, to save him from himself. It was all about timing. She wanted him to at least pretend he was going to follow through. If he didn't act his part how could she play hers?

"I feel," he was saying, "I don't know, different this morning."

"You haven't smoked your morning bowl, that's all. Let me pack it for you." She broke a sticky green bud and pressed it into the metal cone, filled the bong with fresh water. "And maybe you don't even need a new flag, hm? Why not use the bloody one? More symbolic."

"Tink," he said. He stood, and took her face in his hands. He searched her eyes. "Tell me what's going on. I look at you and it's like I don't know you anymore. Are you okay?"

Was *she* okay? Why the hell was everyone asking?

"Fine," she said. "I'm fine." But he stayed there. He didn't budge.

Faced with his intensity, his focus and quietude, this unaccounted-for presence, she wanted to bolt. She would get the rope, the handcuffs. She was on a roll. She wouldn't give up her momentum. She turned her head, her whole body from him.

She couldn't look at him right now. Not like this. She'd break. She'd tell him everything. She flicked the espresso machine on, packed the grounds for a double, added water, and pulled the lever. A present from her father when she turned eighteen, it was already showing its age, and it moaned as it forced the water over the grounds. The smell reached down to her bones, her blood; it filled her.

She made a double shot for Valiant, too. He needed it more than she did.

Leo was talking and she only half heard. He was talking about eggs. Tiny red eggs in a nest. She was getting pieces of his dream. Like Sappho's poems preserved in the mouths of mummified crocodiles, like those fragments that survived. Everything was tastier in pieces, more mysterious. There was all that white space around them. Room in which to doodle and drift, blanks you could fill in yourself. "Blood-orange," she heard him say. "It was sky and water in one. I could breathe and swim through the tops of trees."

"Like a bird-fish," she said, to show she was listening.

Valiant, having changed from his robe into his riot-wear, joined them at the round wooden table littered with the ashtrays filled with ash, with the sketches of Leo as Zero the naked savior, and with the fruit too soft to eat—green shrunken apples and oranges collapsing in on themselves like dying stars.

She and Valiant drank their coffee. Leo drank his tea and smoked, taking a break in the story of his dream to inhale, to hold the smoke in his lungs. He passed the bong that wasn't a bong to Gwen who straightaway passed it to Valiant who packed it with fresh dope and smoked. It seemed to calm him, enough so that his hand was steady when he lit another cigarette.

"You were on the edge of something," Leo said to Gwen, and

it was as if he'd reached into her chest, grabbed hold of her heart and squeezed. He'd always had this ability—to know just where she was, to intuit it.

"A cliff. No," he said. "It was a house. It was where we lived, but it was old, ancient, with these high walls. And you were on the edge of it. On the roof. And it was crumbling, the wall, the whole structure was falling, turning to a desert. You were alone, walking on the sand, and I was—" He laughed. "I was this mouse and you picked me up. You were so, so benevolent, Gwen. You were this gorgeous giant."

A wave of exhaustion washed over her. She didn't want to be benevolent, nor did she care to be huge. Leo was talking and she closed her eyes, letting his voice mix with her need for sleep. She felt the kitchen sway, as though they were on a ship, a ship far out at sea. She opened her eyes. Leo was silent, and so was Valiant, everyone in their own world, all right here, at one table. There was mist around them, that rare morning light in which the sun's rays, made visible by the smoke, had dust motes dancing inside them. Swirling. And it hit her. This moment wouldn't return, not ever. Not the sun through the soft, burned Los Angeles air, through their torn window screen. Not the two scrubby faces she adored. Not the coffee steaming. 1992 would be gone before they knew it. It would be another year. And she'd be someone else. She'd be a mother, if she dared. And where would Valiant be? How much longer would he hold on—to the body he tried so hard to destroy—hold on to the flimsy sunlight and spare Los Angeles oxygen, so the tunes only he could hear might come through him and into the world? How much longer? And what of Leo? Would this be the end of her time with him? Would she drive off one night and never look back? Or would he stay in her life for years? He was all artist, sitting here in his white

Thomas Jefferson shirt, maculate with drops of tea and blood and smudges of cannabis ash. Yes, with his ringlets loose to his shoulders, with his easy smile, he looked beautiful.

The morning held in this lull a sense of possibility. The three of them could go where they liked. For now, they were due south. But they were free to change their course. They could head east, or west, or north. Anywhere, really. But for this instant in which there was quiet, in which there wasn't any wind, only a pale yellow light surrounding, buoying, filling them, they were still. Suspended.

"You know," she said from deep inside the mist, her voice sounding far away, "we might as well tell you where we're headed."

Twenty

THE LIGHT MADE Leo look almost holy. As if the smoky rays were planned, all part of the set of a film—*Zero, Messiah for Our Troubled Times*—a parody no doubt. And this, the scene in which Zero, the Los Angeles ascetic, complete with his beard, with his parched lips and the dark circles under his eyes, is overcome by his vision.

She picked up Valiant's camera and brought Leo's dilated pupils into focus. And then her mind was far ahead, ten years or so, and she knew this was something she would remember, as she filled an album with images of the three of them, affixing the photos to the blank white pages with little black paper corners she'd have to lick and press into place.

When a friend dies at a young age, leaving the world at a time when your life—the life you will come to feel is your real life—is just beginning, they take that other self, the person you were, with them. She imagined this would be the case with Valiant. He would take the old Gwen with him, on a trip from which neither would return. And something else would happen, too. Years in the future, when she'd look back and examine her life in segments, she would come to view this one in particular less

with a sense of continuity than of transformation. The cocoon
from which her butterfly emerged. But for her friend this time
was his butterfly stage. Unless, perhaps, she could widen her
gaze and look from a greater distance, at a range that included
the unknowable, the dark side of the moon—that place he would
disappear to.

She understood that by the time she developed this roll of
film and filled a scrapbook with the photos she was taking now,
the Count would have been gone for years. And this day in her
memory would be patchy. She would remember how they'd tied
Leo up for the hell of it, everything a photo op. And after another bong rip or so, he was more than game. For him it was a
relief to submit, to be bound and taken from the city—and from
his plan—by force.

In the frame, his chest was bare and wrapped with rope. He
held the bloody flag in his hand and looked up into the rays, as if
he could see the sun, could look straight at it, as if those rays had
reached inside and subsumed him, and the sun could no longer
burn the retinas of his eyes. She pressed the button, heard the
shutter open and close. In the next shot, they were on their way.
Leo's chest was still tied with the rope, but now his wrists were
cuffed and he was being led through the courtyard by Valiant.
Fifi's leash was hooked to the cuffs and Valiant gripped the other
end of the leash, pulling Leo along. In his arm, Valiant held Fifi
with a gesture that said she was his prisoner, too. He looked
straight at the camera and sneered—an old Western, silent film,
villainous sneer, the kind one pictures embellished by a handle-
bar mustache. It was a lark, a riff, a moment thieved and pock-
eted. But taking the photo, she noticed how the thin skin of his
cheeks wrinkled too easily, and his features were too large for
his face.

Gwen looked for Barry, to photograph him, but he wasn't patrolling the building, nor was he on his balcony. Walking away from the Cornell, she glanced back, and thought it seemed a little forlorn and vulnerable, a little lost without him.

It felt as if, stealing into the city by first light, they were the only people left, the last of the Angelenos. Valiant stumbled along, the leash on his wrist, holding Fifi and the remainder of the six-pack. Leo, in his knickers and bare feet and handcuffs, was freed from himself and glad of it. And Gwen with the suitcase in one hand, the camera in the other, felt invisible, ghostly.

Pink by pale pink, pink by gray, quietly the City of Angels watched them saunter up the sidewalk toward the car. Prone, Gwen thought, like a concubine, her smile showing no teeth.

How many times had they walked down this street, the four of them? And yet this particular stroll felt different. She felt a vague, persistent heartache, as if this time was reaching its inevitable close—the end that had been there all along but had been hiding, waiting in the shadows of the theater's wings for that final cue, to pull the rope, to make the curtain fall. And she knew she would remember the quality of the light, *this* light, and how, like diaphanous veils, it both concealed and revealed. The light was kind, and the neighborhood looked pretty in it. Too pretty. The way things look that are past—not passing, not going, but gone.

When they reached Jin's, which appeared to be open, the door flung wide to the day, Leo declared he was hungry. "Fine," Valiant said. "I'll stay out here." And he opened a beer and settled on the curb with Fifi on his lap. Gwen took the leash, hesitating a moment before entering. Leo shuffled in after her. Behind the counter, Jin was watching the news. A few of yesterday's donuts—a maple bar, a plain twist, and a bear claw—sat behind the glass of the donut display case. The donuts were sweating, beads of perspiration on their skin of frosting.

"Morning, Jin," said Leo with a grin that in the context of what had happened there the night before made him look if not insane then certainly naive, as if hailing from some remote island.

Jin squinted his bloodshot eyes at Leo and turned up the volume on the TV.

The L.A. Riots: Day Three. The whole world was watching. A woman leveled her gaze at the camera. *Hundreds have been injured and thirty-three are dead or missing on the third day of what authorities now call the worst civil unrest in Los Angeles history.*

Just thinking about the fires made Gwen thirsty. She paid Jin for a couple gallon jugs of water. He gave Leo the donuts for free and poured Gwen a coffee, setting it in front of her with furtive, downcast eyes. He looked exhausted, his spirit as crumpled as his shirt. In his kind, soft voice he said he hoped the National Guard would make it to their neighborhood, hoped today would be better. But she could tell he didn't believe it. He turned back to the TV. He didn't ask what they were doing or seem at all surprised by the rope or the handcuffs or the leash on Leo instead of the dog. Had it been a normal day, she doubted he'd have asked. This was, after all, Los Angeles.

Munching the donuts, his hands still in cuffs, Leo led Gwen and Valiant to where he'd parked the car, in the Jewish neighborhood with the houses that must have cost a million apiece, the little houses with high, pointy iron fences and bars on all the windows. The street was so quiet it might have been the dead of night, and it felt more like a set than a real neighborhood. As if the town had somehow shrunk, it seemed to exist just for them to leave it.

Now Valiant took photos. He snapped a shot of Leo tied up in the backseat of the car, and one of Gwen as rescuer, untying him, unlocking the cuffs and, holding his head in her hands, trickling water from a plastic bottle into his mouth.

Gwen threw the old suitcase into the trunk, and they were off. Leo sat in the backseat with Fifi on his lap, and Valiant in the passenger seat, reclining as far as it would recline, popped open another Bud. "Really?" Gwen said.

"Breakfast of champions." Valiant grinned and settled back, his dark glasses shielding him from the shock of the sun.

"Just keep it down, okay?"

With Gwen, as always, behind the wheel, they were driving and all the lights were green. It was fate. The city wanted them to leave.

She rolled all the windows down, because the sky looked almost blue. But the air was parched. Her mouth was dry, and her eyes burned. She checked them in the side-view mirror. She looked stoned. *Objects in mirror are closer than they appear,* it said. But there are things that don't appear in the mirror, things you can't see. The smoke-smell, like a hangover, was there, just as the city for all its stillness was tense, holding its breath. Waiting for a wind to lift the anger and its residue, to send it. And she realized, she hadn't, this morning, seen or heard a single bird.

Up ahead a Humvee rolled down Pico slow enough to own it. On closer look, she saw it was crammed with boys in camo. White boys and black boys, she noticed, and a few of them brown. Before yesterday she wouldn't have thought twice about skin color, but now she wondered how those black boys felt, riding into L.A. in uniform. With the white and the brown boys beside them, they were the face of the U.S. government, bringing order, the illusion of control. The boys were holding—she didn't know what they were called—long, muscular black automatic weapons.

"M16s," Leo said.

Valiant hadn't moved for blocks, but now he crooked his head up. The Humvee was one lane over. He lowered his sunglasses on his nose, gazing over them at the boys, all golden in the sun, and so close. "My, my," he said, his drowsy eyes dancing.

The Humvee turned down Fairfax, and he lay back down, a grin on his face. "I had a marine once. It was on the beach. I'd dropped acid and I was wandering. Moonlit summer night. Somewhere in the middle of it all, he was over me on the sand. Jesus, he was a vision. He was something. Gone with the sun. Never did tell me his name."

She'd heard the story. The gorgeous marine he'd had on the beach. He was just out of high school, singing in the gay lounge in Laguna Beach under the pseudonym Johnny Fontaine, the character in *The Godfather* patterned after Sinatra. Those were the heydays, he'd told her.

1981, 1982. Before.

Before anyone realized, at least. They'd called it GRID back then, he'd said with a sad smile. Gay-Related Immune Deficiency, but it didn't stop anybody. He could have picked it up anywhere. There was no way of knowing. He'd slept with so many men, men just passing through town, and that marine who might have been Jason of the *Argo* for all he knew.

Alongside them, an ice cream truck played "La Cucaracha," and she felt like they were already in Tijuana. The red, white, and blue bullet pops, Fudgesicles, sundae cones, the strawberry shortcake ice cream on a stick, Pink Panther and Tweety, even a plain old ice cream sandwich caught her eye. The side of the truck was filled with possibilities. And her stomach was growling. Food. Ice cream in particular. When had it sounded so good? They came to a stoplight.

"Leo." She pressed a five into his hand. "See if you can get his attention. I want anything. Get an ice cream sandwich, or the strawberry ice cream on a stick, anything."

"Oh, oh, I want, I want!" Valiant chanted. He was a child, clapping his hands. "I want a chocolate banana bullet."

Leo got out of the car. Gwen saw the driver stiffen and look from Leo to Valiant, askance. Leo must have mentioned Gwen—figuring the girl factor would win them points—because the driver glanced at her and when she waved and smiled he waved and smiled back. He was missing a tooth. He was Latino, older, with the sort of dark, soft, wrinkled skin her grandmother had in her later years. The light turned green and a car behind them honked and Leo dashed into the backseat with five different ice creams wrapped in plastic.

"My lady," he said, offering her the bouquet of ice creams.

"This one's mine," said Valiant, and took the bullet.

Gwen chose the strawberry shortcake and the Fudgesicle, leaving Leo with the mint-chip ice cream sandwich and Tweety. She tore the plastic from the strawberry shortcake with her teeth and took a bite. She could feel Leo's eyes on her, his disbelief.

"It's good to see you eat, Tink," he said.

"We can share," she said. "If you want a bite of these."

"You want bites of these?"

She grinned. "You know, I just might."

They took the 405 South. La Cienega was out of the question, and the freeway was a holy, beautiful sight—empty, with only a smattering of cars. It was a shining river and they were in it, floating in their little rowboat downstream, floating away. When the roads were jammed and she was headed out of the city, she'd feel a bright urgency with its dull undertone of panic clawing at her stomach. As if she might not make it out before the city folded closed like a game of Monopoly and she'd be stuck inside, condemned to move her little silver car past Go, to circle the board for eternity, bounced about by Chance and the roll of the dice. Or else, she'd fear an earthquake, the big one, in which the city would shake and collapse and be swallowed up by the hungry earth below it, the earth that demanded payment, retribution. There was something about the latter fantasy that she liked—justice, she supposed. Only she didn't want to be here for it. She wanted to be elsewhere, wanted to read about it in the papers—the same way she felt about the riots.

But now their leaving was so easy, it seemed to her like some kind of a trick they were falling for. The witch's house of gingerbread and candy—that false sense of relief that came too soon in the story, and signaled trouble. If things weren't hard, something was wrong. Or maybe—she took a breath, tried to feel it, to believe—maybe this was how it worked. Life. There were openings, sometimes, unexpected fissures in the architecture of the known, and if you stepped inside them, things happened. You didn't have to force them. She told herself she could let go, trust the open road taking them with it.

They passed Sepulveda. She could see the sign—LIVE NUDES. They were sure to be closed today. But tomorrow? She was supposed to work a night shift.

Her stomach churned—like in the old days, before she'd worked there, before she'd stripped at all, when the club, as she'd passed it, had called to her, had pulled at her body as a magnet pulls at metal. She'd been scared then, and because she was scared, she knew it was something she had to do.

The fear she felt now was different. It wasn't about going

there, but about being able to leave. To leave the club, the city. The cash and the weed, the girls and Tony. Dancing. To leave it all for good.

She handed Leo the rest of the strawberry ice cream on the stick.

"Really," he said. "I thought you'd finish it for sure."

"My eyes were bigger than my stomach, I guess."

"I'll take it if you don't want it," the Count said. He was licking the last of the chocolate bullet.

"There isn't much, really," Leo said, and sucked the ice cream down.

She gave the unopened Fudgesicle to Valiant and stuck her head out the window. The wind helped. And the smoke-smell was gone.

The time had come for music. She took the cassette tape of Bing from the player, slid Billie into the socket. Her grandmother's favorite. *God bless the child that's got his own.* It was the song she'd taught her to dance to. Gwen had been seven, and she'd spent the night at her grandparents', woken up to the smell of flapjacks and maple syrup, her grandfather in the kitchen in his plaid flannel pajamas, and her Nana Lotta in the living room in her long black silk nightgown and her brown, bare feet, dancing to Billie Holiday with her eyes closed. The long silver hair that she wore in a bun when she went out hung in smooth waves down her back. She'd taken Gwen in her arms, picked her right up, and swayed with her. Feel the beat, she'd said. In your heart, in your blood. *Mama may have, Papa may have, but God bless the child that's got his own, that's got his own.* That's you, she'd said. What you have, *tu corazón, tu espíritu, todo.* It's all you.

They passed the oil refinery, Long Beach, and the cities with names that belonged to another time—Garden Grove and

Orange and Cypress—belonged to a time when they were small towns separated by citrus groves, when they weren't all part of one smoggy city that went on and on without apparent end.

They passed Anaheim. Home to the giant mouse in the diaper. And Dumbo, and Goofy. Home to Peter Pan and Wendy and Tinker Bell. It was Leo's favorite place. As a kid, he'd loved it so much, he'd wanted to live there. On a second-grade field trip he snuck away and hid in a cave on Tom Sawyer's Island. The class had gone back to school without him. They hadn't even realized he was missing, and by the time his mother had returned from her job as a nurse, it was too late. Disneyland had closed. When he told Gwen the story, he said he'd lived there a week before they found him—which was probably how long a night felt to a seven-year-old. His mother told her the real story later. She said that night was the longest of her life, and, after that, she didn't let him out of her sight. She kept him as close as she could.

In the rearview mirror, Gwen watched him watch the Disneyland exit go by.

"Don't even think about it," Valiant said.

"But . . ."

The Count narrowed his eyes, his mouth set.

"Okay, okay, Tijuana it is," Leo said. "But roll up the window, will you? I have a little something."

"How stupid are you?" Gwen said. "We're going to Mexico."

"God, Gwen, relax. It's just one joint. We'll smoke it now. Roll your window up."

"Yes." Valiant smiled, nailed her with his stare. "Roll up the window, darling, will you? I want to light a cigarette."

Damn him. She wasn't going to let him smoke her out because *he* couldn't wait. She wouldn't be pushed. She'd tell Leo when she was ready to tell him. She glared at Valiant and rolled her window up. "Light up," she said. "By all means."

No sooner had the car filled with smoke than she rolled her window back down. All the way.

"Turn the music off, would you, Gwen, dear? I have the chorus to a new song. It should round out my next album. Leo, maybe you could write the verses?" She shut off Billie, and Valiant sang.

> *Fly, fly, my darling.*
> *Darling, darling, fly.*
> *Why cry, my darling?*
> *Darling, bye, bye.*

Leo hummed along, improvised lyrics.

> *Though your beauty makes me wince,*
> *And your voice is smooth and low,*
> *It's time I left and since*
> *I'm going where you can't go.*

> *Fly, fly, my darling.*

The freeway curved and she felt the air cool. The sky was cloudy. No, it was a mist, blowing inland. She smelled ocean, saw fields of mustard flowers, and beyond them, through the low cloud, she could feel the Pacific like a cool giant hand on her forehead.

To the left of the freeway, on a west-facing hill up ahead, lay a cemetery, acres of green littered with white headstones. A sign read SUNSET VIEW.

"We picked out our plots—my parents and I," Valiant said.

"My brother said he'd want to be with his wife. Somewhere with more room, in case their own kids want to join them. But we're going to be here. Close to home."

Valiant seemed fine with this fact, almost wistful. But to Gwen it was oddly unsettling, this sort of knowledge—the precise location of one's body for years, decades, centuries to come, until the collapse of the good old U.S. of A., or the extinction of the humans, and maybe even after that, until the sun got so close the earth itself burned up. That was a long time for one's bones to be in a box, a box sealed off from even the soil, and the thought terrified her.

Her mother had known she'd wanted to be cremated. Sipping her wine, she'd talked about it. As if her death were imminent, she'd said how, when she left, she wanted her ashes to be thrown into the sea. She wanted to not leave a trace. So Gwen's father had rented a boat and they'd set off from Long Beach Harbor toward Catalina. They'd divided her ashes in half, said a prayer, and watched what was left of her body billow and sift into the ocean.

"It looks nice," Gwen said as they passed the cemetery.

"It has an ocean view," said Leo. "What more could you want?" The ache in his voice caught her by surprise. In the mirror, she saw he was looking at the ocean, his eyes full of tears.

The Count tossed his lit cigarette butt out the window. "Yeah," he said. "I need to pee." Not take a piss, what guys say. But pee. "I need to pee," he said. "Pull over?"

Twenty-one

SHE VEERED INTO the right lane and took the exit.

Just beside the road was a wooden stand with a painted sign that said FRESH STRAWBERRIES THREE DOLLARS. She pulled to the curb, took cash from her purse, and stepped from the car into the sea-fresh air. The strawberries called to her. They were in the normal green plastic baskets in which she was used to buying them, but these berries were small—the size of raspberries. The woman selling them smiled. There was something about her. Something quiet and easy. She was like no one Gwen knew—except, maybe, Brett, were she to place her here, in the open air.

The woman told her to taste a berry. They were grown without pesticides, she said. In a sling over her shoulders, against her chest, a baby slept. It made a mewing sound, barely audible, and Gwen tried not to stare. She couldn't tell if it was a girl or a boy. It had hair that made her think of shucking corn, of those shiny strands that clung to the corn and, when you yanked them off, to your hands. Corn silk, wasn't that what you called them? The baby had a tiny nose, and now she thought it was a boy, his little red lips sucking at the air as he dreamed of what must have been his mother's breast, as big as his own head, of her nipple in his mouth, and milk filling his body with the warmth for which he'd search the rest of his life and not find.

Gwen bit into a strawberry. It was the best fruit she'd tasted in years. Sweeter, more intense than any store-bought berry. It tasted like it had grown in actual soil, had ripened in the sun.

"Chew the seeds," the woman said. "The vitamins are in the seeds."

She said she would and paid the woman for a basket. Leo was walking Fifi—she could see him by the car—and Valiant was off somewhere peeing. Without a word to them, Gwen strode past a NO TRESPASSING sign and into the fields of yellow flowers. She wanted the strawberries for herself—every single berry, every single seed. She took her time eating one and then another, crunching the seeds between her front teeth, tasting the soil and the sun.

The mustard plants were as tall as she was and she walked down a dirt path that wound through them. Swallows dove and rose, darted and sang. The world was alive. The berries, the flowers, the mist from the ocean. She was a kid again. A kid on a road trip with her parents. They'd gone up the coast to Oregon. And her mother had insisted they stop at every fruit stand. Gwen ate so many strawberries, they'd had to pull over so she could puke. Even coming back up they were good.

She could hear Leo calling, "Gwen! Gwendolyn!"

What did he want?

She ran away from the freeway, toward the distant ocean, her hand over the berries so she wouldn't lose any. Fifi was barking, and she and Leo were running after Gwen. It was a chase, a game of hide-and-seek. She ran until the mustard plants gave way to a bald brim of land, and she looked down. They were on a cliff, a bluff. The outskirts of San Clemente spread below them. And she could see the ocean just past the empty road.

Behind her Leo was panting. She could hear his slow approach as he got closer, put his arms around her waist and rested his chin on her head.

"Hey, Tink. Since when do you just take off? We're in this together."

She stiffened. What did he mean by that? Had Valiant told him?

Down below, she could see into a school yard. It looked to be a preschool. And the kids were taking part in a ceremony, a procession. Was she seeing it right? She looked closer. They were holding the ends of long, wide pieces of ribbon. They were walking clockwise around a pole—an ordinary flagpole, it looked like—and ribbons of every color were fastened to the top of it.

"Leo," she said. "Look."

From up here, the boys and girls were mere specks, the colors of their clothes so bright they looked like confetti. And as they circled, the pole turned from top to bottom into a great rainbow wand, a colossal magic phallus.

"May Day," she said out loud.

"What is it," Leo said, squeezing her tighter, "you need me to rescue you?"

"I didn't think they did that anymore," she said.

"Oh yes. The knight always rescues the maiden." She had to laugh. "Oh," he said, "the kids. You know, I think they still go to school."

"The maypole," she said. "The dance."

She'd been three, three or four. Her mother was on the side of the schoolyard with the other mothers, and she was taking photos, of course. But Gwen remembered it. It was one of her actual memories, she knew, because there was movement to it. She remembered holding the pale blue ribbon and walking around the pole, around and around with the other kids; they'd all worn white and walked in time to music, a flute, she thought it was. Their ribbons were pink, yellow, green, and blue.

Gwen tried to shake it off, or swallow it down, but something inside her was breaking. It was warm and runny like a soft-boiled egg. Her chest shook. She turned to Leo and let him hold her. She wiped her wet face on his shirt.

"What is it?" Leo said.

"The past. It's like it has nowhere to go. It's like that pole. We're all tied to it, we all keep walking around and around. Or else it's like the earth—the earth spinning, but also how it builds up, a layer at a time. It's what we bury. What we succeed in not thinking about, so long as we think it's gone. But it isn't gone. It's never really gone. And then it just bubbles up, like the tar pits, or like pus in a zit."

"It's what I like best about you, Tink."

"My zitty nature?"

"How you just spill sometimes. You bring me to life, you know."

She extracted herself from his arms, walked closer to the edge. She looked past the school yard into the blue showing through the mist; it was pulling her toward it, somewhere she'd not been, which was also where she was going. The movement was both the mist and a propulsion inside her, of blood and oxygen and multiplying cells, a swirling to the surface of what she could keep to herself no longer. She felt woozy. Up was down, and down was up. She was afraid she might fall.

"I'm having trouble," she said. "I'm having trouble with facts."

"That's because they aren't real. They're a desire for irreducible truth that doesn't exist."

She faced him.

"But the fact is, Leo, I'm pregnant."

His face was wiped clean. A blank white canvas. He was looking through her into the field of his own bleary vision where, Gwen imagined, the fact was registering itself—a guest taking the elevator to the room with the number that matched the key in his hand. Turning the knob, opening the door, walking inside.

At last he looked at her. "You're sure?"

She nodded. She was waiting for him to struggle, to fight—for that part of him that wanted fame and freedom and the life of a bohemian to wrestle with this fact that existed for her and, now, for him. Instead, there was the instant of comprehension, and then, as if she'd cut the ribbon on some grand opening, the fiesta was in full swing and she was watching from the sidelines. Leo took her in his arms and hugged her. He spun her around and the strawberries went flying. She thought he might toss her into the air, too—but she wasn't there. She wasn't celebrating.

Why hadn't she kept her mouth shut?

"My God," he said. "We're going to have a kid, Gwen! A family! You know what this means?"

He didn't say it—what she felt when he said *what this means*. She told herself he hadn't said it, but the moment was all wrong. It was false. A scene from someone else's life. Not hers. She was the girl with promise, the girl who could be anything. And if she belonged just to him? If she let his child grow inside her?

"It means—" Leo said.

"It means Gwen's going to get fat," Valiant said. He sauntered out of the yellow thicket of mustard, downing his beer. How long had he been there, listening? "Jesus, kid. I thought you'd never tell him. I was dying."

Leo set her down. "You knew?"

"Leo—" she said.

"What?"

"I had to talk to someone."

"Can't you talk to me?"

She said nothing. There was simply nothing to say. She picked up a few of the strawberries from the dirt, brushed them off, and put them back in the basket.

Valiant wrapped an arm around her and one around Leo and folded the two of them into his chest. "There will be time for this," he said. "Plenty of time." He steered them down the path and toward the car. "Time for you and time for me," he said, quoting. "How does it go, Gwendolyn?"

She sighed. What use was there in fighting the camaraderie of the moment? She picked up *The Love Song of J. Alfred Prufrock* at the lines she liked best. "And indeed there will be time to wonder, 'Do I dare?' and, 'Do I dare?' Time to turn back and descend the stair. . . . In a minute there is time for decisions and revisions which a minute will reverse."

"Where's the peach?" Leo said. "I could've sworn there was a peach."

"Do I dare to eat a peach? I shall wear white—something—trousers, and walk upon the beach."

"Yes!" Leo said. "I have heard the mermaids singing, each to each."

"I do not think that they will sing to me," Valiant said, as if he'd known the whole poem all along.

Back in her car they flew south through the morning until the sun was high and hot, past Camp Pendleton and more Humvees with boys in camo, going the opposite direction, on their way to day three of the riots—if that's what in fact it was. Maybe the city had settled, was lying down and licking its wounds. Without a radio they didn't know and, truth be told, they didn't care. They were far from the city, further every second.

In the backseat Leo was glowing, she could feel it. Like one of those worms, the ones that spin their silk cocoons and glow as they pupate, happy in their own little world. He was singing his freedom song and he leaned forward, massaging her shoulders.

> *I'll be your home, darlin',*
> *Come back again.*

She found she liked the song less now. It wasn't a wish anymore, nor was it a reverie. Rather, it had become, in the space of a single day, a reality. How would she possibly leave?

He brushed the hair from her forehead. "You're going to be such a beautiful mother," he said. "I can't believe it. The mother of my child. Gwen, I wouldn't have dared to dream."

She was silent. Driving. She'd concentrate on that. Moving from lane to lane, passing the slow cars, gliding by them. There was just right now—the three, no, counting the baby inside her and Fifi, the five of them on the 5, traveling through San Diego, traveling south, to Tijuana. She crossed three lanes without hitting the brakes. It felt like dancing.

Leo and Valiant were talking about her future like they were looking in a crystal ball or reading her cards. As if they were in that clear future with her. They were talking, but what she heard was Tony, his voice in her head. *Do you even want a baby? How will you write with a baby?* And Brett. *My fiancé is a writer, a good one, but you have to starve for a while.*

She bit the tip of her fingernail and tore it off. The exposed skin was tender, and she ran her tongue over it. She'd get away, soon, find a place to be alone. *Decisions and revisions.* When would she know? When would she be certain? She heard her father's voice. *What's the plan, Gwen? You have a plan, don't you?* She hated his brusque clarity, felt it as an affront to spontaneity, to creativity. But now, she wished she'd inherited a portion of it. She gripped the steering wheel tighter.

I am in control, she told herself, and breathed the affirmation in, trying to make it true.

"I want to be the godfather," Valiant said.

"I don't think that's something you choose," Leo said.

"Why not?"

"I think it's a fine idea. I'm not saying I don't; it's just, it's something we'll talk about. Right, Gwen."

Right, Gwen. It was a statement, not a question.

She said nothing and no one noticed.

Twenty-two

AT THE BORDER the van beside them, in bold red lettering, said S AND M ELECTRIC—WE MAKE YOU S-M-ILE! "No. Not really," the Count said, and he snapped a photo.

Mexico waved them right in.

They rolled the car windows up. She felt the sweat bead at her temples and slip down her jaw. The heat shimmered off the sidewalk and she saw the town through the waves of hot air as if it were in another dimension from the three of them, sealed in the silver Nissan, as if the people on the streets moved through a substance thicker than mere air and were subject to the push and pull of its tides.

The children with bare feet, their clothes torn and dirty, held cartons of gum in their hands. When the light turned red, they surrounded the car, knocked on the windows. "Wanna buy a Chiclet? Hey, rich American, got a dollar?" More kids washed their windows with rags, filthy soapy water and squeegees. Leo opened Gwen's purse and cranked the window halfway down. He took out her crocheted change purse and handed the children all the dollars folded inside. It wasn't much. Twenty bucks or so, but it was blood at a feeding frenzy. More kids came, and men with sunken cheeks and thin arms—one missing a leg—women with children on their backs, their hands thrust toward the windows.

"Para mis niños," the woman at Gwen's window said. Her lips were cracked, her dark eyes fixed on her through the glass.

Leo rolled his window up.

"Zero the savior." Valiant leaned in, breathing on her, slurring his words. "You know he's never going to have any money, don't you, kid."

"You mean *I'm* not," she said. "It was my money." She didn't tell him it didn't matter—she had the wad of cash in her front pocket. She reached in and touched it, made sure it was there. It was one of the things she liked best about stripping. The fact of the cash, the untraceable green.

She put her foot on the gas. Barely. Then the brake. They moved through the masses, parted them and rolled on to where the people in the dirt lots beside the dirt road were selling plaster statues—Virgin Mary and Saint Francis and Jesus himself painted in pastels—pinks and greens and blues.

"Mary," Valiant said, unlocking his door. "Mary! Stop!"

Gwen was pulling to the side of the road when he opened the door and was out of the car, running, his hands flapping behind him. He returned with a two-foot Virgin Mary in his arms. "My whole life I've wanted a virgin," he said, and he held her in his lap. He leaned his forehead on hers and touched her face with his fingertips, her lowered eyes, her lips. Gwen was trying not to look, not to laugh.

"Please," he said. "Might we have a little privacy?" And he pulled his leather jacket over their heads—his and Mary's.

They drove the narrow, crowded streets, past a woman with a cart selling fresh cold fruit on a stick—watermelon, pineapple, banana, and mango—past the sombrero shop with the giant, ridiculous sombreros for the gringos, and alongside the meat market with the skinned cows and pigs, with the plucked chickens hanging in the warm open air, with the swarm of flies. The traffic was thick and slow and, though their windows were sealed, the smell of the raw unrefrigerated meat, the smell of death, seeped in; she could taste it in the back of her throat and it made her gag. She coughed, put her nose in her armpit to drown out the smell. She liked her own smell, as a rule, but now she liked it even more. Her smell had changed, she was sweeter. She smelled, a little, of—was it citrus blossoms?

Skinny dogs walked the sidewalks, lay in gutters in the sun. "See, Fifi," said Leo, holding her up to the window. "It's another world here. In Mexico, it really is a dog's life."

"Sure," Gwen said. "If you don't mind life on the street, scrounging for food and water."

"A life of freedom. Look around. You don't see a single leash."

American college boys walked out of a cave of a bar. Their arms around each other's shoulders, they were singing. She had come here once, during her college days, her college daze, come with a few girls and a few guys—sorority sisters and frat boys, she wouldn't call them friends—come for those endless shots of tequila, for the Coronas and the cheap margaritas in goblets the size of soup bowls. Who had she been then? It felt like a dream, like she was remembering some character she had played. It wasn't her. It had never been her. She'd played happy-go-lucky. She'd played the ruddy, round-cheeked sorority girl, pasted smiles on smiles. A convincing actress, she had fooled even herself. She'd thought it so easy to forget who she was, to be like everyone else. She remembered puking in a bathroom, happy to have made it to a toilet. And the sun—she remembered how bright it was when they'd swaggered back into the day, how bald the town had looked, the way it did now.

The day was bleached and shadowless, unrelenting as a migraine—the kind of headache her mother used to get, occasionally, and her grandmother more often, a headache that could last for days. Lotta had said once it was her body's attempt to forget, to white it all out. She wouldn't talk about what. Gwen's mother had told her it was Carlotta's youth—the thing she wanted to obliterate—something that had happened growing up in that shack in Globe, Arizona. Carlotta had been the oldest, and her mother just kept having children, a dozen in all—more diapers for Carlotta to change, more tortillas for her to make. Gwen remembered her saying she'd learned to hold a book in one hand, flip tortillas with the other. But she wouldn't talk about the extended family, the uncles and the stepfather, the big, crowded family bed. It was her secret past, what Gwen would never know. But she felt it inside her, in her blood, like a fever; it warmed her skin, quickened her pulse, and made her needful. Her life would be the proof—the proof it was worth it. There was a reason she was here, a reason Carlotta had persisted.

She touched the smooth, oval pendant, rubbed it like a worry stone, or like a tiny bottle with a genie in it. As if the Virgin herself would appear. The Virgin of Guadalupe, protectress of women and children.

Had she hung even then around Carlotta's neck, over her chest, like a lock, protecting?

Valiant emerged from beneath his jacket drenched in sweat.

"Here!" he said.

They were passing a hotel, if you could call it that. The Hotel Suiza, boasting rooms for only twenty-five dollars. She parked the car in front and they stepped into the blanched glare of the sun. The building was one-level, brick, with peeling dirty white paint. Gwen with her suitcase, Leo with Fifi, and Valiant with the two-foot Virgin statue entered the little office at the front of the hotel, where they all stood sweating. No one seemed to be coming. Valiant spied the metal ringer that looked like a boob and tapped the metal nipple with such enthusiasm, again and again, that when the man appeared from the back room looking—with his messed up hair and his scowl—like they'd woken him from his siesta, he moved the ringer pointedly out of Valiant's reach. Gwen paid the man cash for the two rooms before they'd even seen them.

"The dingier the better," the Count declared. And the man and his scowl went back through the door, back, Gwen thought, to his siesta—something she needed, now that her night of little sleep was catching up with her. She felt the small room sway, and the hollow, metallic buzz just under her skin rendered her vulnerable, practically see-through. There was nothing she could possibly hide.

Another man stepped up to the desk, pushed his spectacles up the bridge of his nose, and showed them to their rooms.

The Count had one picture left, so they posed, the three of them, in the hall that looked just like a dimmer version of the outside of the hotel, with its old paint, its metal-framed sliding windows, its brown doors and large blue plastic garbage cans.

It was the last photo she'd put in the scrapbook.

She would remember how Valiant had handed the bespectacled man the camera, saying *por favor* a little too loudly, and how he had leaned on her and Leo, and they'd steadied him as they'd walked down the hall to where their faces and bodies and Fifi and the Virgin had grown small enough to fit into the frame. Valiant stood between Leo and Gwen, and he must have told them to wave, because in this last photo the three of them are waving.

Hello. See? Here we are.

Were.

That afternoon, they found a restaurant, a Mexican diner. Shirt and shoes were required, and Leo said he didn't need to eat, but Gwen went into the little market next door and found him a pair of plastic flip-flops and a Cinco de Mayo T-shirt that said TODAY I'M MEXICAN and they sat down in the restaurant and ate like real people. Huevos rancheros and coffee. It was delicious. Even Valiant ate his whole meal.

Beside the diner was a place called the Bar Del Prado and after lunch Valiant wandered in for a drink. There were a few Americans at the bar. An older woman with dyed-black hair, bright stripes of blush, and mascara so heavy her lids were giving in to the weight sat beside a blond loafing boy drinking Corona from the bottle. The room was cool and dark and Valiant slid into a booth against the wall. The red leather of the seats was torn, with the stuffing sticking out, and she could tell he felt at home. Lighting a cigarette, he settled in. A waitress slept on her feet in the corner of the room. After a while she shuffled over and Leo and Valiant ordered their margaritas with rocks and salt and Gwen got an orange juice—reconstituted, not fresh-squeezed. But this was Tijuana, she reminded herself, she should be happy to drink anything that wasn't alcoholic. The walls of the bar were painted bloodred and were tacked with posters of American girls—G-strings threading their asses, their breasts grapefruit-round, and their long blond hair shiny clean.

Cheesecake, that's what it was called. These airbrushed photos of semi-clad pinup girls. Like the cake itself, these photos were meant to please the senses, not to satisfy the soul. These posters were not meat and potatoes. They were cheesecake. Creamy, sweet. Good with strawberries and hot fudge and whipped cream. If you ate too much, you'd make yourself sick.

Leo was talking, his hands animated with such excitement she was afraid he might spill his drink. "You know," he was saying. "We could just keep going. Explore Baja. Go all the way to Cabo San Lucas. What's to stop us? We're young, we're free."

Valiant raised an eyebrow and looked at Gwen. The ember of his cigarette shone in the gloaming.

She rubbed her thumb across the cash in her front pocket. Hardly enough for a monthlong journey for three across the Baja desert, and Leo was extending the plan, pushing the journey off the continent and onto a boat. "We'll sail to Argentina. And we'll need a strong motor once we hit the horse latitudes. Did I ever tell you why it was called that, horse latitudes? When the doldrums hit and the wind died down and it was hot as hell, the sailors sang their prayers, and when they weren't answered, they threw their horses overboard. Of course, we won't have any horses."

"There's some fine logic for you," Valiant said. He was looking beyond Gwen at the bar, at the broad shoulders of the boy swiveling on the stool, drinking cerveza. When he saw she had caught him, he grinned.

"Leo," she said, now that she had her opening. "How exactly do you propose we pay for this trip?"

"That's my Gwen," Leo said, shaking his head. "The consummate rationalist." *My* Gwen. The possessive irked her. She realized she was scratching her arms and her nails were leaving white streaks. Her skin was dry. She needed lotion. And the razor—once again, she'd forgotten to buy one.

Leo's eyes lit up. "Your car's not in bad shape. We could sell it."

"We?" Gwen said.

"What do you say, Gwen. It's a once-in-a-lifetime chance."

Now Valiant was laughing, a real guffaw, and choking on the cigarette smoke. It took a long time for his coughing to cease.

She watched Leo's hand tighten to a fist. "I'm serious," he said. "Goddamn it. Is everything a joke to you?"

Valiant downed his margarita like medicine, lifted his empty glass and nodded to the waitress for another. "Sure," he said, his face drained of humor. "Everything's funny to a dead man."

"Will you two listen to me for once?" Leo said, and didn't wait for an answer. "If we went on foot, traveled by train, we could experience Baja like Mexicans."

"The poor ones, you mean," Valiant said. "I have an idea. Why don't you go into the Chiclet-vending business. You might have better luck selling chewing gum than you've had selling your music."

The Count was getting mean, and this, she knew, went hand in hand with his level of intoxication. The waitress brought his drink, and Gwen watched him suck the yellow-green liquid through a straw as his finger described a small circle in the air, another round. He was on his way to oblivion, and she planned to be gone before he arrived.

Leo leaned toward Gwen. He put an arm around her and pulled her close. "What do you say? You up for a real adventure?"

She pictured Gandhi on the trains, getting to know the real India, and the young Che Guevara on his motorcycle, exploring South America. She saw the fire in Leo's eyes, so bright it seemed to blind him. She thought of the albatross and the griffin, and of how the two didn't mix. And she thought of the baby inside her, the fact that seemed to Leo already a dim fiction. So much for settling down, getting a job, making a home.

The room was smoky and loud, and Gwen was tired. The woman at the bar was laughing too loud. She had her hand on the boy's leg and Gwen watched Valiant watching, sneering. "Why don't you mind your own business," he hollered to the woman's back, but nobody turned around.

Gwen polished off her juice as the waitress brought their drinks. "To the riots," Valiant toasted, rollicking on the upswing of tequila and corn syrup, and he and Leo clinked their salty rims. She told them she'd be at the hotel. She'd see them there, later. Valiant kissed her cheek and Leo took a gulp of his drink and stood, a goofy, inscrutable smile on his face.

"I'll walk you," he said.

Twenty-three

OUTSIDE THE BAR Del Prado, night was coming on like a hopeless, drunken come-on, tequila on its breath, red neon signs and, outside the shops, strings of colored Christmas lights hung from the eaves like the sad close-lipped smiles of boys who would lure you in with their loneliness, that melancholia you'd try and try to fix.

Gwen and Leo sauntered. He took her hand in his and their arms were swinging. Singsong, like girlfriends in elementary school. She felt that way sometimes. That they were girlfriends. Maybe someday, like Love's husband, Leo would get a sex change. Leona, she'd call him.

Amused by the thought, she saw something moving in the corner of her vision, flapping. She turned. They were birds. Or not birds, but bats. So many of them, filling the sky. Their flight quiet, and quieting. On this clamorous street of cars with their horns and their stereos with the bass turned up, playing their booming Mexican songs, on this street of vendors and markets and bars, a hush had fallen.

Why was it hushes fell, like snow, she wondered as she and

Leo stopped, with the others on the sidewalk and along the curb. Why didn't hushes rise, like steam, or bats?

They stood behind a mother holding the hands of her son and daughter, the kids in their navy-blue-and-white school uniforms. The small boy pointed and squealed. Across the street, out of a four-story, burned-out brick building, what looked to Gwen like an old apartment house, out of a hole in the wall where a brick or two just below the roof were missing, the colony of bats was coming fast. They were pouring into the evening, and they kept on coming. Hundreds, thousands of them. Snaking across the sky, flapping their way west, toward the sinking sun. They watched the bats until they were small and then smaller, until they became the gray, darkening sky.

They walked up the sidewalk to the Hotel Suiza, where, out front, a streetlight flickered, and Leo stopped. The light had the effect of a strobe, and when he pulled her to him and kissed her, it was like they were on a dance floor. His lips were soft. Always they were the soft lips of a girl. A fleshy, full-lipped girl. She thought of Brett, whose lips weren't full like his, but thinner, like her own. Brett, whose face would be smooth, whose body would smell of the spice of a forest floor, and clean as a creek carving through it.

She pulled back, but he kept his arms around her. "I'm not letting you go."

"What is it?" she said. She'd missed something, when she'd been off, in the forest with Brett.

His eyes were watery, showing specks of green in the hazel, and he blinked back tears, shrugged. "Sometimes loving you hurts my eyes."

She rested her head on his shoulder. A three-legged dog trotted by. He loved her more than anyone, and here he was, holding

her how she'd wanted him to for months, or had it been years?
"Dance with me," she said. And under the slow sidewalk strobe,
in the carne-asada-and-fried-onion-laced evening, they swayed.
He sang, low and soft into her ear.

> *I'll be loving you, always,*
> *with a love that's true, always.*

It was her mother's song. The one she'd sung to her when she
was small, before she tucked her in. She'd never told him that. At
least she didn't think she'd told him.

> *When the things you've planned*
> *need a helping hand,*
> *I will understand,*
> *always, always.*

People might have been passing, staring. She didn't care. Her
eyes were closed and it was only the two of them, the three of
them. He was making it possible.

She could feel herself melting, her own tears starting, and
she hated him. Just who was he, exactly, and why couldn't he
decide? How was he this man, this one who took her in his arms
and made her feel safe and loved, when he was the man who
last night was planning on parading into East L.A. naked with
only a white flag for protection, who a half hour ago was ready
to sell her car for a trip down the Baja peninsula, a boat ride to
the ends of the earth, but even more would never embark, not
on any of it?

"I'm tired," she said. And he let her go.

His arms hung at his sides. "I love you."

"I know," she said and left him under the strobe, alone on the dance floor.

She let herself into the room. Fifi was sitting upright on one of the bed pillows with the shock collar around her neck, as if she were modeling the awful contraption. Gwen unfastened the collar and had it in her hand when the knock on the door and Fifi's subsequent bark sent a jolt through her body before she could drop it. A solid jolt. Her hand was buzzing. Apparently the batteries had some life to them yet.

She opened the door to find Leo slumped against the door-jamb. "I thought you might like to know. I'll be back at the Bar Del Prado. In case you need me or something." He fixed her with his hangdog eyes and then turned and shuffled away in his plastic flip-flops.

She felt the usual pull as she watched him go. She should run up to him and apologize. She'd been callous, cruel.

So what. She closed the door.

This *was* the dingiest room she'd ever seen. Decadent, the Count had called it, romanticizing. The floor was linoleum, tan to hide the dirt. The curtains, so sheer they were hardly there, were made from what looked to be old sheets—a faded rose pattern. The pale green bedspread was frayed at the ends, and was blooming with yellowish and brownish stains. The off-white walls had cracks, and large patches where the paint had peeled off and the old brown paint showed. One jagged patch stretched from the ceiling to the bed like a streak of lightning or, rather, its negative. She pulled the bedspread down. The sheets were pink. She pulled them back and searched. For what? Bugs? More stains? She found just sheets, clean sheets, and she slid off her boots and lay down in her jeans and T-shirt on the bed.

Why was she such a snob? The kids today flocking to the

windows of her car had called her a rich American. It was true.
When had she ever gone hungry, other than intentionally? When
had she wanted, really, for anything money could provide?

Fifi jumped on the bed and curled up beside her. The bed
was comfortable, and finally being alone she relaxed, felt the
hard exterior that held her together soften. She had a room to
herself.

She slipped her bra off under her T-shirt. Her breasts were
sore and she held them, lifting their weight. They were like
sponges heavy with water and they filled her hands. She wanted
to feel the child inside her, to feel like a mother—what being a
mother would be like—a baby on her breast, in her arms. But
what she felt, instead, was an ache, a need.

She moved her fingertips over her nipples. She could feel
the heat starting up inside her, the sticky dampness between
her thighs. The feeling took her by surprise. When she'd first
started stripping she'd often made herself come, thinking of the
club and what had happened there, but over time the excitement
had waned. The club had become routine, and she'd grown exhausted. She felt different now. New. She unbuttoned her jeans,
put a finger inside her, pressed it deeper and then brought it to
her lips. It was an umami taste, like coffee—dark, unsweetened,
freshly brewed coffee. Would Brett taste the same as she did?
she wondered. Her own taste had changed, though. There was
the wetness, constant, her own secret spring. And her taste was
stronger, sweeter, as if, while she was busy being a person—
busy walking, breathing, trying to figure out this life that was
no longer her own—she was also marinating, steeping herself in
herself. Like tree-ripened fruit. Dark orange papaya flesh.

Or maybe kiwi. Her hair had grown and was prickly. But the
hair on her labia was more like velvet, the fuzz of a fresh peach.

It was soft. She spread herself, moved her middle finger up and down, as though she were rolling a coin. It sent ripples through her, just the edges of ripples, the barest shimmers of light.

She could almost go there. Slip into that river and let its slow, sweet current take her. Sometimes she could and it was easy, that slipping toward ecstasy—stepping outside herself, becoming vast. Like the times she'd been with women, before Leo, when the pleasure had been pure and acute, excruciating.

But there were times she needed something more, something else, for balance. For depth. Sometimes she needed, like Love, a little pain. She wished she'd brought the toys that would fill her, this way and that, those devices that would cause her to submit, to let go, the miniature rocket ships that would open every gateway and send her with such speed, such urgency, into outer space. She'd have to make do without. She pulled her jeans down to her thighs and spanked herself, like Brett did when she danced. Her cheeks burned. On her back, she was her own puppet. She slipped a finger into the silky, lush interior, used two to part the curtains—those lethargic sister folds—as her middle finger danced center stage, a ballerina on point, making those quick, tiny circles in place.

She thought of *Story of O*—*O* for orgasm, *O* for open, *O* for the circles of lilac light pulsing on the black screen of her closed eyelids, her own private movie house. She thought of O and Sir Stephen, thought of him taking her in front of his secretary, taking her behind from behind. O—so obedient. Her tits out and ready, ready to be seen and touched. Her ass upturned, waiting. One finger, two. All she wanted was to be good.

She shuddered and the world was the *O*, the white space the *O* enclosed. *O* for the oxytocin flooding her brain, fueling these contractions of light. *O* for the orifice that expands to contract to expand—for the birth canal, for the child's head crowning. *O* for the Ouroboros encircling the universe, *O* for the ode to the orgasm, the mode of travel to where—beyond name and place, beyond her hopes and her fears, beyond herself—Gwen was the whole world and she was made just of love. She was drifting in it, in herself. She was the sea, and the small boat, and the girl curled inside it.

From far off, she heard rumbling, a little volcano, Fifi snoring beside her.

Twenty-four

SHE WOKE TO pounding on the door, accompanied by Fifi's piercing bark. The sound yanked her from her dreams, where there had been whales, where one had surfaced, saying, *Hang on, sweetheart,* and had given her a ride to shore.

How long had she slept? What day was it?

She felt drugged. Sleep and dreams had come over her with a vengeance. She woke to the dark room and, in the hall, the sound of retching. She zipped up her jeans and opened the door. The hall was dim and her eyes were bleary, but she could see Valiant heaving margaritas and the remains of what must have been the huevos rancheros into one of the blue plastic garbage cans. The smell came over her in a single, pressing wave of nausea. She plugged her nose.

"It's okay, it's okay. There you go," Leo said, holding his shoulders. He looked at Gwen. His eyes were red. Already the night had been long.

She picked up Fifi and calmed her down as Leo searched Valiant's pockets for the key to his room. He unlocked the door and Valiant stumbled in and collapsed onto the bed. He was holding a half-empty bottle of tequila and it hit the wall but didn't break.

Gwen stood in the open doorway and watched the caregiver in Leo take over. His mother was a nurse, and he had, Gwen had always figured, inherited her way of making a person feel at ease, safe and loved. Tugging at the bedspread and the sheet, with as kind a touch as possible, he rolled Valiant over and tucked him in. He wet a washcloth, wrung it out, and wiped the Count's face, the corners of his mouth. The Count slapped away Leo's hand and mumbled something.

"What did he say?" she said to Leo.

Valiant shouted the answer to the peeling walls. "When did I become such a monster?" And she heard his question ricochet down the hotel's brick hallway.

He flung off the covers, twisted his body down the bed—legs crossed, arms outstretched. He sang sweetly, his voice breaking with each high note. They hung back, by the wall, giving him room.

> *They call you lady luck*
> *But there is room for doubt*

Gwen recognized the song from *Guys and Dolls,* but his voice faltered midflight, like a hurt bird in too swift a wind, and it lent the lyrics a strain, unexpected and tragic.

> *At times you have a very un-ladylike way*
> *of running out.*

He stopped singing. "I should have been the next Sinatra," he said to the ceiling. And then he yelled, "Luck's a fucking cunt!"

"Shut up!" she heard someone yell back.

Valiant lay sprawled and still. He turned just his head toward

Gwen and Leo and squinted his eyes as if to focus. Discovering them there, he brightened. "My friends," he said, the words seeming to take what energy he had left. "I can't keep this up."

He curled into a ball, clutching his bottle of tequila to his heart. The Virgin gazed down at him from her pedestal of a bedside table. His eyes shut and he let out a snore. Gwen flicked the light switch off, but they remained in the doorway, comforted by the rhythm of his snores. And then Leo closed the door with a small click behind them. Like parents tucking in a child, she thought.

In their room, Gwen laced up her combat boots. The weight of their steel toes connected her to the ground and made her feel solid. Under her shirt, she slipped on her bra and fastened it. She didn't want to be naked in front of Leo, not right now, nor did she want to be braless. She wanted reinforcement, protection. And she had to get out of this room.

"Where are you going?" he said. "It's late."

"How late?"

"I don't know. After ten."

"I need a razor. I work tomorrow night."

"Oh," he said, his voice flat. "Why didn't you buy one today?"

"I keep forgetting."

He sat on the edge of the bed with his back to her. The bed sagged like the back of an old, skinny horse he was riding sidesaddle. Not that he was going anywhere. The moment was frozen. It was a depiction of a moment, set in itself. Facing the window with the faded, rose-patterned curtains drawn across it, he was like a man in a Hopper painting, which she figured put her in the painting, too—so long as she was still, looking at his back, saying nothing. When she moved, when she walked to the bathroom and peed, came back in the room, drank water from the plastic bottle and found her purse as he sat there, eyes open, face to the wall, she became the observer, no longer a subject of concern.

How easy it was, she realized, to take oneself out of the picture.

She turned the handle of the door.

"I'm coming with you," he said, in a voice that was so dispassionate, she expected him not to move. But he stood, hooked the leash to Fifi's collar, and followed Gwen out the door.

THE STREETLAMP IN front of the hotel still flickered, all the more strobe-like for the darkness. Fifi pulled Leo forward, tugging on the leash, from smell to glorious smell. And when she stuck to any one spot, he tugged her along. Gwen found herself walking ahead.

The Bar Del Prado had its doors open, and the chatter and fierce, garish laughter smelled of cigarettes and booze as it spilled onto the sidewalk.

She was annoyed and she didn't know why. She walked faster, as if to leave the feeling behind. She didn't want him with her, but she didn't want to be alone, either. She didn't want to be out on the street, but she didn't want to be with him in the ugly, small room. Why, exactly, had she gone along with Valiant's whim to come here? This might beat riots and a curfew, but why hadn't they gone north? They might have driven up to Santa Barbara, or all the way to Santa Cruz, where they could have stayed with her aunt.

Leo was a few doors behind her, but she didn't slow down for him, and he didn't move any faster. The longer they walked, the more glaring the silent distance between them became. They should be talking, coming together, figuring things out. She was tired, she told herself. They could discuss things in the morning.

She passed another bar. A man was leaning in the doorway, his smile lurid. "Hey, pretty lady," he slurred, and she strode back to Leo and took his arm. They turned onto a street where the shops were closed, the street lit just by the moon. The gibbous moon, with the face you could see if you looked closely. But she wasn't gazing at the moon. The street was empty and too quiet. There was just the *click-click-click* of Fifi's toenails on the sidewalk, and Gwen had that tingly green feeling in her stomach that meant they shouldn't be there—on this street at this moment.

"The pharmacy," she said. "Didn't you see one near the hotel?"

"I saw one this way."

"When?"

"When we drove in. Don't you remember?"

She couldn't say she did.

On the sidewalk, a man was walking toward them, his gait somehow purposeful. He was slight, wore a baseball cap. She had an urge to turn and run. To get off the sidewalk, out of his way. She grabbed Leo's hand and squeezed it, and as if he were one of those stuffed animals with a squeeze-activated voice box he started whistling, *Would you like to swing on a star.*

Really? she thought. *Now?*

The man was a storefront away, under a frayed awning, when a shadow dashed from behind them and grabbed him. The two men were struggling and yelling. She heard the word *"chingate."*

Sticking her steel toes to the pavement, she pulled Leo back up the sidewalk, away from them. "Come on," she said.

Instead of turning with her and walking away, he shook off her hand and dropped Fifi's leash and ran toward the men. He was insane. She knew this and still he never failed to surprise her.

Or maybe she was the insane one.

"Leo!" she called. "Jesus fucking Christ!"

He was between the men already, giving them both a shove. She couldn't believe what she was seeing. They were back at each other, the two men, and Leo was in the middle of the struggle. Something in one of their hands caught the light. A switchblade? Two? Their stances said as much. Was this personal? Some kind of duel? Or maybe a drug deal gone bad? But wouldn't they use guns for that sort of thing?

She couldn't see any knife now; it was dark and they were yelling at each other in Spanish, too fast for her to make it out. She could hear Leo. *"Hombres, por favor. Parada, parada. Por favor."* She watched as he gave them another shove apart.

Fifi was at their heels, barking and growling. She snapped at the heel of one of the men and he kicked her. She rolled down the sidewalk and into the gutter and came right back at him. Gwen saw the flash again, the blade. She felt dizzy. Leo was grabbing the man's wrist. She heard a clink and saw a knife skid across the pavement.

Fear had her frozen a few yards from the fight. Another skirmish, close-up and personal. Was Mercury in retrograde? Or would it be Mars? Or Venus. Sometimes her brain amazed her, how it would try to run when her body couldn't. She was alone, pregnant, on a sidewalk in Tijuana, her pocket full of cash, while her boyfriend grappled with strangers. To save them from each other. Like Romeo between Mercutio and Tybalt, Leo was an annoyance. She wanted to punch him herself and drag him back to the hotel. Or let him lie on the sidewalk at the mercy of these strangers he so loved, so cared for that he'd left her side for them.

She was frozen and then she wasn't; she ducked in, toward the men, and grabbed Fifi's leash and yanked her off the man's leg. She saw the knife, within her grasp. Did she dare? She took it and ran, ran as if she wouldn't stop. Back toward the bars, where it was safe. Behind her, through the thin night air, she heard someone cry out, as if in pain, but she was running full tilt. She was saving herself and she wasn't going to stop, not even for Leo.

The street was silent and deserted, like a street in a dream, and there were alleys she didn't remember having passed, dark hungry tunnels. Something in her wanted to turn down one, to hide behind a garbage can. She wanted Leo to try to find her, to go back to the hotel where she wouldn't be and worry. She wanted him to pace, to curse himself for his stupidity. She knew the desire was childish, maybe even petty, but she wanted him to think about what he'd done.

Gwen found herself in an alley—she'd turned without realizing. She was walking fast, forcing herself to slow down, to breathe. Looking straight ahead, her eyes were like the eyes of an owl, taking the world in—on both sides of her—all at once: the plastic bins with garbage pressing open their lids, the metal cans vomiting garbage onto the dirt, and the sewer roaches, long and brown, flickering on the splintered back walls of the buildings. One spread its carapace and flew toward her. She screamed. It landed at her feet and Fifi dashed for it as it scuttled away.

Gwen quickened her pace.

She remembered the switchblade in her fist and tightened her grip on the handle. The metal was warm. She turned the knife in the moonlight. It was shiny and clean, no blood. The handle was black metal. She tried the safety, closed and opened the knife. It was an ordinary pocketknife, not a switchblade at all. But the blade when she pressed it to her thumb was sharper than she'd imagined. She could carve a mean jack-o'-lantern with this knife. She walked, holding the knife by her side, holding it down. Should a shadow shift, she'd be ready—ready in her combat boots, with Fifi, her vicious Lhasa Apso, who would attack anyone who meant her harm, even the roaches.

Leo was all right, she told herself, but the feeling gnawed.

What if he wasn't? What if he were lying on the sidewalk dying?

There had been the cry, just as she was leaving, but it hadn't been long or loud. And besides, she'd taken the knife, or else one of the knives. She wasn't certain how many she'd seen.

Maybe she had been wrong to leave him there—to abandon him. But he'd been the one to leave her first, she told herself, and he was a grown man, a fact she often forgot.

And she had a child to think about now.

She stopped walking forward. She had to go back, had to know he was okay. She turned, retraced her steps, past the garbage cans and the flying roaches, out of the alley and onto the road. She looked both ways, up and down it. Had she turned right, or left? Her heart pounded.

What the hell was she doing here? Nothing was familiar. She looked to the moon, trying to remember where it had been, in which section of the sky, as she and Fifi were running from the fight.

She could kill Leo, she thought. How could he just leave her there?

She turned left and walked. A man passed her, and another, slowing to look at her, staring. Behind her, she heard whistles. "Hey, baby," someone growled. She clutched the knife, imagining how she'd use it, in swift jabs. She wanted to run back to the hotel, but now she had no idea where it was. Still, she walked with purpose, in order not to appear as prey. And then she was there, she recognized the storefront, the tattered awning.

She looked around. The sidewalk was empty, as if nothing had happened.

This meant he was okay—he had to be. He must have gone back to the room, unless he was running down the streets, looking for her.

She'd head back to the Hotel Suiza, she thought. After all, she was the one with the key.

Twenty-five

SHE WALKED DOWN the street, through one intersection and another, and realized she was turned around again. Why hadn't she paid better attention? She'd been lost in her thoughts, depending on Leo to remember the way, and now *she* was lost. She looked back, but that didn't seem like the right direction, either. She walked further, to where the street opened onto a small side street. Maybe they'd come down this one?

Up ahead a door, half-open, spilled red light onto the cobblestones. She would have remembered this. Clearly, she'd once again chosen the wrong street to turn down. But if she kept following it, she just might find a new way back.

She passed the door, heard the pulse of dance music, smelled the smoke and stale beer and felt the familiar pull. Drawn, as always, to the red light—the kind light by which astronomers read their maps, so their pupils, still dilated, can return to the stars—Gwen didn't need any map. Her course was charted by feel. But she could at least ask for directions.

She pushed the door open and walked through a curtain of red plastic beads, like the beads that hung in Valiant's apartment, and beyond them she could see other beads, beads of light, lilac and blue. She walked through the curtain, Fifi on the leash beside her. The room was dimmer than the moonlit street, and as she stood at the entrance, waiting for the room to materialize from the shadows, she felt that she was invisible, like a ghost just discovering she was a ghost.

Leaning against a wall to her right was a man she was sure was a bouncer, and even he didn't seem to notice her. A big man in cowboy boots, his shirtsleeves rolled above his elbows, he smoked his cigarette and stared at the stage.

There was no posted cover charge, no waitresses.

Just the woman on the runway, nude, on her knees in front of two college boys, one sniggering behind the other's shoulder. There was a man on the other side of the runway, just one man, and the woman walked to him. Sauntered. The music was too fast. It made her look large and slow. It made her look weary. Her breasts hung. As she walked, they swung like big cowbells, inaudible.

Gwen saw, in the bruise-colored light, the dancer's stretch marks, shining rivulets above her breasts and over her stomach and her hips. The woman knelt before the lone man, an older Mexican in a worn, dark suit. Gwen watched him lay his pesos on the runway, watched her lean over, close. Her long hair, dyed blond, brought a curtain down around them. But she could see the man hold her dark breasts in his hands, his palms open—as though he were offering her something of value. A gift. He was taking the weight of her breasts, assuming for her the burden of gravity, and lifting them toward his lips. She watched as he took the woman's nipples into his mouth. Her left and then her right. The woman closed her eyes. To be a body, Gwen thought. Only a body.

The bouncer was looking at Gwen now. "You can't have that in here," he said in perfect English, and she realized she was still carrying the knife.

"No dogs allowed," he said.

Gwen smiled and nodded. *"Por favor,"* she said, *"dónde está—"* But Fifi, as though she'd understood the man, faced him and bared her teeth, growling. Gwen scooped her up. "Sorry," she said to him. *"Comprendo. Gracias."*

He hadn't thrown her out for the knife but for the dog.

She walked through the plastic bead curtain back onto the narrow street. It was deserted and she kept the open knife in her hand. She set Fifi down. The moon seemed brighter, almost blinding as she looked at it, like staring into a spotlight. The deserted street was a set and she was center stage, standing on her mark. A girl and her white dog lost in a border town. Only she wasn't in a polka-dotted dress, and she wasn't wearing tap shoes. No music would swell from any orchestra pit. And no one seemed to be watching, except, perhaps, the roaches.

She still didn't know where the hotel was, but she saw another red glow at the end of the small street. The light at the end of the tunnel . . . one never thought it'd be red. At the beginning of the tunnel, maybe, but at the end, one presumed, the light would be white, bluish white, if it had any hue at all. Red wasn't transcendence, but return. Red was home. It was a stove and a fireplace, a cup of something warm to wrap one's hands around.

She headed toward what she now saw was red neon that read PSYCHIC. There was a shop, a window with lace curtains sheer enough to see through. Her nose to the window, she looked inside. A woman slept on a sofa. And another woman with all white hair sat at a table, eating what looked to Gwen like soup. READINGS TEN DOLLARS, the white paint on the window said. Fifi barked at the door.

"Shhhh," Gwen said, pulling her on. You couldn't go to a psychic for just directions. You had to get your fortune read, and that was silly. What sort of person goes to a stranger for answers? Ten dollars to be told she'd die at fifty in a car crash. To be told she'd have three children, or none. To be told she'd be a poet, or not. To be told she'd be with Leo for another year, or twenty, or else for just one more day. Could anyone know these things? Wasn't there free will? And chance, she couldn't forget chance. She passed more storefronts, a Laundromat and a car garage. Who was she kidding? These were things she'd pay to know. And Fifi was pulling at the leash, insisting they go back.

Well, what did she have to lose? Ten bucks was one private dance. And there was more where that came from—at least for a while.

She knocked on the door and Fifi started barking. It didn't matter which side of the door they were on, a knock was a knock.

"Uno momento," a voice said. Through the lace, she could see the woman take her soup into another room before she shuffled to the door in her slippers. Baby-blue velour.

Gwen realized she still had the knife in her hand, the man's knife. She didn't want the energy the knife had to hold—that man's energy—to mix with her own, didn't want the psychic picking up on what wasn't hers. She dropped it on the sidewalk just in time.

The woman opened the door. Her eyes were a piercing blue and they met and held Gwen's with an intensity that, though fitting of a psychic, was disconcerting nonetheless. Gwen resisted the urge to look away. She felt her face flush.

"*Hola,*" the psychic said at last, as if breaking character, her face softening. Seeing Fifi she smiled, showing a gold tooth. "Come in."

Fifi stopped barking. Her tail was wagging and the woman reached her hand down to pet her. Gwen winced, but Fifi only licked her hand. Gwen had never seen her like this. Not with anyone new.

Gwen stood stiffly in the doorway. "Am I too late?" She had meant to say *is it too late,* but it had come out wrong.

"No, *hija,*" the woman said, closing the door behind her. "Sit."

Gwen settled into a soft, cushioned chair and the woman sat across the table from her. The chair was low, and she could just see over the table, where a worn tarot deck lay on a red silk cloth. She felt like she was all of four years old in a world of grown-ups, determined to hold her own.

The woman laughed, her voice husky, inviting, and Gwen felt herself relax a little. Her face was dark and kind. Crow's-feet spread from the sides of her bright eyes like the rays of the sun in a child's crayon drawing. Bifocals clung to the end of her nose. And when she smiled, that gold front tooth gleamed. Her thick hair hung past her shoulders and shone like polished silver. It re- minded Gwen of her grandmother's hair, when she was at home and wore it down, like a good witch. The woman smelled of spices. Or was it the house? Cloves and cinnamon and cocoa—it was the smell of her grandmother's kitchen when her grand- father was away on his business trips and Gwen would spend whole afternoons with her, evenings and weekends, baking and dancing, drinking hot chocolate and eating just-made tortillas. It was when her grandmother had seemed most free to be herself.

The woman on the sofa let out a snore and turned onto her side.

The psychic shuffled and cut the cards and spread them out. "Pick three."

Without hesitating, Gwen pulled three cards from the deck and the psychic turned them over. The Fool dressed like a jester at the edge of a cliff; the Empress with her long blond hair, her flowing dress adorned with pomegranates; and Death, a skeleton on a white horse. The psychic pursed her lips. "Hmmm." She wore a sweater the blue of shallow seas, and it matched the eyes that peered into Gwen's again with such quick accuracy Gwen felt pinned by them. Mesmerized. She was afraid to blink. Afraid if she did she'd miss something. The psychic turned over the Fool and Death, leaving just the Empress faceup. She smiled at Gwen, her eyes twinkling as though she saw something new in her, and she rolled her chair around the table. "Give me your hands," she said, and took Gwen's hands in hers. Her hands, too, reminded Gwen of Lotta; they were like hers, strong and warm.

"*Cierra los ojos,*" the woman said, and closed her eyes. Gwen closed hers and waited. She could hear the ticking of a clock.

"You're not happy," the psychic said. "Too long you're not happy. You stay like this you make yourself sick. Time you—*como se dice*—forgive her, let her go. *Comprende? Tu mamá.*" Gwen could only nod.

"There's someone new. Someone coming into your life. *Tu hija. Qué linda. La veo—en el mar, en la arena.* How do you say—skipping? You're so happy. You're laughing."

Gwen could see it. The two of them running on the beach, splashing through the shallows. Indian summer, low tide and the yellow light of late afternoon. As if in a photo from the seventies. Just a glimpse and then it was gone.

Had Leo been there, too? Sitting on the beach, in the background? She'd forgotten to look for him.

"Who do you see?" Gwen asked. "Just me and her, or is there someone else?"

As if she hadn't heard her, the psychic went on. "Your daughter. She change everything, you let her come. She's here for a reason."

Her words took Gwen by surprise, like a hug she hadn't seen coming. Tears ran down her cheeks. Fat tears. They dripped from her chin. She would have wiped her face but the woman held her hands tighter now. She felt herself choking down sobs, swallowing them like fish that would iridesce in the light, but inside her swam round and round her saltwater, fishbowl belly. Dark sea snakes among the kelp, eels with underbites.

"How," she said. It was all she could get out.

"You have all you need." The woman let go of one of her hands. She lifted Gwen's pendant from her chest. Gwen opened her eyes and dried her face. In the woman's fingers, the Virgin of Guadalupe caught the red light from the window and glowed.

"She is here. *Tu abuela*. Behind you." Gwen turned to look. All she could see was the closed door, painted shiny turquoise. "She used to kiss you, *sí?* Your eyes and cheeks, lots of kisses, your whole face wet, red with her lipstick."

"*Sí.*"

"She loved you like that because she couldn't love your mother. *Tú sabes?* After she was born, she was afraid she'd kill her. By accident." The psychic was quiet a minute, as if listening to something she decided to keep to herself.

"There was no medicine then, nothing to help her."

Gwen wasn't sure what she was talking about. She knew her grandmother had been phobic, afraid to leave the house, that she'd spend the morning and sometimes the entire afternoon in her king-sized bed with her German shepherds on the floor around her. But that was after her mom and her sisters had been in school. That was later.

"She was scared," the psychic said. "That she'd crush or drop her."

The thought of her grandmother being anything less than warm troubled her—it was the opposite of the woman she remembered.

"You knew this?" the psychic asked.

Gwen shook her head. No. She hadn't known about the lack of physical love Carlotta had shown her mother. She wondered what that would do to a person, that absence of mother love.

"She say she's sorry. She want you're not afraid. Blithe spirit, she say. What means, blithe spirit?"

"She'd call me that. I was her blithe spirit. Free."

The woman on the sofa snored again and jerked herself awake. She sat up and squinted at Gwen. *"Lo siento,"* she said. She had long dark hair and wore a flowered dress. She brushed her hair from her damp forehead and straightened her crumpled dress and walked past Gwen into the back of the house.

"Mi hija," the psychic said with a sly smile. She let go of Gwen's hand, wrapped her sweater tighter over her chest. She stood. "Anything else, anything you want to know?"

She thought of the cards, the Fool and Death, and why she'd turned them over so quickly. She thought of Leo, and how the psychic hadn't mentioned him, nor any other man in her life, but he didn't seem so important now. Whether he was with her or not, she had all she needed.

"Which way is the Bar Del Prado?" she said.

"The bar?" She peered at Gwen over her spectacles.

"The Hotel Suiza. Where I'm staying."

"Sí, sí," the psychic said. She laughed and took her by the

arm and walked her outside. They stood in the moonlight, in the balmy wind. "Down this street," she said, pointing. "Two blocks. Right. One block, is there."

Gwen pulled from her pocket the wad of cash. Why was she walking around with all that cash? She'd have left most of it in the hotel room had she been thinking. She took out a twenty and handed it to her.

"*Gracias por todo,*" she said, and the psychic took her face in her hands and tilted her forehead toward her and kissed it. She held her face, peered into her eyes, and Gwen felt her heart lurch—they were her grandmother's hands on her face.

"Let them go, *hija*. They worry. You tell them—you okay. You strong. Tell them move on. Is time." She dropped her hands to her sides and smiled, her gold tooth shining in the moonlight. "*Vaya con Dios, hija.*"

Led by Fifi up the road, Gwen turned to see the psychic one more time. She was stooped over on the sidewalk, picking up the knife. She turned it in the red light, closed it, and slid it into her pocket. If anyone could cleanse the aura of that knife, it would be her. She waved at Gwen, and Gwen waved back and smiled.

She felt like Dorothy leaving the Good Witch and had the sudden urge to skip up the yellow brick road. In spite of the weight of her boots, she felt light as the tapping of Fifi's toenails, as the moonlight on the pavement. As if she might fill with helium and float into the night sky, tethered to earth by just the leash, by Fifi, her anchor. She wanted to take off all her clothes and dance. To drive to the ocean this second and cartwheel on the sand. However ridiculous this desire was, it belonged to her body, and what could her mind do but laugh? Yes, the very thought made her giddy.

And Leo? She knew he'd escaped the brawl, knew he was

fine—like the Fool card she had drawn, the Fool of which he was so fond, who could walk right along the edge of a cliff and not fall because the little white dog at his side would pull at his pant legs or nip at his heels to keep him from stepping over the edge.

Of course, she'd taken the little white dog. Maybe she was the Fool tonight. She felt like a fool, buoyant and hopeful, ready for the next escapade. Nevertheless, Fifi was his. If she left him, he'd get the dog. How could he be Zero without his little white dog?

Zero with his quick-lived schemes. "Quixotic" was the word she'd use to describe him, were she ever to write it all down. "Quixotic," from "Quixote." Wild, imaginary, and so beguiling, his gold-flecked eyes wide open, dreaming, his smile, infectious. He took her with him, or used to—his body a lean urgency, his words spinning an intricate tale. He would dance her to his newest utopia, an island frothed and floating, name her both queen and treasure. *Il mio tesoro,* he'd croon. And then the music would end, and she'd find herself in a smoggy city, in an apartment with piss-stained carpet and roaches, rent to pay and groceries to buy. The practical one, the drudge, she was, along with Fifi, the anchor to his boat, the anchor he managed still to pull up here and there to sail the pirate-ridden seas. But how long could she be that for him? The bottom of the ocean was a lightless place. She shrugged off the thought. It was bringing her down fast and she wanted to stay off the ground awhile.

Maybe from here she could see where it was she needed to go, and see, too, how to let go—how to let them go—Carlotta and her mother—how to send them each off into the abyss she couldn't think about just now, couldn't fathom anyhow, even if she tried, send them off with a kiss and a hug, the way a mother waves to a daughter leaving home, driving off into the world.

Vaya con Dios, the psychic said. One must trust.

She turned a corner and there he was, in his knickers and the T-shirt, pacing in front of the hotel. In the stutter of the streetlamp he was slow motion. When he saw her, he ran to her and flung his arms around her and held her tight.

"Jesus Christ, you're all right."

"I'm fine," she said, feeling her jaw tighten.

"You left. I turned and you weren't there. I ran after you. I yelled. Didn't you hear?"

"No, I didn't." She pushed him away. Her hands curled into fists and her feet planted themselves in a firm stance. Her body was ready. And the rush of blood was really something. She wasn't shouting. Her tone was low, and meant to connect, the way her fists wanted to. She wasn't thinking anymore, or rather, her body was thinking for her. And she knew why they called anger seeing red. Knew it in a way she hadn't before. Leo was bathed in a red glow, like the strip joint tonight, like the psychic's sign. And she was the bull, drawn.

She stood there, staring at him for what felt like a long time.

"What's wrong," he said at last.

"Nothing," she said between clenched teeth, as if it were a struggle not to reach out and bite him. "I'm fine."

"Stop saying you're fine."

"Fine then, Leo." His name felt odd in her mouth. She sounded like a mother scolding her son. "Here it is. You might have worried sooner, before you jumped in between them. You might have thought before you got in a fight."

"You mean broke up a fight."

"Is there a difference?"

"You wanted me to let them kill each other?"

"What two random men do to each other is none of my business. And with your pregnant girlfriend beside you, it shouldn't be your business, either. Who do you care about more?"

His face fell and she thought he might sob, but his eyes were blank, as if he were busy. Busy figuring. His lips pursed to a sneer. He spat his words. "How can you be so selfish?"

She stared at him. *Selfish.* The word was like a sucker punch to the gut, taking all the air out of her. She walked past him into the hotel, pulling Fifi down the hall toward their room. He grabbed her arm.

"Gwen, look." The sleeve of his white T-shirt was darkened with blood and he pulled it up over his shoulder. "I was cut. See? It hurts. You have to help me."

She studied the cut, touched the skin around it. It was a slash, rather than a puncture wound. It was curved and the clotted blood made it look like a mean, close-lipped smile. It could've used some hydrogen peroxide, or antiseptic ointment, but he was going to be fine.

"I thought I was selfish." She slung the words back at him. "Not so much the type to help."

"I could get hep B, or tetanus. I don't know when I had my shots. You think I should go to a hospital?"

The old Gwen would have broken down; she'd have driven him wherever he wanted to go. But this Gwen only looked at him. In the yellow light of the putrid hall with blood on his arm, he was someone she didn't know. Not anymore.

"What do you think, Gwen? Does it look infected?"

"I think you should have thought of that before you jumped in and left your pregnant girlfriend on the sidewalk," she said. And then she laughed. Not the high, nervous laugh, but a low grounded rumble she hoped would shake him. She couldn't push the thought from her mind. What if. What if he'd been killed. Or what if the men had turned on her. But in his mind, the risk had been worth it. She meant next to nothing to him, in the scheme of things. She turned the deadbolt to their room and walked in. "You're an asshole, Leo. You can go to hell," she said, and she closed the door.

"Bitch! You have a black hole for a heart," he yelled. The words stung.

There wasn't much to pack—her hairbrush and the notebook she carried everywhere and never seemed to write in. But where would she go? She wouldn't leave him, him and Valiant, here in Tijuana. So what was she doing?

It didn't matter. The act of packing was enough. She refolded her sundress, shut the suitcase. She stared at the wall, at its peeling white paint, the old shit-brown showing through. Why had she agreed to come here? What had she been hoping for? An all-day, all-night fiesta? Something to bring them together again, lighthearted and hopeful?

He pounded on the door. "I'm sorry. I'm so sorry," he cried.

She opened it to stop the noise. He was on his knees, his face a blotchy red. He wiped his nose with the back of his hand and stood.

"You're right. I'm an asshole," he said, and noticed the suitcase on the bed. The corners of his mouth were low and his eyes were bright. He didn't turn from her. He didn't yell. He just sat on the edge of the bed and flicked his shoes off. "You can leave me, you know. But no one will love you as much as I do."

"Is that some kind of a curse?"

"If that's what you think my love is. A curse." A tear spilled down his cheek and he wiped it away with the back of his hand.

"Christ, Gwen, can't we just sleep?" he said. He moved her

suitcase onto the floor, clasped her arm and pulled her down with him onto the sheet. "Tink, you need to sleep. Remember how we used to sleep? We were so good at it."

She was exhausted. As if all the late nights were heaped like quilts on top of each other and she were under them already. She couldn't keep her eyes open. "I want to get to the ocean. It's been too long," she said, and even as she spoke she felt herself drifting. He was right. She needed to sleep. His arm was around her shoulders, his stomach to her back.

"You're not just you anymore," he said, hugging her closer. She could feel his heart lulling her. His breath like the tide, like waves on the shore, he was Morpheus taking her out and under, taking her elsewhere. He unlaced her boots and pulled them off along with her socks.

"Tink," he said. "Dream of flying."

Twenty-six

THE ROOM WAS overexposed. The thin, flowered sheet hanging in the window did little to block the sun, and there was the Count, backlit, a vision in silhouette, standing over them, singing in falsetto.

Somewhere, over the rainbow, skies are blue.
And the dreams that you dare to dream really do come true.

Had it come to this—to Judy Garland so early in the morning? This was serious. Too serious. She couldn't fathom it just yet.

She closed her eyes, tried to focus on the buzzing in her ears. She could almost feel it—the dream he'd woken her from. The power in her chest, in her heart, filling her body and lifting her into the sky. It was her *over the rainbow* dream, only she wasn't stuck at a farm but in a city, the crowds moving in on her, so close and thick she couldn't breathe—that part was recurring. She'd had the dream since she'd been a kid. But the rising above the throng, the flying, that was different.

Two flying dreams in two days, ever since she'd found out.

The bed dipped as the Count sat beside her as though she were the sick one.

> If happy little bluebirds fly
> beyond the rainbow,
> why oh why can't I?

This time he hit the high note with ease. She opened one eye. He was still wearing his bandanna on his head, but now he had some makeup on, eyeliner, mascara that was running. Where had he gotten it? He hadn't packed a bag. Had he been rummaging in her purse? She noticed it was open on the chair. How long had he been awake? She'd never seen him this worked up in the morning. She could smell tequila on his breath.

The song over, he sat looking at the lit window. She heard the squeaking of brakes outside, brakes on what had to be a large truck; she could hear a crane lift a trash can, hear rubbish clatter into the truck's open bin. She thought of the roaches she'd freed and wondered how they were getting on.

Leo grunted and pulled a pillow over his head.

Stumbling out of bed, she tugged her T-shirt down, buttoned up the jeans she must have loosened—but not bothered to take off—in the night. They were snug, snugger even than yesterday, if she wasn't mistaken. Not wanting her bare feet to touch the floor, she took her flip-flops from her suitcase and slid them on. She was so parched she could barely swallow. She found one of the gallon jugs of water, took it into the bathroom and chugged while she peed. She brought the water with her back to the bed, where she sat beside Valiant.

"Did I ever tell you how she died?" he said.

It took her a minute. "Judy?"

"Ms. Garland, yes."

"It was an overdose, right? Suicide."

"Accidental, the coroner's report said."

"That's what they said about my mother." She heard herself say it, heard the words slip into the bald morning light. So easy. And then they were there—the truth they stood for was there, hanging in the air between them. And it was all right. Somehow it was all right. This was Mexico. What did she have to hide?

He looked at her, searching, she thought, for that part of her capable of lying. She could tell it was something he'd never thought to look for. "What about the cement truck? How she died and you lived?" he said, still doubting.

"The second part's true. And we'd been in the car together the day she died. It was almost Christmas. All that's true. The cement truck was something I made up. It explained things somehow."

They sat for a while in the quiet. Even the street outside seemed to still, waiting.

"It was pills?"

"A whole lot of Xanax washed down with vodka. My dad was out of town. I found her the next morning." She stopped herself. She'd never said it out loud, never told anyone, not even Leo. She looked at him. He was breathing deeply, steadily, and had the pillow over his head.

"Go on, dear." Valiant put a hand on her back; its weight was warm and calm and encouraging.

She shook her head. If she let it out, she might not stop. The chasm would open and she'd tumble into it. Like being on a high-dive, closing your eyes and going headfirst—not a sleek, toes-pointed dive, but more of a tumble, head over heels, like love.

She leaned forward and that was all it took. She was falling.

"The light—it was like this. Too bright through those flimsy white drapes. Vindictive.

"It was late morning and she wasn't up. The house was too still, too cold. I had goose bumps on my arms and this pit-of-my-stomach hollow feeling. I knocked on her door. Nothing. I put my hand on the cold metal knob and let it stay there awhile. I didn't want to open that door.

"I saw her in the mirror first. There was a full-length mirror. It was where she'd do her makeup, where she'd sit on the awful lime-green shag carpet and make herself pretty. I used to be in such awe of her, when I was little." Gwen wanted to remember her mother's face as it had been when she was alive, when she'd sat watching her work her magic, but she found she couldn't. The face she was seeing now was the face the photographs had captured and not her real face at all.

Valiant took her hand in his and squeezed it. "You don't have to go on," he said.

But she drew a breath and kept telling the story, trusting it would lead her where she needed to go. "She was facedown in a black slip, her hair spread out, like she'd fallen. She looked so small. Even then. Like a doll. And all around her was her makeup. Open eye shadows and blush and brushes. And the weird thing was, she hadn't worn makeup in weeks, months. Maybe in years. She'd stopped going out and hadn't cared what she looked like. And this was like in the old days, when getting ready had been her own private party.

"When I saw she wasn't moving, wasn't breathing, I screamed.

And still she didn't move. I thought she'd move. Thought maybe she was just hungover. I shook her and she was icy. I turned her over. Her eyes were open. Her eyes." Gwen could see them, not like in any photo. She tried to push the image away. She looked at Valiant, into his dark, wet eyes, so filled with life, but all she could see were her mother's lifeless eyes. "I couldn't look away. They'd gone flat, but I stared, like maybe she'd come back. And then I closed her eyelids, with two fingers, like they do in the movies. And I ran and called 911."

Gwen listened to herself talking, spilling what had been bottled inside her for almost half her life. The facts. What it was she'd seen and done. She was outside herself, watching and listening from a distance, on the other side of a tunnel, or through the lens of a movie camera. And she wondered why she wasn't crying. She should be able to cry, she thought. If she were directing she'd make sure the actress playing Gwendolyn Griffin let a tear or two slip down her cheek. Silent, stoic tears, tears of relief and recognition. The scene required them.

Valiant's cheeks were shining with his tears. He was right there with her. Or, rather, he was there, standing in that place of grief she should have stood in, going where she couldn't. He gave her hand another squeeze.

"I felt ashamed. Or guilty. Or something. I should have been able to save her. And I didn't. I didn't save her." It felt strange to say it out loud.

"I'd always thought"—she swallowed—"I'd always thought I could. When she'd cry when I was little, cry so long I thought she might never stop, I'd cry along with her. And when that didn't work, I'd try to make her laugh. I'd stand on my head and make faces. Sometimes it worked, and she'd laugh and hug me like she'd never let me go. But that day, in the car, I don't know why, but it was like I took a huge step back and watched her, and I hated her." That did it. The ice inside her had cracked. Falling into her own watery depths, she went on.

"I hated her weakness. I hated that she looked on my life like it was her second chance or something, and at that moment I didn't care. I wanted her to be happy, but I wanted to be happy, too. I wanted her to be happy *for* me, not *because* of me or something I did. So I just let her cry. I watched her cry and I didn't try to stop her. I didn't say the things she wanted me to say.

"And then." She paused. This was the part she'd forgotten. The part she most didn't want to remember. "She swerved into traffic, into the oncoming cars. I caught the wheel and jerked us back. It was a miracle we didn't crash. She'd have killed me and herself and God knows how many other people."

Valiant hugged Gwen. He pressed her to his chest and held her, and she let go of all she'd been clasping so tightly. "It's okay, it's okay." He said it over and over, and he smoothed her hair back from her forehead, and she sobbed, messy, choking, snuffling sobs.

When she caught her breath, as if it were a fish she'd hooked at last, this portion of the air belonging to just her, she pulled away from him, wiped her tears and snot on her T-shirt. She saw that Leo had turned onto his side and had his back to them.

"You're the big brother I never had," she said to Valiant.

"Big sister, darling." He smiled, and then the smile was gone. His eyes were placid, flat with distance. Like the mountain lion, he seemed to be looking through her to the other side, to that place where he was going. "I'm tired. Really tired. I want to go home."

"Okay, we can leave now. I'm ready."

"Not to the Cornell. I want to go home-home. My parents' place."

"San Clemente?"

He nodded. "I want to stay there awhile. My mother's there, just by herself most days. I miss her chicken and rice. I miss her cool hands and her voice. God, I miss her voice. I've been away so long."

"Okay," she said. "It's okay. We'll leave right now. You'll see her in a few hours."

She excused herself and went into the bathroom, where she splashed water on her splotchy face. In the room she gathered her things into the suitcase. And then she pulled the pillow from Leo's face and sang the little song her mother had liked to sing to her mornings before school.

> *Lazy bones, lying in the sun,*
> *how do you expect to get a day's work done?*

It wasn't the first time she'd tried it on him, and there'd even been mornings it had made him laugh, but now he glared at her with his one open eye and rolled over.

The dried blood on his sleeve looked worse in the morning light. The stain was darker, bigger than she'd remembered. She pulled the sleeve up and looked at the wound. It was livid, in-flamed. She pressed on the skin around it and a bloody pus seeped. She pulled her hand back. "We need to get you to a hospital."

He held up his arm, gazing at the gash in a detached manner, as though he were assessing a work of art—something he'd made and was proud of. He ran his fingertips over it, and wiped the pus on the bedsheet. "It's fine," he said.

"No, it's not fine."

Valiant backed away from him. "It's disgusting."

"I'm taking you to the emergency room," said Gwen.

Leo got out of bed. "My mom's a nurse. Apparently our destination is San Clemente," he grumbled. "We can stop by her place. She'll fix me up."

Twenty-seven

THEY WERE DRIVING for the border before the gringos who'd been at the bars the previous night were out of bed. The town was sleepy still, and almost pretty. It had a morning-after feel, hazy, with bright trash flattened on the sidewalk and a few vendors pushing their carts—fruit, tortillas, sombreros.

At the border, there was only one car ahead of them. Leo was in the front seat and Fifi sat on his lap. Her head out the window, she was sniffing the air. "Oh, shit," Valiant said. "Do they let you bring dogs in from Mexico?"

"What do you mean? She's my dog."

"We didn't have any trouble getting across," Gwen said, but her stomach did a flip. "Here," she said, taking the shock collar from her purse. Leo strapped it on to Fifi. He covered her loosely with Valiant's black jacket and slid her under his legs. They hoped she would look like a shadow on the floor.

She rolled down the window for the agent, who asked if they were American. Gwen told her they were. The woman said she needed to see ID, and Leo and Valiant gave their licenses to Gwen, who handed them, along with her own, to the woman.

When she peered into the car, nobody moved. She was broad-faced, with sharp eyes and thin lips that Gwen found herself wanting to see smile—to see if they *could* smile. She looked at Gwen and then at Leo in his TODAY I'M MEXICAN shirt with dried blood on his sleeve and scowled. She walked to a back window and tapped on it. Christ. Gwen felt the blood drain from her face. And then she heard it—the yip like a hiccup from under Leo's legs. Fifi had been shocked midbark. Gwen held her breath, but all was quiet. She could see the woman in her side mirror, her expression unchanged, a good sign. Valiant rolled the window down. She looked at him, at his driver's license photo and then back at him. With his legs crossed and his arm around Mary, he was the epitome of cool, but this was taking longer than Gwen expected. Leo bit his lower lip. His eyes were wide and blank, as if he'd just remembered something.

If the agent found Fifi what would she do? Quarantine her? Gwen wasn't sure Leo had kept Fifi's tags up to date. He'd never taken her to the vet, not as long as she'd known him. Her tags, however old, would make her American, Gwen supposed, and they'd make Leo her owner. That had to count for something.

The agent handed Gwen back the licenses, gave a slight upward nod, as if expression were precious and she meant to conserve it, and she let them drive past. They sighed a communal *oh* of relief. They were on the other side, in America, where the road was a freeway, wide and clean and smooth, where the signs of upcoming cities were big and plain—San Diego, San Clemente, Los Angeles. And Leo pulled Fifi out of hiding, took her shock collar off. He held her on his lap and stroked her head. "Well, Fifi, you almost got to live the dream."

Was he kidding? No. His face was set as though he meant it.

They were in the desert now, and Gwen breathed it in. Such a particular smell. Creosote. The smell before the rains came.

Its musty sweetness brought with it her childhood, a certain idle solitude, that feeling of wanting something and not knowing what it is, or else wanting nothing but an impossible changelessness.

Everyone slept, everyone but Gwen. Gwen the driver. She yawned. A double, a triple espresso—she'd give anything to have one right now. There was a coffee bar in San Clemente, just an hour away. She told herself she could make it.

San Diego came and went. And then there were fields, green and yellow with mustard flowers, and the ocean all misted over. Fog ebbed and flowed over the freeway. She drove slow in the right lane and opened her window. Breathing the fog, she felt clean, new. She shivered, grabbed Valiant's jacket from the floor and wrapped it around her. It stank of smoke and booze, but it kept her warm.

They passed Camp Pendleton, and the giant nuclear tits of the San Onofre power plant, passed the yellow, diamond-shaped warning signs—the family in silhouette, man, woman, and child with their hands linked, running across the freeway—what to watch for, what not to hit. At the border patrol immigration checkpoint, she slowed to a stop and waited for the line of cars to filter through. In the fog, the waiting felt, to Gwen, otherworldly. As if they were all just souls, bodiless souls, and when they arrived at the checkpoint they'd be escorted to the next stage—the officers wouldn't be officers but orderlies in all white, and they'd take them by the arm to the depot where they'd each enter a womb and start a new life. She looked in the rearview mirror at Valiant, his face gaunt, but peaceful as he slept. He looked to her like an ascetic, as though he'd already given up the world. The cars inched forward. Leo yawned and stretched and Gwen thought of telling him—about the souls and the new bodies, about the orderlies in white. Tell a dream and you lose it, she reminded herself, and she kept the vision just that, a vision. At the stop sign the officer no sooner glanced at them than waved them on. No one in the car looked Mexican enough to bother.

Fifi stuck her head out the window. The salt air blew her long hair back, flattening her face so she was all eyes, black nose, and lips. She looked like a white seal. She stayed there, blinking against the wind, and Gwen thought she saw her smile. Valiant was still out. "He lives over here," Leo said, and she took the first exit and drove up a hill.

Leo hugged his knees to his chest. "Why didn't you tell me? You could have, you know?"

"Tell you?"

"About your mom. You told him but you couldn't tell me?"

"You were sleeping."

"Or trying to." His look was petulant. Sad eyes, the tight jaw. "You can tell me things, Gwen. I'm here for you."

She wanted to believe him. It was why she had stayed with him, she knew—because, despite his erratic tendencies, his eccentricities, he was steadfast. So why hadn't she told him the truth?

He turned from her. She watched the road. What was she guilty of? Everyone has a mask. *A face to meet the faces that you meet.* It was timing, she told herself. She was coming clean with the world now—showing her true face. She wanted to explain, but found she couldn't—couldn't put this shift into words. Words were flimsy, surface reflections, the world as one saw it in still water, marred by the slightest wind. And she was deep beneath the water in her own slow, thick world. Her words would come out in burbles not even she could understand.

The road traced the edge of a cliff; it went on and on. "The long and winding road, huh?" she said, talking against the silence.

Valiant gasped and sat up. He blinked open his eyes. "Fuck." He looked out the window. "Jesus, we're here. I was dreaming. We were on a ride, in a car-thing, you know, on a track."

"A roller coaster?" Leo said.

"Only it went just in a circle. We wanted to get off and they wouldn't stop it. The guy who ran it was laughing and it went faster and faster, until it launched us, the three of us in the car, and the car was a magic carpet and we could go anywhere. We were off the track."

"Where'd we go?" Gwen asked.

"We didn't get that far," he said, laughing, and then coughing too long. "We each wanted to go different places, I think. But it was okay. We had all the time we needed."

His house was the last on a cul-de-sac, and it looked out over a canyon. She imagined that flaming car from Valiant's youth screaming down the hill and soaring into the canyon, imagined the fire spreading for miles. All that light and heat and power. A god—or a goddess—unleashed. She pulled to the curb and parked the car.

"That's my room," Valiant said, pointing to an upstairs window with a royal blue curtain half drawn across it. He hadn't always been obsessed with darkness, then. He'd been just a boy once, one of the few black boys in San Clemente. Baseball and bubblegum. Maybe even girls? He'd said he'd tried them for a while, but it was hard to picture.

They got out of the car. Fifi found a spot in the middle of the yard and peed. Valiant rang the bell and they all waited in the cool, suburban morning. A robin hopped along a fence. Over-head, a flock of gulls circled. One could see the ocean from here, she supposed, if it weren't for the low clouds.

A woman opened the door. She was dark-skinned, short and pear-shaped, wearing a bright, floral housedress. Her salt-and-pepper hair was in rollers under a hot pink scarf. She lit up when she saw Valiant, and her eyes filled with tears. *"Meu Angelo, meu bebe,"* she said. "I was worried. I've been calling, didn't you get my calls?" She hugged him, coming up not quite to his shoulders. He picked her up and squeezed her. She turned her head, Gwen thought, away from his smell—cigarettes, tequila, and vomit, days of not showering. They all had to stink. They'd probably grown accustomed to it.

"Maria, I want you to meet Gwen. Gwen, Maria."

Gwen put her hand out, and disregarding it Maria pulled her to her pillowy chest. She smelled of dryer sheets, of powder and perfume. She let Gwen go and took Leo into her arms. *"Meu caro,* it's been so long." She pulled back and looked him over. "What are those," she said, "knickers?"

"Part of a costume," Leo said, blushing.

"Theater?"

"Something like that."

"Maria," Valiant said. "I was hoping to stay, for just a while. A few days."

"Naturalmente, Angelo, you'll stay. You take a hot bath, I wash those clothes. You have a bag in the car?"

Valiant shook his head. "Just Mary," he said, and Leo carried her over and set her on the stoop. "For you," Valiant said.

His mother beamed and hugged him to her again. "You stay as long as you like. I'm making coxinha."

"And pão de queijo?" Valiant said. Gwen thought he might jump up and down.

"Come inside," she said to Gwen and Leo. "You want some cookies, tea?"

"No thank you, Mrs. Valente. We should get going," Leo said.

"All right, love. It's good to see you." She turned to Gwen, held her in her gaze. "Thank you, dear."

"For what?"

"For bringing my boy home." Her eyes brimming again, she turned and went into the house.

The three of them stood in the quiet, as if no one were willing to break it.

"Well," said the Count at last. "I guess this is it."

"What are you talking about? You're coming back," Leo said.

The Count nodded and tried to smile. He gave Leo a big-hearted hug. And somehow she knew this was it. The last time she would see him.

"It's been fun," he said.

"Shhh," Gwen quieted him. It was too much. All of it. She wasn't ready. "We have time," she said, as if saying the words would make them real. Looking out, toward the ocean at the low-hung layer of clouds, her chest felt heavy. She should have been there more for him. He was right—she'd been selfish. She turned so he couldn't see her tears.

He put his arm around her, bent to her height, and rested his head on her shoulder. "Hey, kid. It's okay. You two will make amazing parents. You will. Think of what a spiffy job you've done taking care of me." He gave her a squeeze and whispered into her ear. "My camera's in the car. I want you to have it. Develop the film and send me copies." Unable to speak, she nodded.

Like the Count that he was, he took a step back, bowed, and kissed her on both cheeks. "Your baby, girl or boy, will be a knockout." He put a finger under her chin and lifted it. "Those Grace Kelly cheekbones. You should have been—"

"A movie star?" He nodded. "I don't know," she said. "I think it's better this way."

She wanted to give him something. A present. "Someday," she said. "I'll write a novel, about us. The three of us."

"All right," he said, smiling for real now. "That sounds all right. But promise me one thing."

"Anything."

"It has to have pooping in it. No one ever poops in novels."

They all looked at Fifi, on the side of the yard, pooping on the pansies.

Twenty-eight

THE CAR FELT hollow without him. She pulled away slowly. They were heading back down the road, toward the ocean. The street curved, but just before the house was out of sight, she stopped. She could see, in her rearview mirror, the stooped figure of Angelo Valente. He was leaning on the railing as he climbed the few steps to his front door. She wanted him to look toward them and wave, but he didn't.

She watched the door close behind him, and she drove down the hill.

Leo reached under his seat and pulled out a small plastic baggie. "Ready for another trip?" he said. "An uncharted waters sort of trip?" He shook the baggie and the shriveled brown pieces danced inside it.

She looked at the bag and then at him. "Not really."

"Really." He was grinning like the Cheshire cat, as if he were already lit. He opened the bag and sniffed. "Smells innocuous enough."

"You brought that into Mexico? What were you thinking? Or do you think?" She tightened her grip on the wheel, faced the road because she sure as hell didn't want to look at him.

"It isn't like it's cocaine. They're mushrooms, for Christ's sake. They're a vegetable. Or else a fungus. Is a fungus a vegetable? My point is, we might have been cooking a risotto for all the border patrol knew."

He was turning a piece in his fingers. "Amazing how inedible this looks," he said and popped it in his mouth.

"You remembered, didn't you, at the border. You'd forgotten about them." She was putting it together—his sudden look of terror and the fact of the mushrooms. And she'd been worried for Fifi. She was glad she hadn't known.

"Oh, God, I'd forgotten." He was chewing, chewing, his mouth puckering and his eyes watering. "What do we have to drink?"

"Here." She reached behind his seat and handed him her last gallon jug of water, half full.

"Will wonders never cease," he said and washed the mushrooms down. He'd long ago learned not to touch her water, learned firsthand that the goddess could be fierce. Still, he had enjoyed the comment. She snatched the water from his hands.

He took his time chewing another few pieces, as if he were *trying* to taste them. He swallowed them dry. "They really do taste like shit," he said, beaming, and he dropped the baggie in her lap. "For you, my dear."

"Are you serious?"

"Jesus, Gwen. Since when did you turn prude?"

She stopped the car in the middle of the empty, winding road. She looked at him.

His face was blank. "What?"

"Really, Leo?" she said. And then it dawned on him.

"So you're pregnant. God, Gwen. What'd you think, I forgot? It's not like it changes anything. Think of all the hippies that dropped acid pregnant. Their babies were fine. You yourself were born in the Summer of Love."

A car behind her screamed to a stop, honked. She drove on.

"That doesn't mean my mom did drugs."

"This is just mushrooms. It's a—"

"A fungus, I know. A fungus from a cow pie. Lovely." She put the baggie of mushrooms in her purse.

She turned down the main drag to the ocean. "Make a left here," he said. "And a right. We can park at the end of my old street. The beach access is free."

They drove down a row of apartments that looked like they belonged to the seventies. At a beige duplex, he told her to stop. She pulled over, yanked the parking brake up. It was the apartment he'd grown up in, he said, where his mom still lived.

"Why haven't I been here?" Gwen had met his mom before, but it was at the Italian deli down the street. She'd loaded Leo up with parmigiana and salami, olives and pasta, so much food they'd lived off it for a month.

"It's small," he said. "Two bedrooms. Brown shag carpet wall to wall. I didn't think you'd want to see it."

"She needs to look at your cut. Let's go up." She killed the engine and opened the door and—before she could stop her— Fifi jumped from the car and bolted toward the apartment. Leo caught her at the bottom of the stairs. Holding her tight, he got in the car with her.

"Start the engine, will you?"

"No." Gwen stepped from the car and crossed the lawn. She shouted back at him, "You need antiseptic, something. You said she was a nurse."

"She is."

"Well—"

"No." Jutting out his jaw, he was a toddler embracing the word. "No. I told her I'd be on the news, and I went to Tijuana instead. My son the bum, she'll say." He laughed it off. "And anyway, I can feel the mushrooms. The world is blooming! Come on, Gwendy, let's go to the beach."

"It's *your* arm," she said, and got in the car and started the engine.

Looking back at the apartment, she pictured his mother alone in her apartment, glued to her TV, waiting to glimpse her son. "I bet she'd just be happy you're alive," she said, and released the parking brake. She drove to the end of the street and parked the car in a cul-de-sac in front of a little Spanish-style church.

Without a word of explanation, Leo was out and running down the stairs to the beach. She pulled a sweater, a sundress, and a bikini from her suitcase and did a quick car-change. She tucked her notebook into her purse, put Fifi on her leash, and locked the doors.

She had the feeling she was in a strange land. The sea was misty and still, and descending the cement stairs was like walking through a series of veils. She could make out the faintest notion of the pier through the mist, and as she turned down the sidewalk she saw, taking shape further on, the little seaside shops—a bikini/T-shirt shop, Pizza By the Slice, a mini-market, and a café with a wooden sign that said ESPRESSO hanging from the awning. She was saved.

There were round tables for two on the sidewalk and she sat at one alone. Leo had vanished into the fog. She might as well enjoy her coffee; after all there was nowhere she had to be.

She sat in the white, wet light, thinking of the mushrooms in her purse and the baby inside her. Things inside things. Hidden. The town was hidden, the ocean, too. And the people—that was it, she realized, what was so odd: she hadn't seen a single person. The street was deserted. A few cars had passed her, but she was alone on the sidewalk, alone at this café with her little white dog. It was a Saturday morning, so where were the people? Were they in their homes, afraid the riots might spread, break out in this beach town of surfers and bikini girls and older, retired folks? The thought struck her as ridiculous.

A girl appeared—as if she were the result of a magic trick— out of the thick air. Wearing black-rimmed glasses, her dark hair cut in a pageboy, she was bookish, with a hint of the mischievous in her smile. She'd make a good stripper—one with a literary pseudonym. Anaïs, or Colette, Gwen thought, watching her jot her order—a triple espresso and a croissant—on her small pad.

The waitress looked at her a second longer over her glasses, her eyes dark and pretty, and she left.

Where she'd been, Leo now stood, glowing, the curls of his hair tightly wound.

"Darling," he panted, "it's beautiful down there. You have to come. Be a good girl and eat your drugs and come down. My *God*," he said, looking around. "I feel like a kid again. Like a king."

"King of the apple blossoms."

"Yes! That's it! Gwen, there's so much I want to show you. This was my playground."

She opened the Ziploc bag. It smelled earthy, the way the soil in the middle of a forest might smell. "Listen," she said. "I'll make you a deal. If I join you down there, you have to promise me something."

"Anything."

"This will be the last of it. For a long time."

"Last trip to Neverland. Got it, Tink. Now, damn it, come

on." He grinned. "There's that cave I want to explore with you, in the boulders."

"And one more thing," she said. "Sit down." It was hard for him—his body was like a spring, ready to burst into the day, to leap and to run—but he sat at the table and she took both his hands in hers. "Leo," she said, "this part's serious," and as she said it she knew. She felt the truth settle, felt it sink into the hollow centers of her bones, and while she could have sobbed, she watched herself finish saying what needed to be said. "By the end of this, this excursion, I'll know. If we're together, then we'll give it a shot. If we're not, then we're not. And if we're not"—she swallowed, made herself say the words—"it's over."

"What about the baby?"

"I'll raise her on my own."

"You're serious."

"I am." She was someone else saying this, someone she didn't recognize. Someone she couldn't help but admire.

"Well," he said, "you seem decided." His dilated eyes were consumed, she could tell, by visions, his ears by voices calling him on. He stood and took Fifi's leash. If she got the baby, he'd get the dog.

"But Tink, I want you to know that I love you. I'll always love you." He kissed her forehead, and she felt a warm river move through her as she watched him leave.

His love had never been the question.

Twenty-nine

SHE HELD THE mushrooms in her fist, looked at them on her open palm. Five pieces in all. Hard and rough and brown, like something that would fall from a tree in autumn—oddly shaped, dried-up seedpods. They weighed next to nothing. And yet so much hung in the balance. On the one hand psilocybin, and on the other—her world where she was right now. And where she was—well, it was hard to say, exactly. She was in the middle of a low cloud, drifting amid the possibilities. She wanted clarity—absolute, incontrovertible. She wanted to be grounded and sure—sure of her next play. Think strategy, she told herself, don't listen to your big, dumb mess of a heart.

In the fog her hand all but disappeared and the mushrooms seemed to be floating. There wasn't any tag on these fungi that said *eat me*. She could put them back in her purse and watch Leo from an easy vantage. She could sit on the shore and meditate. She could exude the illusion of calm assertion. Maybe she could even fool herself.

But the mushrooms were here, here in her hand. And Leo was right about one thing. They were just a fungus—a fungus that might help her to see.

She smelled them again. Their bitter odor made her salivate, and her stomach turned on itself. The old trip returned in a flood of colors, images, feelings.

She remembered the quality of the light, the indistinct brightness that had held her in its trembling mystery as though she were inside the body of a huge, slow, deep-breathing animal. She remembered the terrible, ever tighter enclosures and the expansion that had followed and that she'd felt born into, as if she were brand new.

She let herself enter that day again, let it all come back. It had the quality of a dream, or of a scene from childhood, cast in a sepia light. It had been at Laguna Beach, just north of here, where they had eaten the mushrooms, more than a year ago. It had been October, the fog thick as it was today, the sand fine and white as ash and the sea like milk—shining, cold, frothy—and far, too far across the slow sand. She had taken a step, and another, and the sea had been no closer; for every step she took it took two. She looked for Leo but he had disappeared somewhere up the beach.

She remembered how the mushrooms had come over her in waves, each one bigger than the last. The world had groaned like a giant intestine, pulsing, contracting and expanding. And her own insides had done strange things, flips with twists.

Heading through the white morning to find Leo, she'd stumbled through the icy surf. She found him hidden between boulders, at the far edge of the shore, and she crawled back, behind him, into the shade of the boulders, her body convulsing and her heaves dry. She held her sides and rocked like a sick child until Leo held her and rocked her and they rolled off their towels onto the damp sand.

She had felt like she was dying, like they were dying together in their shared dream.

And inside her something had raced, something afraid of the darkness, the mouth closing around her—as if she could escape, could crawl out of her body writing in the sand. If death were a mouth, it had shut around them and was swallowing. She could hear it humming as if they tasted good.

Down, down, Alice in the hole, the slow fall. She clung—to the sand, to Leo's hand—her fingernails digging in, as if they could save her.

Stupid girl, her mind had insisted. The mushrooms were poison and you took too many.

Leo held her and she held him, but she was alone in the hole, in the stomach of her mind, in the fear of losing herself. She felt her body dissolve, the molecules separating, making room for the Other—for the Great Unknown—to enter. So this is how it feels to die, she was thinking, when she heard singing.

Leo's song had become the blue of deep oceans, and she moved her fingers and her toes, stretched her body between them. She could still see him sitting on the sand, singing with his eyes closed, a whirling Middle Eastern chant. And the sun and sand and sea were inside his song. She was in it, too, running inside the music, tearing off her jeans and T-shirt and meeting the waves head-on in just her bra and her panties. They had been the only people on the long stretch of beach, and she sent the water with her cupped hands skyward, where it caught the sunlight, each drop a bright bead, and all of it alive, all of it rainbow, the whole spectrum hanging like a garden in the air.

Leo's eyes had seemed a universe of their own, shining, flecked with gold and green, gold-green and green-brown. His pupils were tunnels, and inside them she felt his heart thrumming, his good heart. He was more than she had thought, much more. Lit from inside he was a luminary, a cathedral with its stained glass glowing, or else a plain old house with its windows open and into which she'd found herself eager to peer.

All that day the sand had glimmered with fool's gold and quartz. The day had seemed long as a lifetime, and in it she'd known the truth. She didn't have to waste her youth working some stupid job. She had known the stones were dreaming her into existence, those shining boulders that held the beach in place.

And she could become anyone—anyone she pleased.

So she'd quit her day job, her desk job, her file-and-answer-the-phone job for $7.25 an hour, and she'd ventured out, into big bad Los Angeles, and found herself a job stripping. Her life had changed. The fungus had helped her to see the possibilities.

But now?

She couldn't do it. She folded the air from the bag and zipped it closed. The mushrooms had never really been an option. She had another, a different, journey to take. Her waking dream would be lucid and the magic in her life, real.

Thirty

THE WAITRESS BROUGHT the croissant and espresso, and Gwen shoved the baggie to the bottom of her purse. Here were the almonds and dark chocolate from her pregnancy-test purchase—almonds for protein and chocolate for joy. She tore off a chunk of the fresh croissant, stuck a slab of chocolate inside it, and dipped the corner of her makeshift chocolate croissant in the espresso. She closed her eyes and let the taste fill her body. She took her time eating, savoring the flavors.

As she watched the fog thin and lift, revealing patches of blue—sky and ocean—her thoughts found Leo. She imagined he was down the beach, inside his beloved cave, singing. Perhaps by now he'd emerged and flung himself into the waves. Wherever he was, he was in his Neverland, where he was happy.

She could get in her car right now. She could leave him.

The sudden notion terrified and then thrilled her.

But it would go against the pact she'd made with him. *If I join you*, she'd said. *At the end of this, I'll decide*. But she hadn't joined him. She hadn't taken the mushrooms, which meant the pact was broken, and she didn't have to tell him a thing.

If she took off, when he came down from his trip, he could walk to his mother's place. Gwen wouldn't be stranding him, she'd be leaving him where—if he decided to—he could make his way back home. And if she left right now, she could go to the Cornell, throw everything she owned in her car and leave town.

But where would she go?

Not home to her father. Returning to Phoenix, pregnant and without a man, returning to the house she grew up in— even the thought made her stomach turn. What would her father say to his country-club pals? And anyway, she wouldn't raise her daughter under her father's roof, in a house that was less a home than it was an extensive hotel suite. She tried to picture the house as it was now, but she had a hard time seeing it. In the years since her mother's death, her father had added nothing to the place. Rather, he had served as a nega- tive force, emptying the rooms of what had once been there. He threw out her mother's clothing, her makeup, her hats and her purses. And then, when Gwen left for college, his need to banish her spread to the study, where he stripped the walls of her photos, cleared the shelves of the books her mother had loved. Old hardbound collections of Yeats and Whitman, Keats and Woolf and Hemingway. Without telling Gwen, he'd given them to charity. Seeing the shelves empty, Gwen wanted to scream and throttle him, to punch him until her numb body felt pain, until she could feel again. Instead, she'd embraced the numbness. She had turned to ice and taken a vow of distance, which, given his own emotional sovereignty and the fact that he hardly looked at her, she was sure he hadn't noticed. Even her bedroom became a shell of its former self. She had taken the things she cared about—her clothes, the typewriter, her cigar box of treasures—and the rest of her belongings he'd boxed in the garage. Only her bed remained, along with an empty bureau. It had become little more than a guest bedroom. He'd done what he had to do, she told herself. But one thing was certain: the home she'd grown up in was no longer her home.

She needed a fresh start, somewhere other than Phoenix or Los Angeles.

She thought of her aunt in Santa Cruz. Sam the bohemian, who made her living painting—canvases, murals. She painted her own version of human, dreamy and kind, with wide-set eyes and Renoiresque bodies, who inhabited a land where animals were equals, a human who seemed led more by her heart than her head. She and Loni had an apartment a block from the ocean. Every room was painted a different vibrant color—orange, purple, red. She'd visited them once, a few years back, when she'd needed a break from Leo and the city. Santa Cruz was a place Gwen could live. A quirky ocean town. A place that was far from L.A.

It was also Brett's hometown.

She sucked on the last square of chocolate, looked around her. While she'd been imagining a new life, the world had taken shape, born from the cloud of possibilities. It was crisp and clean, and she could see the horizon, blue on blue. Closer in, though, the water was a brownish-reddish color, more like a muddy river than an ocean.

She asked the waitress about it and the waitress gave her glasses a nudge so they sat higher on her nose. "Well," she said, "the phytoplankton are blooming."

"Phytoplankton?" Gwen said, happy for the diversion.

"Plant plankton." The girl smiled. "It isn't toxic or anything."

Gwen downed the rest of her coffee and the girl went for the check, leaving Gwen alone with her thoughts. Could she really leave Leo? Her breath was shallow, her heart skipped ahead. If she were ever going to do it, now was the time.

Thirty-one

SHE PAID THE check, tipping the waitress twice what she needed to, and walked to Frank's Mini-Market to buy the razor already. And water, she always needed more water. You can take the girl out of the desert, but you can't take the desert out of the girl. That was how Leo explained her obsession. Though really it was so much more. Water was essential, pure. The source of life, her mother had taught her, and renewal.

Outside of Frank's, the *Los Angeles Times* with its headlines was front and center. *King Case Aftermath: A City in Crisis.* She picked up a paper, feeling strangely guilty. Los Angeles was in crisis, and what had she done? She'd skipped town. When the going got tough, she'd split—just like she was thinking of splitting from Leo.

She skimmed the front page. *Bush Ordering Troops to L.A.; Police Struggle to Get Upper Hand in Turmoil; Unrest: Deaths Placed at 40, Eclipsing the Watts Riots; Injury Total Is 1,899 Since Outbreak of Violence Wednesday.* Her eyes stuck on the number: 1,899. Nearly two thousand people were hurt badly enough to go to a hospital. She realized she was light-headed, and she leaned on the door-jamb.

She opened the paper and read on: *Looters, Merchants Put Koreatown Under the Gun.* She thought of Jin—the man who had, for years, filled their donut, their cigarette and vodka, their bottled water and aspirin needs. She hoped he was all right. He had the things he cared about—his family, his business—right there in the heart of L.A. He couldn't just take off, the way they had. She wondered if he was still guarding the store with his gun.

Her eyes skimmed the page. *Authorities were gaining the upper hand for the first time in three days of the worst urban unrest in Los Angeles history.* There was a photo of looters and a store with smoke pouring from the windows. It was La Brea, the caption said, a few blocks from their apartment. She had breathed this very smoke, watched it fill the air not two days ago. And here she was, on a quiet morning and from a safe distance, reading her life. Some part of her still didn't believe it had happened—in Los Angeles of all places.

For the years she'd lived there the city had lain docile and half-asleep under an entropic smaze of promise. It was the land of dreams that really could come true—not just America, but Hollywood. Had even she—somehow—been still hoping? For what? For some big break to come, not for herself—she'd quit that game before it quit her—but for Leo, for the record contract that would give the world (and, more important, her father) the chance to see in him what she had seen all along. And now the dream was gone. There was nothing more to hope for.

When Wrong and Right Blur. Looting Assumes Trappings of Justice if System Is Seen as Failing, Experts Say. Did it really take an expert, she was thinking, when it occurred to her—she'd been one of the looters, which meant this article was referring to her. And in her case, wrong and right *had* blurred. She had been caught in a war zone. Normal laws were out the window. She'd needed water and gas. She could have left some cash on the counter, but for whom? How did she know the cash wouldn't have been taken by someone else, she reasoned, wondering where her theft fell on the karma scale. She would tip double for a while, she told herself, until it evened out.

Some Residents Flee to O.C., the next headline read. She had to laugh. Here she was, safe behind "the Orange Curtain." But how many people had gone all the way to Tijuana to escape the grid gone haywire? She supposed they'd been the minority, since popular opinion didn't view Tijuana as any kind of haven.

Dusk-to-Dawn Curfew Continues. So, no work tonight.

"You buy, miss?" She looked up from the paper. The man behind the counter with his wide, white-toothed grin and his dark eyes reminded her of Jin.

"Frank?" She was aiming at flirtatious, but she knew she'd missed. She was in a serious frame of mind. So why the automatic urge to flirt? Why the instant smile, her eyes crinkled at the corners? She despised that tendency in herself.

The man shook his head, smiling. She folded the paper and replaced it.

A City in Crisis. Her eyes held the word. "Crisis," from the Greek *krisis*, meaning decision. By the end, she'd know. That was what she'd told Leo. She would make a decision.

She searched the racks for something more to eat, something for later. If she kept herself from getting too hungry, she could avoid the nausea, or at least keep it to a minimum. All the food (if you could call it that) was sealed in plastic, shrink-wrapped in shiny-clean need, the quick fix of the mini-mart. Zero was a candy bar, and the ineluctable tide of time was summed up in the black and pink candy-coated licorice capsules boxed and labeled Now and Later. Even the Milky Way itself was sealed and shrunk to fit the hand, the mouth, to fit the life for which the modern human hungers. The high strain of the too-bright fluorescent lights was getting to her. Screw food, she'd get her water and her razor and get out.

She found a bottle in the back, under the glowing rainbow of sodas. She took a razor from the shelves. Eventually she'd work again. It might not be tonight, but it would be soon. She couldn't dance for very much longer; one more time, she figured, to say good-bye and to earn what money she could. It would be the end of the fast cash. Another semester and she'd have her degree, she'd be able to teach, but until then, what would she do, what *could* she do, being pregnant? And once the baby was born, it would take two—one to watch the baby and one to work. And if she left Leo, who would that other one be? It was hard to imagine Leo with a steady job, but maybe, if he felt paternal, he'd grow up. Or else he'd be the one at home, cooking and whatnot, and she'd be the one with the job.

Seeing the first-aid section, she thought of the knife wound, and she felt guilty all over again. She should have taken him to the hospital when he'd been willing to go. She added bandages, hydrogen peroxide, and antibacterial ointment to her purchase. She handed a twenty to Jin's twin who was *not* Frank, and when he gave her back her change, she smiled, but not so much as before, and stepped into day.

She could feel the sun on her skin. It had to be afternoon. One or two? She didn't own a watch, she never had. For as long as she could remember, she'd had her own relationship with time. She couldn't fall asleep to the ticking of a clock, nor could she write to one. Rather, she preferred to regard time as a fluid—water or oil, depending on her mood. She was afraid if time lived on her wrist, it would replace her very pulse, and she wanted to move to her own rhythm.

She crossed the street and the railroad tracks and was on the warm sand, her flip-flops in her hands and her toes sinking. The small flag flying from the pier flapped in the breeze. Today it was yellow, meaning caution, rough water. The waves looked big enough, but not jagged, nor wind-tossed. They were falling in even lines. Looking beyond the red waves to the horizon, she turned the past few days over in her mind, returning to the dream she'd not resolved. There was more to it. More than she'd had time to make sense of. Her mother's words repeated themselves. *You have your whole life.* Gwen had her whole life—which meant, she now saw, that her life was whole, and not any of it, not one jot, could be removed for the rest to exist. For *her* to exist—which was what she wanted now, to be here on this earth, right where she was, walking through the cold shallows. How much time had she wasted trying to throw her life away?

She stepped on a shell, half buried in the sand, a white, spiral shell. She picked it up, shook off the sand and held it to the sky. There was a hole spanning the length of the shell, a window through which she could see the spiral, the pink, glossy tongue curling in on itself, tighter and tighter, disappearing into the spire. The sky brightened. She turned the shell so its smooth interior shone, and then tucked it into the pocket of her sweater.

Leo stood by the boulders. Wearing just his knickers—wet and, like his legs, covered in sand—his hair dripping with the ocean, he looked like an illustration from a book of fairy tales come to life. He was the prince dressed in rags, having sailed through centuries in search of his one true love. His cherub necklace flashed in the sunlight. And he, too, was golden, his face turned toward the sun, his dimples and curls soaking in the light as if his body might burst forth with new life—with wings maybe. He had made it home. It was clear this was where he belonged.

When he saw her he ran to her, his arms wide. He lifted her like a child into the air and set her back down. "Tink!" he said. "Tink! You came. I didn't think you'd ever be here."

"I'm here," she said. His eyes were wild, his pupils big, and she imagined he was seeing the world through a crystal prism rainbow. Inside it, she was sure she appeared consummate, glowing and sublime.

"You know what you look like, Tink? You look like a queen. Will you be my queen?"

She hesitated, unsure of her answer, but as he kept right on talking she realized it didn't matter. He was in monologue mode. Her answer was assumed and she was playing the part of the girl in his story, the girl who was queen because he'd dubbed her as such.

"Listen, listen," he said. He took her hand in his, their fingers interlacing. "Close your eyes." She heard the tide rush in and back out again, taking the small rocks with it, enfolding them with a great hiss, like breath exhaled through the teeth.

"It's so easy," she said.

"*Sprezzatura,*" Leo said. "Studied carelessness. There's no better music than this."

"It's just itself," she said more to herself than to him. And then she had to be in it. She wanted to feel the ocean around her, moving her as it moved.

"Tink," Leo was saying. "Do you feel it? Do you feel the sun? It's a star! Think about it. The sun is a star—so close we can feel its heat on our skin."

She dropped her purse and the bag from the mini-market. She pulled off her sweater and sundress and ran for the waves. Stumbling into them, she could hear, behind her, singing. "The sun is a star, a star, a star," he sang. And then she was swimming, feeling strong, amphibian. Her legs snapped open in a frog kick and her arms parted, too, pushing the water back behind her, and she was sleek and primeval, parting the curtains of water and kelp, moving to where, deep beneath the churning waves, the water was still and quiet, asleep, maybe, on the ocean floor. The yellow flag had to be wrong. Up again, she floated, and her eyelids thinned to tissue-paper lanterns—the sun seen through skin, bald and sanguine. She squinted through the reflection shining off the water and saw Leo, tiny, sitting in his place in the sand.

She realized she couldn't touch. She'd gone further than she'd thought, gone out with a current, a riptide, and out here each wave was bigger than the last. Like everything else, she thought. You make a choice you think is right, you move in a direction, and before you know it, you're treading water in some mad effort to stay afloat.

Wave after wave, she swam down, to the deep colder water, and kicked hard toward shore. With a rip, you move sideways, she remembered. It was what her mother had taught her. To get out of it, you don't swim straight in; you move parallel to the shore.

She caught her breath again, quick, before the wall of water, fast and high, collapsed in on her. She went under, but it took her anyway, took her with it—heels over head over heels—into its tumble and churn. Letting her breath go, slowly, she waited for the calm. Up for air, she opened her eyes to a wave. And then it was on her, sucking her down, into its whirl. Strands of kelp, impossibly long, snaked around her waist and tightened their grip. She pulled them off, gasping water.

Flotsam and jetsam are gentlemen poeds. The line of the poem came to her, these lines from poems at the oddest times. The lines themselves like flotsam in the ether, floating in and out of brains like memories, floating like her, at the mercy of the ocean. She was no more real than a line from a poem, and she could be gone as easily, forgotten, pulled into the black, into the depths. She was flotsam.

In a lull between waves, she saw Leo, still sitting on the sand, singing most likely, although she couldn't make out his flapping jaw, and the song she was in was all ocean—hiss and churn and slap. He was looking out, but did he see her? She waved and he waved back. *Not waving,* she thought, *but drowning.* She'd have laughed if she'd had the energy. She yelled and he didn't budge. He sat there.

Leo alone in the sand—what was wrong with this picture? Something was missing.

Fifi. Where was Fifi?

Gwen was closer to shore now, in a current swift as a river carrying her up the coast. She let it take her, let herself be taken. She reached down and found her toes could touch the sand, thank God. Her toes and fingers had lost all feeling, but she wasn't done with the ocean. Not yet. She liked the speed of this ride. She was in the blue, and the blue was in her; it was a truth she now understood. The depths—the icy, lightless, breathless black—she knew were inside her, too, they'd be there always, but it wasn't where she needed to live.

She could let the current take her. She could be buoyant. She could float.

She rode the river down the cusp of shore, and the houses on the shoreline—the row of beachfront houses with their clear storm walls, their bay windows facing the wide, windswept

Pacific—the houses drifted by like seconds, like hours, brief days, like years when you look back and see all you might have done. In these houses, no one seemed to be home. The houses looked lonely, and she thought she could enter one like Goldilocks, just open the door and go inside, help herself to a bowl of cereal, look in the mirror, and find she was home. In the mailbox, the letters would be addressed to her. Gwendolyn Griffin. Letters from the magazines that wanted her poems at last. And in the moment she thought it, she knew she'd got it wrong. The houses weren't what might have been, but what would be. A life by the sea, maybe not in a beachfront house, but in some apartment like Sam's up the street on a hillside, a life with her child. The life of a writer, on her own terms—a life she'd know was hers by the words she'd put on the page.

She looked back down the beach. Leo was gone. He was a dark speck blending with the sand and the railroad tracks.

Gwen stepped from the water and walked up the incline, lay down flat on her back on the warm, dry sand, her hands outspread. Her body felt heavy as it soaked up the heat from the sand and the sun. She was, she realized, beginning to take up space. To take, to seize, to claim . . . to claim space. *I am here*, her body declared and would declare. I am here. It was nothing less than an affirmation.

I am here.

Thirty-two

FIFI LICKED HER face—her lips, her cheek, her eyelid. It was dusk. Orange dusk. She must have fallen asleep. Overhead, a few palms rustled in the light breeze—like hula dancers flicking their hips, she thought. And here, barking and wagging her tail, was the little white dog, the dog she'd lived with long enough to call hers. Fifi with her leash dragging the sand. She took it, brushed the sand from her backside, and they ran along the tideline, kicking up colors—orange and blue, pink and green—the colors of gasoline, quick and ardent.

Fifi pulled her faster, faster. Gwen could see him, the shipwrecked prince, tiny at first, like an action figure, and then coming clearer, coming into focus, full-sized and made of flesh, running toward them.

He was yelling. "Tink, Fifi!" A hundred gulls or more huddled on the beach between them flapped and flew and took to the sky, circling. And then Leo was beside her, breathing hard. "Tink," he said, "Tink," and his eyes were bright. "I thought you—I was watching and then—you were gone. You and Fifi. I was alone for a lifetime. And I didn't like it, Tink, not one bit." She searched his eyes and found they had the ocean in them, all that orange fire. He pulled her close and squeezed her like he'd never let her go.

Feeling the warmth of him, melting with it, she wondered how he *hadn't* managed to find her. Had he looked?

He took her hand and they walked down the beach, back toward the pier. "Tink?"

"Don't call me that."

"Why not?"

"Because we're at the end of the play now. We're at the end and that's when Tinker Bell takes the poison that's meant for Peter, because she wants to save him. But she can't save him. I mean, she does, in the play. In the play, she almost kills herself for love. I'm not going to do that."

He was quiet. She saw the gulls land behind him. "I thought we were at the beginning," he said at last. And she found herself wishing it were true.

They stood in the shallows and watched the sun at the edge of the deep end redden to a bright coal and sink. The clouds flushed and darkened, and the sky turned a pale, watery blue. Gwen spotted a bird out there, its far silhouette. A large bird, not flapping, soaring. It was following a boat, riding its current of wind. She thought of the albatross, the boat ride to Sausalito. She thought of her father, at home in his study, on his first Scotch by now, and she longed to hear his voice.

A girl was coming toward them, passing them, turning her quick cartwheels on the hard sand. She couldn't have been more than seven. She wore a loose dress that fell over her face each time she was upside down. She was followed by a couple, holding hands, talking and laughing. They wore sweatshirts and jeans rolled up to their calves. They smiled at Gwen and Leo and said hello. So easy. A life by the sea. She took Leo's hand

and pressed it. In return, he gave her hand a squeeze that was somehow weaker and briefer than she'd wanted.

Looking over the ocean to that farthest line, where the lighter blue met the darker, she thought she saw a sprig of water, a burst, so small from this distance, this edge where the waves swallowed her feet and Leo's and then rushed back, leaving them covered with sand. There was nothing, and then she saw what appeared to be another spray of water. She pointed. "Do you see?"

"Whales," he said.

"Whales?" she said, and she tightened her grip on his hand, and said, again, "Whales," to feel the wide word in her mouth, the inhalation of breath it seemed to necessitate.

He let her hand go and began to talk in earnest now, and she listened to him from a great distance. "God, it's been years," he said, and she was, she realized, years away, far into the future, looking back on the moment, the father of her child talking about when he'd been a kid. She tried to notice things, the way he spoke with his hands, gesticulating, the way his face reflected the calm gloss of the afterglow. "When I needed to be alone," he was saying, "I'd come out here, out to the pier. I'd run to the very end, to where I couldn't go any further, and the ocean would take it, all of it. I'd feel so small by comparison, all of my worries, my anger, none of it mattered. And I remember seeing the whales. I pretended I could hear them calling me—like we knew each other, across all that water."

They were back to where she'd dropped her purse and purchases. She found her jug of water and drank from it in big gulps. She changed from her suit into her dress and drew her sweater around her. It was getting cold.

"Let me see," she said, reaching for Leo's arm. The wound was sealed shut. Less livid, it seemed to be healing. Even so, she doused it with hydrogen peroxide, and when the fizzing stopped she smeared it with the antiseptic ointment and covered it with a bandage.

Leo had spent the afternoon gathering driftwood. There was a cement ring beside them and a pile of wood beside that. And now, in the center of the ring, he leaned twigs together in the shape of a teepee, and the bigger sticks over those in the same shape. He took his time perfecting the design, as if it wouldn't all go up in flames.

Looking out at the blackening sky, at Venus, low and yellow over the dark water, she found she was thinking of a snake, or a poem with a snake in it—the Ouroboros encircling Brett's arm (which was also a poem), her arm moving as she danced, serpentine. Gwen felt in her purse for the notebook and her good fountain pen, the one her father had given her to show his support for her writing. In the gloaming, she put pen to paper. Hardly able to see her own scrawl, she wrote as it came to her, line by line. It felt like an exercise in trust—this writing in the near dark.

> *She will come on the stilt legs of the heron,*
> *watch you with one yellow eye.*

Venus, the goddess of love, winked at her, but planets weren't supposed to flicker.

> *She will slow the beating of your heart—*

She wrote the line and like magic her heart slowed. Her heart was the languid breaking of the waves. It was wide open like that, like arms before a long-awaited embrace. She watched the waves, the way they phosphoresced as they crashed, turning a brilliant green and glowing. The sky was dark, and she could no longer see the page. She closed her notebook, twisted the lid onto her pen. But she'd written. At last she'd started something new.

Leo balled up newspaper and stuffed it into the structure like batting. His thumb flicked the wheel of a lighter he'd found in the sand, flicked it over and over, until a flame appeared in the dark. The paper caught quick, as did a few twigs, but the big pieces of wood only smoked. He kept at it until the fire took, enough for a small glow, and they sat close, warming themselves. Sparks lifted into the cooling night. As he stoked the fire, she watched him with a fondness she recognized as maternal. And mothers must let go, she thought. In the flickering light, his hair a tangle of ringlets, his hands and his face smudged with ash, he was the beautiful boy he had always been, would always be: happiest in his freedom, squatting beside the fire and poking it here and there with a stick, tossing in new balls of newspaper for extra flare.

He hadn't eaten all day, and she was hungry again, so she left him to his fire, walked to the Pizza By the Slice shop beside Frank's and brought back four big slices of pepperoni. They devoured them, agreeing that pizza had never tasted quite so good. They fed Fifi their crusts and she rolled in the sand and curled up beside them.

When the fire had dwindled to coals, they lay back, Gwen's head on his arm. The stars had come out, the marine layer of moisture having lifted and somehow cleared. The moon had yet to rise, and in the deep sky there were more stars than she'd ever seen. The sky was cloudy with them. And she thought she could see, in the Milky Way galaxy, the snake with its mouth ajar, its tail inserted. Here on Earth, they were a part of it, part of this very galaxy. Galaxy from the Greek *galactose*, meaning milk, which her body, all by itself, would soon make—as if she were the universe, she thought, and she focused on a dark portion of the sky, feeling its mystery as though it were her own.

Leo was talking and his voice—or was it the stars?—made her eyelids heavy. She fought to keep them open, waiting for that one shooting star. "We can only exist in a thirteen-billion-year-old universe," Leo was saying. "We come from the stars and it takes time for there to be enough atoms from all these stars to make us. An eleven-billion-year-old universe would be too young, and in another twelve billion years, it'll all collapse into itself and then, maybe, there'll be another Big Bang, and we'll start all over again."

Her eyes were shut, she'd been drifting. She willed them open, and just as they focused there it was—the falling star. Not very long or luminous. Just a tiny fleck of light falling from a corner of the sky. Her falling star.

She made a wish.

Thirty-three

SHE HEARD THE gulls' cries and the slow, rhythmic crashing of the waves, and she lifted one drowsy eyelid. Dawn had brought the fog. Soon she'd become aware of just where she was and the fact that she'd slept all night on this bed of sand, but for a moment longer the dream hung like an overlay on the fog. She couldn't pin it to any characters or actions. It had the texture of dissolution, a thread she'd held in her fingers as it frayed and thinned to air. Less narrative than lyrical—like the ocean that had risen in the night, nearly taking them with it, and was now retreating, leaving in its wake a stretch of flat, abandoned sand—the dream left in her a sense of anguish. Loss in the form of an emptiness that nothing and no one could fill. She felt hollow, and rather than dissipating, the feeling intensified with the realization that she was more or less alone. Fifi lay on the sand beside her, but Leo was gone.

Her purse was splayed open, and a few of its contents—her brush, her notebook and her pen—were spilled onto the sand. The violation sent a jolt of panic through her. She checked to see if her wallet was still there and it was, along with her cash. The baggie that had held the mushrooms was there, too, only now it was empty. Mystery solved.

Leo was out in the fog again, spending another morning in Neverland.

She stood up, brushed the sand from her legs. Crouching behind a boulder, she lifted her dress, squatted in the soft, dry sand and peed. The morning was moist as a good kiss, and colder—her favorite sort of morning. Beside her purse was the jug of water, nearly half left. She drank, and walked down to the ocean.

Looking into the fog, she could see as far as the nearest wave—the red-brown curl and the ruddy foam, so very different, she thought, from the pure white from which Aphrodite had sprung. Still, the ocean was the ocean and she had to get in it, to immerse herself and come out new. Groggy and inspired, she ran back to their tousled camp and changed from her dress to her bathing suit. She walked into the ocean one slow step at a time, feeling each inch of her calves and her thighs as the gelid water shocked them to life. Behind her, Fifi followed the tideline up and back, barking at the waves.

Out of the mist, a red wave rose and crashed. Another followed close behind it, dissolving to milk at her waist, and then she saw him in the low cloud. He had never been much of a swimmer, but now he sputtered, he floundered, he sank. Perhaps he was calling her name, but all she could hear was the roar of the waves. From where she stood, she felt the riptide tug at her legs. It was stronger than it had been the day before. The waves grew big and bigger, folding in on each other as the tide rushed in and, more fervently, out again. Thick with kelp, the white water surged and hissed. He waved at her, flailing his arms.

Not waving, but drowning.

Perfect, she thought. Now it was his turn. The Fool on the edge. But where was his little white dog to keep him from tumbling off the cliff? Gwen could no longer hear her bark over the ocean.

The low cloud moved past them, shoreward, and in the clearing she could see a swatch of red fabric flying from the pier. Red for warning: danger. A notch up from yesterday's yellow, it was a signal she was sure he'd missed.

She yelled for him, and the ocean folded her voice into its fervent, hissing body. She wanted to turn around and head for shore. After all, no harm could come to the Fool. The sea would save him. It had to. And she had her child to think about. No, she insisted, she'd go no deeper.

Here was a wave and she caught it. The surge hurled her toward shore, her arms out in Superman fashion, as though she were flying—how her mother had showed her, her mother who had taught herself to swim, who'd mastered Lotta's fear of the water and made sure Gwen had loved it, seeing that she was on the swim team every summer, that she had strength and stamina. For what? To let this man she loved drown? She turned back to where he had been, but the fog had closed in again. She could see just as far as her hand.

Panic shot its numb, breathless electricity through her stomach and her chest, down her arms and legs. She realized that he might actually die and she was the only one who could save him. "Leo!" she called. The ocean answered with its thunder. She was a survivor. She'd survived her mother's death, she'd survived the riots, and she'd survive this, too. She swam under one wave and held her breath. Another wave moved over her and pushed her to the ocean floor. She thought of the child inside her and she felt powerful, capable of any feat. She fought her way up through the seething water and gulped air. With the next wave she was down again, where the rip seized and sent her out further. It was yesterday all over, only worse. No sooner had she thought it than she knew. This would never happen again.

If she made it out of this ocean, she would leave him.

She swam parallel to the shore—one fierce breaststroke after another. The stroke had won her a blue ribbon once, and she could almost hear the crowd of parents and children yelling, cheering, her mother's voice over them all, and she darted under the surface until the riptide had lost its hold and she was free. She saw him, further out still, but close enough to reach. Another wave swept him up and she swam to where it would fling him, her eyes open in the teeming ocean. The salt stung but she found him, a dark mass in the plankton and the kelp. Flotsam. The sailor sunk when the ship had foundered. Their ship. What was no more. She wrapped her arms around his waist, pushed off from the ocean floor and kicked. He was deadweight. She needed oxygen. She gripped his wrist with her hand and reached the surface, sucking in the air. The ocean swelled and gathered and curled around them. She took one stroke, two, and then lost her hold.

Either the ocean would take him, or it would let him go. She'd done all she could.

The wave spat her out in the shallows, in a foot of water on the hard sand. The red-brown foam hissed its last and subsided. Beside her, in a patch of clear ocean, he sat, coughing up water and gasping the air. There was a brief moment of sun. It reflected off the rippling water and danced over his body like cool fire. He shivered. His arms shook and he pulled his trembling knees in the wet black knickers to his chest and held them. The tide went out, leaving them on wet sand, and then it rushed back in, rushed past them. His skin was pale and his hair hung in limp clumps over half his face and down his back. A strand of kelp was caught in a tangle. She crawled to him. On her knees, she took her time loosening the hairs around the kelp enough to tease it out.

This is the last time I'll touch his hair, she said to herself, as if to give the subsequent act of her leaving weight, as if to make it real. The tide moved out, then in again. A lone sandpiper wading in the shallows jabbed his long beak into the sand. She pulled the kelp from Leo's hair, popped a bladder between her thumb and finger and hurled the foot-long strand behind her into the ocean.

He seemed not to notice the gesture. His eyes were wide, staring into the fog. "Fucking amazing, Gwen. The light. I saw it and it was beautiful, like they say, only it wasn't just white, it was a goddamn kaleidoscope. Made of every possible color. Jesus. I could die just to go there, just to see it again."

"Be my guest," she said, and she stood and walked from the ocean to their camp. She was numb. She couldn't feel her fingers or her toes, and she couldn't feel emotion, either. Not sadness, nor anger, nor fear. She changed into her dress, took off her wet bikini under it. She pulled on her sweater and wrapped it tightly around her. Warming her hands in the pockets, she felt the shell and closed it in her fist.

She saw a single jogger, a woman in a dark sweat suit, emerge from the fog and disappear back into it. We get these glimpses, she thought. Brief openings in the curtain. For just a moment things are clear. Things are themselves and we see them for what they are.

She watched Leo stumble toward her and collapse at her feet. Still breathing hard, he was on his back, his head on a pillow of sand. "I'm just going to nap here. For just a minute," he said, and shut his eyes.

From where she stood, she memorized his face—the curve of his dark eyelashes, the Roman nose, the soft pink lips with the center dimple that inscribed them with a pout. In his exhaustion, his body held a dreamy and exquisite languor, but she no longer desired him. Rather, she found herself assessing the lines of his limbs and face as if to draw them—his smooth uncomplicated forehead, the round, ruddy cheeks, the thick black beard she now saw had a handful of whiskers the color of tinsel, and the locks of his hair like the ribbons on a gift, the kind you take between your thumb and a single blade of scissors in order to curl the ends, to make the present pretty.

The end was different from what she could have imagined, which made the beginning another thing, too. The night they met, when she remembered it, had an antique yellow hue, as if the scene had been lit by candles. It hadn't, of course. They'd met under a streetlamp in front of the movie theater. She'd been alone, waiting, and Leo had come with their mutual friend, the actor who had set them up. A blind date. The movie was Spike Lee's *Do the Right Thing*, and she'd sat between them. She remembered how uncomfortable the movie had made her feel, the actors hurling their names for each other's races straight at the camera. For Gwen their anger had felt like a slap across her face. After the sting had subsided, she had looked at Leo in the movie light. In that hesitation, before returning to the screen, they had drunk deeply, and the silence of their drinking, Gwen had thought, was the song of a lifetime, an eyelid wide, between blinks. Now she saw it wasn't a lifetime, but a lovely youth, one slow morning hour of dappled light and remembered dreams. The kind of hour that burns off like fog in the sunlight.

"Dream of flying," she whispered.

She watched his lips curl to a smile. He looked up at her, and what she saw in his eyes was a gleeful satisfaction. "God," he said. "Maybe I did die. You're glowing. You have a halo, Gwen. You're an angel." His smile widened. "I'd be dead if it weren't for you," he said. And she understood what had held her for all these years wasn't her fear of being alone. Or it wasn't just that. It was his helplessness. So long as he couldn't get by in the world without her, she couldn't leave, because leaving meant abandoning him. The truth, though, was that she was not his mother. She had never been his mother. And now that she was going to be an actual mother, she could no longer pretend to be his.

She wouldn't make him choose. He'd be free to grow up when he was ready, even if that time was never.

"Good-bye, Leo," she said.

"You going for coffee?" he asked, rising to an elbow and looking at her. His eyes red from the salt water were green and shining. "I'd have a cup. A large. One sugar, one cream."

She thought of the horses on those boats in the doldrums, the horse latitudes. How did the sailors do it, she wondered. Throw a horse overboard and watch its hooves hit water, pound and tire, and not just one horse, but a team of horses? It came down to survival. Die of thirst or else lighten the load to catch the wind and move.

Her purse over her shoulder, her bikini and her flip-flops in her hand, she bent down and kissed Fifi on the head. Leo sat cross-legged, like a swami, staring into the mist as if he were seeing visions. He opened his mouth and a chant filled the air between them. *Aaahhh*, he sang. The first vowel, born in the depths and rising. She knew he wouldn't hear, but she said again, "Good-bye." The gold angel over his heart caught the sun sifting down now, warming her back, and she turned and was walking before the tears ran onto her cheeks and dripped from her nose and chin. Walking away, her feet and legs, her whole body was heavy. She could still turn back—but even as she thought it she knew it was part of a fiction, a story she'd told herself for so long she'd begun to believe it. The fact was that the two of them together in the world had never worked. Leo belonged to his own world. His was an island, where he leaned his back against a palm tree, played his pan flute and sang and the fairies circled and danced.

She heard again what he'd said that night in Tijuana—no one will love you as much as I love you. Perhaps it was true. But her steps were quickening now. They were finding their rhythm. She was moving through the fog or the fog was moving through her and the moving was the thing. Moving accrued momentum, sloughed off inertia. Walking fast on the hard wet sand, she dropped everything and turned a cartwheel, another and another, gaining speed. She stopped, dizzy, and faced the ocean, the spinning motes of mist. She walked into the water. It lapped the hem of her dress and she stood in one spot as the tide covered her feet in sand. She looked up and down the beach. No one was around. Facing the waves and the endless ocean, she opened her hands and stretched her fingers and her arms wide and she opened her mouth and screamed, and the fear and the anger awakened from their slumber rose up inside her molten and seething, and she screamed again, screamed until she had nothing but emptiness—emptiness and a child—inside her.

She grabbed her things, crossed the sand and the street, and passed Frank's and Pizza By the Slice. Smelling espresso, she ducked into the café, and the girl with the glasses and the pretty eyes pulled her a double shot, and Gwen downed it and paid her, tipping double again for karma and luck.

She climbed the stairs from the beach and stopped at the top to feel the holiness of the place. She gripped the metal rail and closed her eyes. As if the world were a ship and she were on its prow, she leaned into the wind, feeling her body, her miraculous body with two hearts inside it—one loud in her ears and the other quiet as a birthday wish you close your eyes to make before blowing out the tiny wax torches of the years.

There, in front of the little Spanish-style church, stood a phone booth she hadn't remembered seeing. Inside it a black phone dangled from its cord. She hung it up and then took it in her hand again, slid two quarters into the silver slot and dialed the familiar number. He picked up after two rings.

"Dad? I just wanted you to know I'm fine. And there's something else," she said, and she told him everything.

"Ah," her father said. "Now isn't that wonderful news."

Thirty-four

GWEN HUNG UP the phone.

Outside the church an old woman was sweeping. She wore a long black dress. Her silver hair was pulled back in a bun. The church had one door, arched, wooden, painted a dark red. It was ajar, and Gwen found herself drawn to the simple building. She asked the woman if she could go inside. *"Sí, niña,"* the woman said. She smiled and Gwen noticed that she had a gold front tooth, just like the psychic. The detail gave the moment a holographic, synchronistic feel—a stone skipping over the smooth water of time.

It was a memory, the gold tooth in the mouth of her great-grandmother, Maria, and Gwen three or four, the last time she saw her before she died. She was sitting on her lap as she sang in Spanish, her voice low and craggy, and the song sweet. She'd looked old as the earth—the branching wrinkles in her face, her clouded eyes, and how her mouth as she sang was like a mine, full of darkness where her teeth were missing, and full of treasure.

And in this instant of the stranger's smile, Gwen knew it was right—the fact that she was on this morning standing in front of this church talking to this woman. It was just a flash and then it was gone, but the realization cast a new light on those other moments out of which her life was made. With the slightest adjustment—this shift in view—it all lined up. Not in a straight start-to-finish sort of way, but more like a circle. By walking ahead she was sure to reach the beginning soon enough. It would look different because she would be different, and it would wait for her with the patience of an old friend.

Gwen closed the door behind her. The church was cool, damp, and dark. A chill ran through her. It took her eyes a minute to see. The room was tiny. There were five rows of wooden pews. And on the wall there was a fresco of Mary. With her red and gold and green veils, her brown skin, she was the Virgin of Guadalupe. In front of her a table held white candles in red glass jars. A few flames swayed, and red light danced across the Virgin's downturned face, across her hands parted over her heart. A sign said DONATIONS, ONE DOLLAR, beside the matchsticks and the metal collection box.

She folded a dollar into the slot, lit a candle. This was for Lotta. She sat on the pew and felt the stillness of the room and the stillness inside her. "Hail Mary, full of grace. Blessed art thou among women, and blessed is the fruit of thy womb," she said. And although she was praying to Mary, she was praying to Lotta, too. Blessed was the fruit of her womb, which meant her mother was blessed. Even if Lotta had been afraid to touch her, afraid she'd somehow kill her, she was blessed.

She fed a second dollar to the box and lit a candle for her mother. Looking into the face of the Virgin she thought she could see her mother's face, that slight smile on her lips. "I miss you, Mama," she said, and she felt the abyss inside her yawn, felt the tears come, but this time, she could also feel the love. Something in her chest lightened, and she found she was listening to a song in her head. *I'll be loving you, always. With a love that's true, always.* It was her mother's voice, singing her to sleep, and it was the song she would sing to her daughter.

Thirty-five

THE CENTURY LOUNGE was warm and red, like a womb. It was a dream of a palace of curtains, the girls appearing and disappearing in the shadows, flitting like moths toward those smaller chambers furnished only with light, chambers that could hold two people like a confidence, where girls danced for just one pair of eyes, for a song. Through the showroom, she moved among whispers. *Hey, mister? Wanna see? Follow me.* She moved, only she didn't flit. She was slow and deliberate, like a snake, winding among them—the girls and the strangers—feeling the ground under her heels, the ground under the carpet, under the wood and the cement, feeling the pull, the ache of gravity, and happy to linger in the twilight, watching, one last time, Brett, flushed and trembling, on her knees as she arched her back, and her breasts, the curve of her neck held the red light, and glowed.

Tony tapped her on the shoulder. "One last?"

He had found her, found her out.

Blushing, she took his hand and led him to the private dance booth, the one on the side, their booth, where he sat with his hands clasped atop the desk-like ledge, where she fed the token into the slot and the light hummed to life. Between them, there was a vague, remembered heat—her bare, hothouse orchid (now crowned with its new leaf of short brown hair) and his itch to touch. Only now she embodied mystery, *the* mystery. She felt it as a kind of power. She was electric, charged, having claimed the direction her life would take. She arched and twisted, contracted and splayed, but he didn't dare risk—didn't even consider—contact, now this aura of impenetrability shielded her like invisible armor.

Nirvana was playing, which meant Devotion was dancing. And she was up next. Her final set.

She looked at Tony, wan and sad. He was smaller, older, with deeper wrinkles than she'd realized.

Their song was over and the light clicked off. She pulled on her G-string and her black slip and stepped out of the dark booth. They stood beside their table, arms hanging at their sides—the moment, their silence, too long and hard to break. She said nothing. She leaned toward him and kissed his cheek, and he pulled her in for a hug.

"What'll I do without you?"

"Find the next good thing," she said, and smiled to nip in the bud a real tear.

"Here," he said, pressing a roll of bills into her hand. "For expenses." She opened it—the bills were hundreds, and the roll was thick. She gave him one more hug.

"I have a poem," she said. "It's going to be published, in one of the really good journals. I'll send you a copy if you give me your address."

He pulled a pen from his front shirt pocket and scribbled his address on a napkin. "I'm happy for you," he said, but his eyes were moist. She watched his slow walk toward the front of the club, toward the door. Thin and a bit bent, he looked more alone than ever, and she wished she could take his arm in hers and walk him to his car.

Lady Madonna, children at your feet, Richie Havens sang, and she hurried backstage, past Devotion and Love getting high, between the red curtains and into the light, just as Joe's voice, smooth and low, advertised her finale, her farewell. "And on the main stage, it's Stevie. This is the last night she'll dance on this stage, guys, so treat her right."

She walked the stage like she owned it. With a swish of her hips, she let one strap and then the other slip from her shoulders. She felt the black silk slide down her body and pool at her ankles, and she stepped out of it and danced in just her G-string for a roomful of people—for one final set she danced. She spun around the pole. Gripping it with her thighs and her hand, she leaned back in a dip, and saw the showroom upside down. The faces that faced her seemed to be drowning—their mouths slack above their dull eyes. But then the Friday night crowd was always drunk and cheap.

Just today the curfew had been lifted. L.A. on the mend meant business as usual. The city was rebuilding itself. Citizens were helping the shop owners fix things up. The politicians were talking. There'd be federal aid for more jobs—jobs for minorities, they were saying. The outlook was hopeful. But the thrill of being alive? All that energy the chaos had unleashed? Had it really been stilled by the rush-hour traffic already, swallowed up by mere routine? Or was being alive to that extent exhausting? We're creatures of habit, of comfort. Routine is safe. The vacant eyes of the mouth-breathers—there was nothing Gwen in her birthday suit, no matter her soaring spirit, no matter her spunk, was going to do about that.

She pulled herself upright. She was done with the dance,

with this sort of dance. She'd moved beyond the desire for strange eyes on her, remaking her in the image of their fantasy. She didn't want to be this man's student or that one's teacher. She didn't want to be the secretary or the ex-wife or the girl next door. From this time on, her sexuality would be her own. She wanted off the stage, out of the light, where Brett might brush by, their bare arms grazing, where she might turn, take Gwen in her arms for a waltz, her laughter lavish, voluptuous as wind chimes bejeweling the air.

Behind the curtains, she found herself alone backstage, and the quiet was strange. She thought of the dream of her mother bursting into petals of pastel light. She thought of the kiss and took her time. Maybe Brett would walk right through that door, she thought, and her heart beat so she could feel it. She slid off her G-string. Naked, she looked herself over in the mirror. Her face was already fuller, and her cheeks were pink. Really, her whole body looked fuller and pinker. Since she left San Clemente, she hadn't stopped eating. Munching. She'd stocked up on snacks—soda crackers and peanut butter and sweet pickles. Her stomach growled. She wanted something now, to keep the nausea at bay.

One more song, one *last*, as Tony had said. She licked the arches of her brows—Brett's move. *All the gang has gone home*, Rickie Lee cried. She couldn't wait any longer. In just her pearls, she strolled into the light.

Say good night, America, Rickie Lee sang. *The world still loves a dreamer.*

Good night, then. Good night to the red light, and the flushed curves of flesh. Good night to the hours past midnight and the hum of LAX, to the girl on her own in the city's hub, its spokes whirring like the hands of a too-quick clock. Good night to Brett and Love and Devotion. And good night to Los Angeles, to the dreams she'd had and who she thought she'd be. Good night to Tony, and to Mr. Cooper. To the matches struck in the dark, the cigarettes glowing. Good night to Valiant and to Leo and to the Cornell.

She'd packed up her things—her mother's silk slips, her books of poetry, the Underwood, and the cigar box. She packed what was hers just today. It was all in her car. Leo hadn't so much as called, and Valiant must still have been with his parents. Tonight she'd head up the coast. Sam and Loni were expecting her. She'd drive through the night and arrive by morning.

The song was short. *I'm standing on the corner, all alone*, Rickie Lee sang, and she realized it was over. There hadn't been time, time to take it all in, the room, the mirrors, the men. She should have picked something longer.

She turned to these last bars of music around the pole, and froze—leaning out, her head down and in profile for the audience. She held the pose as the song gave way to silence, a brief lull. And then she picked up the dollars littering the edge of the stage like so many pale, crushed flowers.

Backstage, she sat in her pearls between Love and Devotion. Love wore pink chiffon, and with the white boa draped around her neck she tickled Gwen's back as Devotion packed the pipe and offered her a hit. She shook her head.

"You're leaving?" Love said.

"She's pregnant," Devotion said.

"Lord, if I got pregnant," Love said, and got to her feet. "And I guess I could. He has to wait a year before they'll lop it off."

"You've said," Devotion said, and lit the pipe.

"Well, *anyhow*, if I got pregnant, honey, I don't know what I'd do. I can't imagine not dancing. It's who I am." Towering over them in her heels, she parted the curtains and walked onto the stage. Gwen could hear Streisand crooning "The Way We Were," and she imagined Love moving in circles, her circles moving.

"What *will* you do?" Devotion said.

Gwen stood, brushed the filaments of carpet from her butt. "I'm moving. Up to Santa Cruz. I have an aunt who said I could stay awhile, until I figure things out."

Devotion exhaled smoke, and leaned back on an elbow. "Doesn't sound half bad, getting out of this dump."

"Nice!" The voice was breathy, someone Gwen didn't recognize. She turned to see a new girl, a young redhead, farm-truck fresh, in her white lacy bra and cutoffs frayed clear to the seams. "God, this stuff smells good!" she said and reached for Devotion's pipe. She giggled and took a drag. "There's this guy, over there in the corner. Mr. Cooper, I think he said. He'll pay you just to talk."

"Tell him Stevie says good-bye, will you?"

"Stevie? Sure. But he'll pay you—"

"I know. If you could tell him for me."

"Yeah, sure. Stevie."

"Thanks," she said.

She visited Joe, who gave her back her music. "I can't talk you into staying, can I?" he said.

"Not a chance," she said, and left him for the dressing room, where she changed into jeans and a T-shirt. She took her lock off her locker, pulled out her costumes, her white and black lace, her plaid gingham dress, the little-girl church socks. She stuffed them into her carpetbag of a purse and put her fake pearls in there, too. She found the Virgin of Guadalupe necklace and fastened it around her neck.

She could smell spice and she turned. Brett stood in the

doorway in her black bra and her G-string. How long had she been there, watching?

She walked to the mirror and sat down, put her feet on the counter. She took a lipstick from her purse and applied it with her finger. Her lips shone berry-brown, the exact color, Gwen thought, of her nipples.

Her own lips were dry.

"Could I?" she said.

Brett turned the lipstick up and Gwen touched her pinky to it, dotted the color onto her lips. She looked in the mirror to see, and Brett's dark eyes held hers.

"You could kiss me now," Gwen heard herself say, "and no one would know."

Brett smiled and patted her lap. "I'm up next song."

Now or never, Gwen thought.

Her hands went cold, her heart pounded in her throat. She sat on Brett's thighs. Her breath was cinnamon and smoke. Her eyes, up close, were dark as a night sea and she—they—were floating, the two of them, in a canoe across a glassy surface. Brett ran her fingers through Gwen's hair, not catching a single tangle. She tugged at the roots and tilted her head back, just a little, her face toward hers.

Gwen closed her eyes. Her lips and the slip of tongue—it was soft, it was seamless and sweet and slow, as though they had all the time in the world. Their tongues were the rounded fruit flesh of her dream, plum and peach. Apricot. Brett bit her lower lip, and electricity shot through her. Gwen was dissolving right here in Brett's strong arms. She felt small, and protected. She was a snail, and Brett was her frail shell. "You're shaking," Brett said, and held her tighter. She kissed her eyelids.

Gwen opened her eyes. With her fingertips, she traced the

faint Ouroboros around Brett's smooth arm. She wanted to stay here for just another moment, another breath.

Brett kissed her forehead. "I should go," she said.

Gwen nodded. She couldn't speak. She'd been blessed—blessed by the goddess. Gwen climbed off her lap and Brett stood.

She lifted the Virgin pendant from Gwen's heart. "Guadalupe," she said. "She watches over unborn children and their mothers. I'm glad you have her." She set her back on Gwen's skin.

"I want you to have this, too," she said. She took the black velvet choker with the silver moon she'd made from around her own neck and fastened it on Gwen. They faced the mirror. Brett's moon hung between Gwen's collarbones. Gwen took the crescent in her fingers, turned it so the stones caught the light.

"Lapis lazuli," Brett said.

Gwen nodded. "To help you remember your dreams. And moonstone."

Brett grinned. "For new beginnings."

"I'm moving to Santa Cruz."

"Santa Cruz, hm? Good town."

Her music was playing—Leonard Cohen's "I'm Your Man." "Listen," Brett said. "Here's my number. I'm going home soon. I've got to get out of this city." She laughed. "I need some time away from my fiancé." She pressed a slip of paper into Gwen's palm, closed her fingers around it. "Call me sometime."

In the doorway, she turned, glanced at her over her shoulder. "I'll see you, Stevie."

"My real name's Gwen," she said, needing her to know.

Brett's eyes flared with mischief.

"I'm Carmen," she said, and Gwen watched her vanish into the red pulse.

She laughed out loud in the empty room. She should have known. Brett, Carmen—maybe she was all fiction. She opened the piece of paper. There was her number. She ran her finger over the black ink, the small, slanted scrawl.

It was real.

She tucked the paper into her change purse, for safekeeping, and slung her bag over her shoulder. She walked the hallway without looking back. The red glow was inside her now.

It took the weight of her whole body to push the back door open to the night, to the warm L.A. night, its low clouds glowing with the lights from the streets like a huge cocoon the whole city was inside, as if all of Los Angeles might turn, along with her, into some newly winged thing. She walked to her car, fit her key into the lock. The engine hummed to life. She turned onto Century Boulevard, turned north onto the 405.

She rolled her window down and Billie Holiday sang her through the night.

The clouds thinned and vanished and the sky was lapis lazuli. And, later, the waning gibbous moon rose—so fat and orange, and then blue-white. She followed the shining thread of road through the lit fields and thought of Stevie, the girl she was leaving behind. She wasn't perfect, but she'd taught Gwen a thing or two, like how to walk with her shoulders back, her head high, her naked heart lighting her way through any dark room. She had shown her how to bare not only her body, but her beauty, and how to love herself—bruises, blemishes, worries and all.

WHEN LIGHT SPREAD from behind the hills and filled her rearview mirror, she was off the freeway, heading west again, nearly there. The road was only two lanes, winding through the mountains. A bright wind blew through the redwoods and the air was sweet. She rubbed her swelling belly with the palm of her hand, ate a Saltine cracker. Rounding a corner, she saw, twinkling in the distance, the blue of the ocean—where her mother's body, her ashes, lay, but didn't rest. Rather they pulsed, they flowed, they traveled always on tides through the world. Dazzling against the pale curtain of sky, the ocean left its ghost of light dancing in her vision, shimmering in the road before her.

At the side of the lane, along a creek, a woman had parked her car. She bent toward a spigot, where she filled a plastic jug with water. Gwen pulled over. She got out of her car and stretched. The woman was young, Gwen's age maybe. She wore a prairie skirt and a peasant blouse and not a spot of makeup. Gwen watched her fill jug after jug. When she finished, the spigot was still running. There wasn't any off switch. It just ran.

"Can you really drink the water?" Gwen said.

The woman smiled an easy smile. "It's the best water around."

Gwen filled her own empty bottle with the cold water and drank it down. The woman was right. It was the best water she'd tasted, ever. She filled her bottle again, twisted the lid on, and watched the water in a single silver stream fall to the ground.

Acknowledgments

I'D LIKE TO give thanks to:

Melissa Berton, Laraine Herring, Mary Sojourner, and Mike McNally, for reading my various drafts. Your insight was invaluable.

Susan Lang, for her Hassayampa Institute, whose community of writers gave me a sense of support and purpose at a time when I most needed it.

My teachers, especially Stephen Yenser, Ellen Bryant Voigt, and Larry Levis, for feeding the fire.

The Wonder Agents of 3 Arts—Richard Abate, whose faith in my writing proved both impetus and inspiration, and Melissa Kahn, who spun her magic and found such a fine home for my book.

Editor extraordinaire Jessica Williams, for her hard work and keen eye, and all of the amazing people at HarperCollins who helped to bring this book into the world.

My family, for your constant love. Hannah and Max, my song and my reason.

And finally, I want to thank Ty Fitzmorris, who believes.